The Messenger Conflicted

conclusion to the Messenger prequels

Joel Pierson

iUniverse, Inc.
Bloomington

The Messenger Conflicted
conclusion to the Messenger prequels

This is a work of fiction. All of the characters, names, incidents, organizations, and dialogue in this novel are either the products of the author's imagination or are used fictitiously.

iUniverse books may be ordered through booksellers or by contacting:

iUniverse
1663 Liberty Drive
Bloomington, IN 47403
www.iuniverse.com
1-800-Authors (1-800-288-4677)

ISBN: 978-1-4759-9393-6 (sc)
ISBN: 978-1-4759-9394-3 (e)

Printed in the United States of America.

iUniverse rev. date: 06/10/2013

Acknowledgments

As the Messenger series comes to a conclusion, it's time to look back at the exciting and challenging road it's been. Considering that *Don't Kill the Messenger* was intended to be a standalone, I never imagined I would be here, at the completion of my sixth book in the series. But good characters are like good friends—you just want to spend as much time with them as you can.

My thanks this time to everyone who's read the books and taken the time to tell me their thoughts. It made a difference. Special thanks to Juliet Youngren, who's shared her thoughts on each work in progress, reminding me when something didn't quite make sense. If only someone would do that for all aspects of life!

Thanks, of course, to Dana, who contributed greatly to the storyline. We wanted to write this one together, but life got in the way. Still, her contributions made this a strong farewell to a series that's meant a great deal to me over the past five years.

About the Author

Joel Pierson is the author of numerous award-winning plays for audio and stage, including *French Quarter, The Children's Zoo, The Vigil, Cow Tipping,* and *Mourning Lori.* He also co-authored the novelization of *French Quarter.* How he has time to write is anyone's guess, as he spends his days as editorial manager at the world's largest print-on-demand publishing company. Additionally, he is artistic director of Mind's Ear Audio Productions, the producers of several popular audio theatre titles and the official audio guided tour of Arlington National Cemetery. If that weren't enough, he also writes for the newspaper and a local lifestyles magazine in his hometown of Bloomington, Indiana. He stays grounded and relatively sane with the help of his wife (and frequent co-author) Dana, and his ridiculously loving dogs.

The Messenger Trilogy

Don't Kill the Messenger
The Messenger Adrift
Messenger in a Battle

The Prequels

Instant Messenger
A Messenger So Dark
The Messenger Conflicted

Messenger, arise! Know thyself! For thou art lost.
Free thy mind and go forth to find those who need thee.
Long shall be thy days upon this earth,
and blessed thy mission be.
Yet, be vigilant and avoid misprision in all things.

—Found in a cave outside of Jerusalem, 1763
Author unknown

Chapter 1

Monday, October 1, 2007

Tristan

I should introduce myself, but I'm not exactly in the best position to do so. My name is Tristan Shays, and I'm thirty-four years old; this much I know. Beyond that, I begin to get hazy on a few particulars—like precisely who the hell I am. And before you start thinking, *Amnesia? Oh, how lame! What is this, "As the Days of Our One Life to Live Turn to the Guiding Light"?,* let me point out that I have suffered a closed-head traumatic brain injury. At least, that's what I was told. I don't actually remember the injury, and from what I hear of it, that's probably for the best.

The personal details currently in my possession are a combination of what remained pre-injury and what was shared with me by my caregiver and lifesaver, my cousin Ephraim Shays. It was he who got me to safety after my injury, he who brought me to the best doctors in the region. It's been a full month since my nine-day visit to comaville, and details have been very peculiar in returning. Oddly, they're coming back to me in chronological order. So, at present, I know more about my childhood than I do about my life of two months ago, which is frustrating, in that I don't really need to know what my third-grade teacher looked like. My current occupation, list of friends, and social obligations, however, would come in pretty handy.

Ephraim's been very helpful, as much as he can, with the more contemporary bullet points. He and I weren't close before my accident, but he knows enough about me to tell me some of what I need to know. Apparently, I was on a voluntary leave of absence from a management position in a corporation that makes LEDs—light-emitting diodes, those very bright light bulbs that seem to be popping up all over the place. More than that—and this is the part that even I found surprising—my father invented the damn things years ago, and somehow, even though he's dead, I still get a fraction of a cent every time an LED is put in *anything*. So, at the risk of sounding snooty (which I don't think I am), I'm loaded. As in embarrassingly wealthy. I won't quote a number here, as that would be gauche, but let's just say I could take Europe out to dinner, pick up the check, and still have enough to leave the tip. And because of the LED royalty thing, I don't even have to go to work to sustain it. Which is actually good news, because even five and a half weeks after my injury, I still get tired very quickly, which feels crazy after sleeping for nine straight days.

This is what makes Ephraim such a godsend. He took a leave of absence from his job, just to take care of me. He's been living in the guest room of my house in Ocean City, Maryland, and he dedicates each day to helping me with whatever I need. Good thing, too, because in all these weeks, I haven't heard from a single family member or friend, which leads me to believe I'm either a wealthy recluse or a colossal dick. I truly hope it's the former and not the latter.

I'm told that I've never been married and I'm not in a relationship now. Both my parents are gone, and I don't have any siblings. My memories of childhood confirm this. What troubles me, though, is my apparent lack of a social circle. Ephraim doesn't know me well enough to know who my friends are, so he can't help there. I seem to have lost my cell phone, and I must have been very type-A about my e-mails, because the first time I checked my e-mail account after my injury, I had nothing archived. I should add that part of the fun of rebuilding your life after a comprehensive memory loss is the realization that everything you need access to requires a password that's now long gone.

I'm fortunate, in that my memory loss wasn't complete. I didn't wake up to a world where I couldn't recognize a computer or a television or a car. I remember how to drive, how to use technology, which end of the toothbrush goes into my mouth. What's missing are the little details that make me *me*—who my friends are; where I've been for the last month; why I took a leave of absence from work; who my former colleagues are. I wish I'd kept a diary, so I could read over these details and make them a part of me again.

Ephraim tells me not to worry; the memories will return, he assures me. Apparently, he's done quite a bit of research into this type of injury, as he suffered a similar injury himself years ago. In the next month, he says, I should be myself again. It can't come quickly enough for me. On top of this is a pervasive and nagging feeling that I'm forgetting something very important, something that I should know, despite my injury. It's about my … I don't even know the best word for it, but "purpose" comes to mind. I feel like I have a purpose, something that drives me; something that led me to leave my management job for another path. I've been trying very hard to find it, sitting alone for hours, working to clear my mind of all other thoughts, but it won't come. I don't want to bother Ephraim about it; he's got enough to do. But the thought is so important, and the lack of an answer so troubling, that over lunch today, I have to ask him.

"What do I do?" I ask him at the dining table on the back deck of the house.

He lowers the butter knife he's holding and asks, "What do you do about what?"

We're having lox and bagels. I didn't realize I like lox and bagels, but learning that I do has been a pleasant experience. I clarify my question for him. "No, I mean what *is it* that I do now that I've taken a leave from my job?"

He smiles a little at my question, trying—I am sure—not to look impolite for doing so. "I wondered if you would ever ask."

"I've been trying to remember. Really trying hard, to the point where some days, it takes up most of my day. I didn't want to ask you, because I find myself falling into a pattern where I'm asking you everything. And if you hand me my memories one by one, I won't have the benefits of working to get them back. But this one … it's eluding me, and it feels like it's very important. So I decided to ask you. Do you know what my purpose is? How I spend my days?"

He pauses long enough to take a bite from his bagel, which he's loaded up with cream cheese, thin slices of smoked salmon, Roma tomato slices, slivers of red onion, capers, and lemon juice. "I'm not surprised this part is elusive. It's part of the nature of your injury. The area of your brain that keeps track of your identity was badly damaged, and your purpose of late, as you call it, is closely tied to that identity."

"So you do know what I do?"

"Yes."

"You're welcome to shatter the suspense at any time," I tell him.

"You're a philanthropist," he answers matter-of-factly, after which he sips an iced coffee.

"That's it? A philanthropist?"

"Yep."

"Why didn't you tell me before?" I inquire.

"You didn't ask. Besides, I wasn't in any hurry for you to rush back into it. Fact is, it's fairly dangerous."

I'm surprised by this. "What, writing checks to needy causes is dangerous?"

He looks at me, his expression instantly stern. "That's not the kind of philanthropy you engage in. You travel. You help people, using your resources to assist those who are in need. And sometimes it gets dangerous. Your injury, the one that very nearly killed you? It was a result of your philanthropy."

"Tell me."

"No. Not yet."

"Ephraim, it's my life, my past. Just because I don't have access to it at the moment doesn't mean I'm unable to handle it."

He looks unfazed by my insistence. "This isn't a casual decision. Nor am I undertaking the role of guardian. I just happen to know something about the human mind and psychological trauma. Your mind can't recall the details of your injury yet, because doing so would be harmful to your health. For now, it's protected, much like a scab over a cut. Pick at the scab protecting your mind, and I assure you, it will never heal. The memories will return, Tristan, and when they do, I'm sorry for what that will do to you. For now, the less you think about it, the better. Let yourself heal and become stronger. Then, when you're ready, you can deal with those memories. At that time, if I can help you, I will."

"Well, if you're gonna be all *reasonable* about it," I offer sheepishly.

He gives a little laugh at my faux petulance. "Believe me, dear cousin, I of all people know that you are a grown-up and what you're capable of. I also know, as few others can, the extent of damage that was done to you. The time may come when you'll be able to return to your philanthropic work. If so, I'll do what I can to help you. But don't rush things. A lot of medical professionals would have offered a very dim outlook on your chances of surviving what you survived. For now, consider yourself on medical leave. An extended vacation, if you will, to enjoy autumn on the Eastern Seaboard, with a trusted family member in residence to attend to your needs."

"All of which sounds great. I just can't help feeling restless. When I remember who I was, I get the sense that I always had to know exactly what was going on. I hated to be out of the loop on anything—least of all my own life. And that's what I feel like now, like I walked in half an hour late to the movie of my own life story."

"Then today, let's go for a drive," Ephraim says. "Around the area. Maybe it'll stir some familiar sights. I'll even take the wheel, so you can be a passenger and look around."

"Thank you. I'd like that."

Within the hour, we are in my car, venturing into Ocean City for a drive. It's not like I haven't been out of the house since I came home from the hospital, but previous excursions have been very task-oriented: go to the grocery store; go to the doctor's office; pick up something for the house. I feel like Ephraim has been limiting my exposure to the world around me. I'm sure it's for all the right reasons, protecting my delicate psyche, like he said. But it does make me feel like the special-needs nephew of the family. *Mustn't say anything to upset Tristan after his incident.* Does Tristan get a vote?

It's a beautiful day, with plenty of sunshine and mild temperatures. Tourist season is over, so the town is back to its off-season population, which is just fine by me. Tons of parking, no crowds. *Boy, I do sound like a recluse. Gotta work on that.*

As we travel the streets of my hometown, I look for familiar sights but find, to my dismay, that very few of them stir any recollection. We pass a little restaurant called The Golden Door, and I get a flash of remembrance. "I think I've eaten there," I say, hope returning to my voice. "I think I go there frequently."

"That's good. I don't know if you're right, but it's a good sign."

We drive on, and on the highway outside of town, I see a billboard for Hellenic Pride Cruise Lines. It shows a massive, gleaming-white ship against a brilliant blue ocean, along with the words, "Your adventure is waiting." Instantly, it evokes a feeling of tranquility in me, but a few seconds later, other sensations rush in to take its place. In my thoughts I see a computer screen displaying a page from the company's website. Pictures of Alaska. Then a woman in a white dress, standing with me on the deck of a ship. Accompanying these thoughts are sharp feelings of pain racing through my head.

"Tristan, what's wrong?" Ephraim asks, concern in his tone.

"The ... billboard. It stirred some memories, but I don't know what they mean."

"Try to get them out of your mind for now. They may be related to things you're not ready to think about yet. Focus on something peaceful. Green grass, blue sky."

As strange as this sounds, I try it, and the images fade, taking the pain away with them. "That's better. Thank you. I'm sorry; it was causing some physical pain. Not one of my favorite things."

"I would imagine. I can take us home if you'd like."

"No, not yet. Please. I'm enjoying being out. Could we go …" I hesitate.

"Go?"

"To my company. Where I worked before all this happened?"

"I don't know if that's a good idea. The billboard brought up painful memories—literally. I'm not sure you're ready to see your former workplace."

"Just the building, the outside. Please, I'm hoping it'll be associated with good, safe memories."

He thinks about it for a bit and then says, "All right, the outside of the building."

With that, he takes us toward Salisbury, Maryland, and the place where I wish I remembered working. It is roughly a forty-minute drive, during which I have no other painful or troubling memories. Ephraim remains relatively silent during the drive, perhaps allowing me to sit back and simply absorb the surroundings. I'm okay with that. This area is beautiful, and honestly, I don't know what to say right now. He and I have spent a lot of time together in the last month. A little time alone with my thoughts is a good thing.

In Salisbury, we turn into an industrial complex, and I see ahead a building ten or more stories high. The sign at its apex says Shays Diode. No other names are in evidence; this whole thing is the company my father created. Even though I used to come here every day, it now looks monolithic and alien, a tower of steel and glass, filled with people trying to bring light to the world. How did I fit in? A management position, Ephraim had said, but in what capacity?

As we pull up to the building, Ephraim asks, "Does it look familiar?"

"I think so, but I can't decide if that's because it does or because it should."

"In time, memories will come back to you."

"No time like the present," I reply. Without another word, I unlatch my seat belt, fling open the passenger door, and sprint for the building. Through the open door, I hear Ephraim call out, "Tristan! Come back! Shit."

Out of the corner of my eye, I see him reach over to close my door and then head to an available parking spot. Seconds later, I dash inside the front entrance and find myself in a huge, modern lobby. Instantly, I'm struck by the size and the strangeness of it. My entrance is abrupt, and I realize that the dozen or so people in the lobby have all stopped what they're doing and are now staring at me—and I at them. It's unbelievably awkward, and I feel like I should say something.

"Sorry, everybody. Sorry."

I'm utterly unprepared for what comes next. One by one, the people in the lobby speak to me. These faces I do not recognize light up at the realization that I'm among them.

"Mr. Shays!"

"Tristan?"

"Sir, you're back!"

"Admiral!"

Admiral? Did I miss something?

Then, to make a strange moment stranger, they all start clapping. Honestly, genuinely clapping their hands at the sight of me. I really have no frame of reference or even the slightest idea of what to do, but something tells me these people learned of my injury and they're glad I'm okay. *Got to acknowledge that.* "Thank you. Thank you, everyone. I'm feeling a lot better. I wish I could say I've come back to stay, but I've got a lot more recuperation ahead. I just wanted to see the old place and make sure everybody's doing okay."

From around a corner, I hear a loud voice ask, "Tristan, is that you?"

I see a Hispanic man moving toward me at a good clip, with a big smile on his face. It's obvious that he knows me, and I wish like hell I knew who he was. As he approaches, he adds, "It really is you. They said you had a bad head injury and you weren't well enough to see people. It sure is good to see you, to know you're all right again."

I look at his face, trying my best *not* to look like the mayor of Whothefuckareyouville. As I stare at him, a name comes into my mind. It doesn't sound outside the realm of possibility, so I take a chance and say it. "Esteban?" In hindsight, I wish I'd said it *without* the question mark, but you do what you can, right?

"Yep, it's me. I'm very glad to see you on your feet again."

Out of the corner of my eye, I see Ephraim frantically enter the building. He quickly comes to my side. Mercifully, he makes very little fuss, considering his dismay at my escape efforts. "There you are," he says pleasantly. "We agreed we'd take things slowly today, remember." He puts a hand on my shoulder that feels as much like capture as comfort.

"I just wanted to see everyone," I reply.

"Hello," the man in front of me says, "I'm Esteban Padgett, the CEO of the company. I don't believe we've met."

"I'm Tristan's cousin. I've been taking care of him since his injury."

"Well then, we all owe you a debt of gratitude," Esteban says. "None of us would be here if it weren't for this man."

His voice begins to stir up the murky waters of my memory. I picture Esteban sitting with me in my kitchen, having dinner. This is followed by other visions, including a woman with a gun. I shake my head to clear it, but I'm momentarily overcome by the pain in my head.

"I think we'd better get him home," Ephraim decides. "Thank you, everyone. Tristan will be back once he's feeling a hundred percent again."

Holding on to my arm, he leads me out of the building and back to the car, helping me into the passenger's seat. After taking his place in the driver's seat, he speaks in a tone far less pleasant than before. "What the hell do you think you were doing back there?"

"Trying to assert some control back in my life," I answer.

"Believe it or not, the restriction of your activities isn't random or arbitrary. I am trying to keep you away from anyone and anything that will be damaging to your healing process. I respect your autonomy, but when you dash away from me like a petulant four-year-old, I'm forced to play the role of stern guardian, which is not one I relish."

I should apologize, I really should, but fuck that noise. I go where I want. That's *my* name on that building. Instead, I switch gears. "So, from the reception I received in there, I'm guessing there's something you aren't telling me about my position with this company."

He starts the car and backs out of the parking spot. "You may have been the CEO once upon a time."

"I see. And this little tidbit was redacted because ...?"

"Relevance. You stepped down from the position, handing it over to your buddy, Padgett, so you could do your philanthropy work." He navigates us back to the road to Ocean City.

"Which brings me back to the other hidden topic of that philanthropy. It appears I had a pretty sweet gig back there at Shays Diode. Just what was it that would make me give all that up?"

He drives in silence for a minute, staunchly defying my request for information. Finally he asks, "When you looked at Padgett, you saw something, some memory, didn't you?"

"Yes."

"What was it?"

"I'm not sure. I saw him in my home, having dinner with me, which was fine. But then I saw him in danger. A woman was holding him at gunpoint, and I was there too. I think I was trying to talk her out of hurting him. It didn't make sense, and it caused me pain."

"It caused you pain because it's related to parts of your life that you're physically not ready to examine yet."

"Yes," I say, "but the picture in my mind of me trying to protect him—obviously, it worked because he's all right now. This ... this is going to sound like a strange question, but ... am I—am I some kind of ... superhero?"

A strange silence fills the vehicle for several painfully long seconds, before Ephraim bursts into barely controlled laughter. How he is able to drive despite this outburst of hysterics is beyond me. "Super— Oh my, that's good. Okay, you got me, Tristan. I can't protect your secret identity anymore. By day, you are mild-mannered millionaire playboy Tristan Shays, but by night, you transform into Captain Diode, defender of the downtrodden, and supplier of energy-efficient lighting."

"A simple *no* would have sufficed," I reply, trying unsuccessfully not to pout.

"I'm sorry," he offers, the laughter starting to taper off. "But the mental picture was too good to pass up. No, my dear cousin, you are not a superhero, which is good, because the hours are lousy and the pay is dismal. What you are is something quite different, and when your brain promises to leave you alone, I'll tell you about it."

Wednesday, October 3, 2007

Monday's escapades result in a definite cooling between Ephraim and me over the next two days; not outright hostility, but a dimming of trust, which is difficult to deal with, as much as I need to rely on him. On the scale of unforgivable offenses, my stunt at the office can't rank terribly high. *I entered the lobby of my workplace—oooh, thirty days in solitary.* Equally disturbing to me is Ephraim's insistence on meting out the details of my life in rationed doses, as if an overabundance could physically harm me. It seems unlikely, yet he's so very smart, and he hasn't been lying to me, so I have reason to believe him.

If I look at things rationally, I have to admit that everything he's done has been with my health and my best interests in mind. So why is there something buried deep inside of me that doesn't want to trust him? He's in my dreams sometimes. In some, we're walking through a museum together; in others, it's an airport. It feels significant, but like so much of my recent past, I feel like my thoughts have been put in a food processor and turned into mental pesto. I haven't worked up the nerve to ask him if the dreams of the museum and the airport are significant. Maybe I don't want to seem like I'm doubting him. Or maybe I don't want to know what the explanation would be.

Just after 11:00 in the morning, I'm transferring the laundry into the dryer when I get a strange sensation. My right knee begins to hurt, which is odd, because I know I haven't done anything to injure it or even stress it. Hell, if I were any more sedentary of late, I'd need a helper monkey. So the knee pain is unusual, and it is beginning to increase in intensity, to the point where I'm not sure I'll be able to stand on it much longer. I make my way haltingly toward the living room, but I realize I'm going to need help.

"Ephraim!" I'm not sure where in the house he is, so I call with enough volume to reach most of the rooms.

In seconds, he races downstairs to my side. "What is it? What's wrong?"

"I'm not sure. All of a sudden, my knee started hurting terribly for no reason."

"Shit." He puts an arm around my shoulder and allows me to lean all my weight on him, effectively becoming my right leg as I struggle to the couch. "Okay, stay calm. Sit up and elevate that leg."

I do so with some difficulty. "What's happening? You look like you expected this. Is this related to my head injury?"

"Not exactly. I look like I expected this because I did expect it. I didn't know when it would return, but I knew it would."

"Return? You mean I've gone through this before?"

"Yes. Many times. You remember the philanthropy I talked about? You're about to find out about it firsthand." He grabs a pen and a pad of paper from the end table. "Now, I need you to breathe regularly and stay as calm as you can. In a moment, you're going to see things …"

"See things? You mean hallucinate?" I ask through the pain.

"No, not quite. You're going to receive visions. Names, faces, addresses, maybe a date and time. I just want you to say aloud everything you see."

"What is this?" I ask, very disturbed at what's happening to me.

"It's your gift, Tristan. Your gift and your curse. Yours and mine both. You've been given time to heal, but clearly, someone believes you're ready for service again."

"Service? I don't …" Before I can finish that sentence, I do see visions in my head, just as he described. "Ohhhhhhh, owwwww. Here it comes; I see something."

"What do you see? Leave nothing out."

"I see a building full of people. Maybe a hotel. No, wait, they're all older. It's a nursing home. The residents are sitting down to eat in a common room. But … something's wrong; something's out of place. I smell something. Smells like sulfur. No, like gas. There's a gas leak." The images fill my mind as if I'm standing in the room, watching it happen. In an instant, the scene turns to horror, and I cry out.

"What is it? What happened?"

"An explosion! A fire! Everyone was trapped—there was no time."

"Tristan, stay with me. You should have an address in your mind. Where is the nursing home?"

I concentrate. "It's 4268 Transept, in Bethesda."

"Good. You're doing well. Now tell me, when will this happen?"

"At 4:30 this afternoon. What is this? How can I know this?"

"Is there anything else? Any other information that you see?"

"Owww, no. Just what I told you."

"Okay, that's fine. You did well. Rest for a few minutes."

To hell with rest. I want answers. Angrily, I rise from the couch and grasp him firmly by the lapels of the button-down sweater he's wearing. "Tell me what's going on, God damn it!"

Before he can answer, the pain and weakness in my knee return, and I quickly find myself losing my grip on his sweater and tumbling to the floor. My menace now deflated, I'm forced to add, "And if it's not too much trouble, could you help me up, please?"

He internalizes his well-earned laughter and simply smiles pleasantly as he helps me to my feet and then back to a seated position on the sofa, explaining, "It's going to hurt until you're on your way to warn them."

"Warn them?"

"There's some orange-pineapple juice in the refrigerator. Can I bring you a glass while I disrupt your entire worldview?"

"Yes, please."

Three minutes later, a glass in hand for each of us, Ephraim sits beside me on the sofa and begins the story of my life. "You and I share a calling, Tristan. An ability that you've just witnessed, something very few people in this world can do. Periodically, and without warning, you will receive visions in your mind of impending danger, sometimes to a friend or family member, other times to someone you've never met. These visions will always come in time for you to contact these individuals and warn them of what will happen. Unfortunately, you're part of a subset whose visions are accompanied by intense pain as a motivator to deliver the warning. The pain will begin to subside when you commit to delivering the warning, and the closer you get to your destination, the more the pain will subside."

"Destination?" I ask. "The phone is three feet away. Couldn't I just call this nursing home and say there's going to be a gas leak this afternoon?"

"You certainly could. Many of us take that path, but there's a catch: the likelihood of success is directly proportional to proximity. Think about it—an anonymous voice on the phone, speaking of danger that won't happen for hours or days? Most people would dismiss that as the words of a crackpot. But if the messenger travels for two hours or six hours or ten hours to deliver this message, allows the hearer to see his face, hear his voice, know the urgency of the warning—it can make all the difference. How many people were killed in the vision you just saw?"

"Dozens. Fifty or more."

"It's a staggering responsibility. I know. I did it for many years, until one day I said *no more.* Somebody got the message, and now I'm done with it."

"Free of it, I think you mean," I correct.

"In one sense, yes. But in another, I'm stripped of my responsibility. The knowledge that my actions can directly save a life. Sometimes I miss it."

He speaks of these things so calmly, so matter-of-factly. I can barely wrap my mind around them. "Would *why me* be too pathetic of a question?"

"Understandable, certainly. And there actually is an answer to that question, but I think I've blown significant enough quantities of your mind for one day. Besides, we have a little road trip to plan. It's about a three-hour drive, so we should get organized soon. I'll go with you."

"Thank you. And I'm sorry about the whole grabbing-you thing."

"Quite all right. No harm done."

"Unless you count my pride," I quip in reply.

"Indeed."

One lingering question remains, and as he turns to get ready, I verbalize it. "So … this is what I do now?"

He stops and turns back to me. "This is what you do now."

"I gave up the presidency of my own corporation, one my father built up from nothing, so I could receive anonymous warnings and then drop everything to go and save the lives of people I've never met?"

"That's about the size of it."

"Was I … was I any good at it?"

"One of the best," he replies before heading up the stairs to his room.

This is my path. It seems unlikely at best, impossible even. Equally troubling is my lack of knowledge of this path, the absence of memories. If this has overtaken my life, why wouldn't I have any recollection of previous trips, past warnings? What happened to my brain that this crucial part of my past—of my *present,* for Christ's sake—is closed off to me? I know I should feel honored at the privilege of preserving human life this way, but at the moment, all I feel is an imposition. Not the most noble of sentiments for someone in such a position of honor, but it's what I feel.

What will they say, these people who run this nursing home, after I drive two hundred miles and show up at their door, warning them to evacuate all the residents in anticipation of a gas leak and explosion that won't occur for hours? I know what I would say: "How would you know?" It's a question I dread; what possible answer could suffice? *"I have visions."* That's nice, but the twenty-first century has engendered a generation of skeptics, embracing science over mysticism. That's all I bring to the table, after all, mysticism. Prophecies and visions, crystal balls and tarot cards—

A memory stirs. Tarot cards. A hotel room somewhere. I'm seated in front of a deck of tarot cards, getting a reading, I presume. There's someone else in the room with me, a woman, I think, but I can't see her face clearly. I look down at the deck and see several different cards, but one stands out—a card called The Hanged Man—which, for some reason, appears several times. I try to focus on who's in the room with me, but I can't see the face, which brings with it a fresh round of pain in my head, alternating with the pain in my knee. I abandon the pursuit of the image, and the pain in my head begins to subside.

Ephraim comes halfway down the stairs to interrupt my thoughts. "Tristan, wheels up in ten minutes."

It's time.

Chapter 2

Wednesday, October 3, 2007

Ephraim

I know what you're thinking, so you don't even have to say it. *Look out, Tristan! Ephraim's lying. Don't trust him.* I'll grant you that it's a logical train of thought, given my previous encounters with him, but there are two sides to every story, and it's only right that I should tell mine. Suffice it to say that things aren't always what they seem, and people aren't always what they appear to be on first glance. I don't think of myself as evil; I don't know. I'm not a fan of such labels. It could be argued that I work for evil people, but even that isn't mine to judge.

At the moment, there's something far more pressing to attend to: keeping a nursing home full of people from being barbecued. Oh, and if you're thinking that the Social Darwinism Commission would consider that a prime demographic for letting nature take its course, you're right on the nose. One and a half million Americans are in nursing homes, essentially waiting to die. Their younger relatives, wracked with guilt for their elders' comfortable incarceration, visit sporadically out of a sense of duty. They dread the sterile white surroundings, the muted sounds of prolonged suffering, the smell of antiseptic competing with urine and blood and every other fluid that can leak out of a failing body. But mostly they dread the reminder: *You too, someday. Tick, tick, tick.*

It's an uncomfortable truth, but such are my thought processes. Part of my burden is looking beyond compassion into long-term practicality. I simultaneously see the transience and the permanence of human life—which is less of a contradiction in terms than people think. Most fail to distinguish between human life and *a* human life. I know the difference well, and it colors everything I do.

So it is with considerable restraint that I agree to accompany Tristan on this mission of alleged mercy. Were it not for the obvious pain that besieged him, I would be tempted to tell him that his visions were just a hallucination, spawned by his earlier head injury. Let the place explode; let the people go to their rest quickly, rather than through slow lingering. But no, the forces that employ us have decided that Tristan Shays is well enough to fulfill his calling once again, though it very nearly cost him his life last time.

He needs me there; I understand this. I also know the extent of his injuries—probably far better than he does. Had I arrived at Gnothautii headquarters even three minutes later, I likely would have had no chance of saving him. Foreknowledge does have its advantages; I've known for years that I would be there, in time to rescue him from the people who would try to steal his final breath.

For the first several days of his coma, the doctors at Johns Hopkins were unsure if he would ever awaken. The damage done to his brain was that devastating. In theory, the Gnothautii's procedure could actually have helped Tristan. It would have involved creating a disconnect between the part of his brain that was active during his visions and the part that processes pain. They were skilled enough surgeons to free him from that part of his burden. But then Karolena stepped in. (Speaking of evil.) Few people in this world genuinely scare me, but Karolena is at the top of the list. Most people, no matter how devious, how wicked their designs, they're driven by some explainable motivation. Maybe it's power, greed, bigotry, religious fervor, personal ambition, revenge;

it's something that can be examined and described and attributed. But with Karolena, she's like a destructive force of nature, like a storm that doesn't care who it kills. That's something you can't fight, something you can't beat. And she set her sights on Tristan Shays, for reasons that defy explanation.

My raid on Gnothautii headquarters wasn't a proud moment. Some people were killed who probably didn't have to die. They were following orders, after all, although when the orders are that insidious, I tend not to accept that as an excuse. But I couldn't leave any witnesses who could identify me to Karolena. She knows who I am, and if she found out I took down her operation, it would not end well for me. *End,* yes; *well,* no.

My thoughts are interrupted by Tristan coming down from upstairs. I'm surprised and gently amused to see a fire extinguisher in his hands. The expression on his face suggests that he's uncertain of the wisdom of carrying it. I try valiantly not to laugh openly at him, but something in my face makes him ask, "What?"

"Just wondering the reasons behind your choice of equipment there."

"In case we don't succeed in preventing the fire," he answers simply.

"Ah." I take the extinguisher from him and place it on the table. "You're thinking ahead; that's good. I respect that, and I mean it. But since we're in training mode, I'll share a few constructive reasons why it probably won't be a good thing to bring with you. Reason one: As you may have noticed, it's heavy. Heavy and bulky. We want to travel light, and lugging around a twenty-pound metal cylinder with a hose on it could potentially slow us down. Reason two: It sends a bad message. We want them to feel like we're there to prevent disaster. Walking in with an implement that's needed only if we fail undercuts our display of confidence a bit, I think you'd agree. And reason three: If things go pear-shaped and we need a fire extinguisher, I'm pretty sure they'll have one or two there for us to use."

"I suck at this," he says.

"Hardly. You're just out of practice. Come on, I'll drive, and we can work on that self-esteem of yours in the car."

I'm happy to do the driving to get us to Bethesda, Maryland. At this point, Tristan needs to focus. While it would make sense for me to take the lead on this mission, it wasn't assigned to me—a detail I noted with some interest, as he and I have been given a number of identical assignments in the past. But this is my chance to observe him in the field as he gets back on his feet. I need to monitor his progress following the head injury—determine if he's truly ready for this. I won't let him get too deep into the weeds; a failure at this critical juncture could permanently damage his confidence, after all.

Traffic is light for an early Wednesday afternoon, which is good. Less to distract us. "Tell me what's most pressing in your thoughts," I invite.

Tristan thinks a moment. "I'm frustrated because even though you tell me I've done this before and I know what I'm doing, it feels so unknown, so unfamiliar."

"Understandable."

"And what? They couldn't start me off with a cat stuck in a tree? It has to be deep-fried senior citizens if I fail?"

"Would it help if I told you that our employer wouldn't send you if he didn't think you were ready?"

"It should help," he says, "but given that I'm still scared shitless and 90 percent sure that I'll fail, it's cold comfort."

"I know you're looking to me for what to do today, and I will be there by your side for this, but the majority of what happens has to come from you."

"What?" He sounds distressed at this announcement. "Why?"

"It's your first time back at this, and it's important for me to know how much of it you've retained …"

"I can answer that right now," he replies. "None of it. I'm going into this with no recollection of what to say, no memory of what to do, and that terrifies me."

"Use that fear. When we get there, let it motivate you."

"Please tell me you did not just say that. Let my fear motivate me? Next you'll be telling me to buy your inspirational tapes for just thirty-nine ninety-five."

"Scoff all you want," I answer calmly, "but it's good advice. You, my dear cousin, overthink things. It's your trademark. Today, you need to put that thinking aside and *feel.* Fear lives inside you at a very primal, instinctive level. Tap into that, and you'll know what to say and what to do—better than if you spent the entire drive working things out."

He laughs a little at my words. "Huh. Instinctive level. You sound just like ..."

At that, he stops. My heart stalls for an instant at his hesitation, as I wonder if his memory will let him go there. Though it's gently dangerous, I prompt him just a little. "Just like who?"

With my peripheral vision, I watch the conflict unfold on his face. My words have clearly triggered a memory, but his eyes tell me he doesn't have access to it. "I don't know," he finally answers. "Someone I heard once. Talking about instinct and emotional response. Sounds like a lot of new-age malarkey to me."

I let it go. He can only be talking about Genevieve Swan, and as much as I hope the words would trigger a breakthrough, this isn't the time. Courtesy of my own manipulated brain, I know that his memory recall is coming. I've lived through it, though it's yet to happen. And I know that it will be very painful and very necessary. Just not today.

His words need a reply. "Entertain the possibility, at least. Since I'm determined to be a heartless bastard and not hand you a script, at least try tapping into that reserve of emotional response. Humor me?"

"Promise me that when we get there," he says, "if I falter, you'll back me up so that no one gets hurt."

"I promise—on the condition that you give it your best effort first. If that doesn't work, I'll do everything I can."

I know that my plan is unfair to him, bordering on cruel, but in its own way, it is a kindness. It would be very easy for me to take charge of this mission, say and do the necessary things, while Tristan stands back and watches; but I have to believe that he was chosen for a reason, that he needs to be the one to help these people.

There's so much I want to tell him, so many things I'd like to explain. He's been through a lot of shit, some of it because of me. And I know some of what's to come. Things he couldn't possibly imagine. What could I tell him, though? We go through our whole lives never knowing what tomorrow brings. Sometimes, through a defect in the way of things, we get a glimpse of our own future. I got the whole picture—how I'll live, where I'll go, how I'll die. And before you go thinking that's fascinating knowledge or that it's in any way comforting, let me just say that it's not.

The remainder of the drive to Bethesda is rather quiet. I know there's more to say, but not here and now. On Tristan's face, I see a similar desire for conversation, but he suppresses it too, hopefully to focus on tapping into those instincts inside of him.

At 3:45 in the afternoon, we turn onto Transept Street and enter the parking lot of the Magnolia Orchard Senior Care Facility. We still have forty-five minutes before the place is supposed to turn into a geriatric inferno, and everything looks damnably normal. I wish life were like the movies, and a building would give off an aura of evil and foreboding before tragedy strikes. But no such luck. Only Tristan and I know what awaits this place and the people inside it if we're unsuccessful.

Tristan gets out of the car and stands staring at the entrance to the building like it's the gates of hell itself. As for me, I'm reading the place as if I'm holding the owner's manual. *Three-story brick building with lots of glass windows. Brick is better than wood frame, as it won't burn as quickly as wood. But we're dealing with a potential explosion here, rather than a regular structure fire, so the brick becomes a pile of missiles, and those lovely windows turn into knifelike shards waiting to slice through anyone within reach. Three-story building means two floors of residents above the ground level, and more than likely a limited number of elevators. With only forty-five minutes, evacuation would be a logistical nightmare; probably flat-out impossible. That takes it off the table, leaving prevention as our only option. Which means we have to be quick and convincing. If we're not, there's no room for plan B, except to get the hell out of there without getting caught in the explosion.*

I look over at my cousin, try to read the thoughts behind his expression. Since they're not talking, I have to ask. "Tell me what you're thinking."

"I didn't have lunch," he says quietly. "I realize I'm a little hungry."

Not the answer I was hoping for. "Look at me," I say, standing right in front of him. I personally hate it when people do the "look at me" thing when they speak, but just this once, I think it's necessary. "You need to focus. I've got your back, but you're the one to make this happen today. Right here, right now. I've surveyed the scene, and our one option is preventing the explosion. Are you with me?"

"So you don't think they might have a cafeteria?"

He's using humor to defuse his fear, which would be absolutely adorable, were it not for the scores of members of the Greatest Generation who will be horribly immolated if I don't get him focused.

"Tristan, when this is over, I'll get you all the pickled herring and tapioca pudding you can eat. For the moment, however, I need your mind on other things, so I'm afraid the only thing I have for you at present is this." Without another word, I draw back my open right hand and deliver a powerful slap to his face, strong enough to knock him backward against the car door. For a few seconds, he looks stunned—literally and figuratively—but he quickly recovers and looks at his wristwatch.

"It's 3:45," he says. "We don't have a lot of time."

"Welcome back," I reply with a little smile. "And you're quite correct. What's the plan?"

He thinks a moment, but not too much, I notice. *Good, he's paying attention.*

"The explosion is going to be in the boiler room, in the basement of the facility. We need to get to it first and stop it from happening. But I'm guessing there's no way we could find it on our own, let alone get to it unaccompanied. So that means we're going to need help. But who?"

"You tell me," I reply.

"Janitor?"

"Aim a bit higher."

"Director of the facility?"

"Maybe a little too high. Think keys, access, and knowledge."

"Facilities manager," he says. Sounds like a winner to me.

"Good. Be confident, and don't take no for an answer."

We enter the nursing home by the front door and go immediately to the reception desk. Behind it is a woman working on a computer. After a few seconds' delay while she finishes a task, she looks up at us and asks, "Can I help you?"

I remain quiet, inspiring Tristan to step up, which he does with a nearly imperceptible hesitation. "Hi, good afternoon. Is there a way we could speak to your facilities manager? I'm sorry, we don't have this person's name."

"Do you have an appointment?" she asks, quite reasonably.

"I'm afraid we don't."

"He doesn't take sales calls without an appointment."

Tristan interrupts her, politely but firmly. "Ah, I see. This isn't a sales call. It's a matter of public safety, and we'll just need a few minutes of his time."

"Safety?" she repeats, with an expression that doesn't suggest an abundance of impending cooperation. "Safety like how?"

"We received a call from a staff member who was concerned about the level of natural gas on the premises," he says, struggling to stay calm. "Our group works quietly with facilities managers when we get these calls, so we can take care of the issue before it becomes a problem."

"There's procedures we have to follow."

"I understand that, and I respect it," Tristan says, lowering his voice, "but take a look around you. You've got residents out in the halls. Family members visiting them. Our goal when we inspect a site is to keep things very quiet, not cause any concern, any panic. We find that on almost every occasion, we're able to take care of the problem before it gets out of hand and anyone has to expend the slightest amount of worry. So what do you say? Do you suppose you could arrange for us to meet with your facilities manager for just a couple of minutes?"

She looks frustrated as she answers, "He's on a break right now. With something like this, I have to run it past the director first, and then, if she ..."

This is taking too long. It's time for me to interrupt. I pull a small, rectangular electronic instrument out of my pocket. "This device," I say to her, "detects levels of natural gas in the air. A green light means a healthy level. Yellow means elevated, and red means dangerously elevated. Let's take a reading, shall we? Right here at your desk." I press the button, and a red light illuminates on the face of the device and into my palm. She and Tristan stare at it, until she stands and says, "I'll go find him. Please wait here."

The receptionist hurries away from her desk, and I place the device back in my pocket. After a moment, Tristan quietly says to me, "And that would be a ...?"

"Laser pointer," I answer.

"Mm-hmm. Always gives off a red light, I trust?"

"Oh, yes."

"Thought you were letting me take this one."

"I am. I just brought the props."

"What do we do when he gets here?"

"Convince him," I answer calmly. "In a tone of helpfulness. We're his friends, and this is all routine business. Clear?"

"Clear."

The receptionist returns three minutes and forty-two seconds later with a short man in a blue button-down shirt, who looks like his name should be Tony. "I'm Tony Parker, the facilities manager," he says. "Renee tells me there's a problem?"

"Nice to meet you, Tony," Tristan answers without introducing himself. "Not a problem; more of a concern. Someone at the facility smelled natural gas, and they called us to come and take a reading. We found elevated levels and decided we should speak with you."

"And where are you from exactly?" he asks in a very defensive tone.

Tristan's answer doesn't come immediately, so I step in, offering the most non-threatening name I can concoct. "Safe-Air Industries. We're a state nonprofit group, offering assistance to facilities managers like yourself."

The innocuous name does nothing to soften his suspicions. "I've never heard of you."

"That means you're running a tight ship around here," Tristan offers quickly. *Kudos to the cousin on swiftness of bullshit.*

"Who called you?" the irrepressibly charming manager asks, sounding ready to pick a fight with whichever octogenarian squealed.

"It's anonymous," I answer. "I assure you, no one's here to bust anyone's chops. We want what you want: the safety of this building and its residents and staff. Give us two minutes of your time, and no one even has to know that we were here."

Despite the kindest smiles on both of our faces, Tony the facilities manager still looks like he wants to take us out to the parking lot, kick our asses, and steal our lunch money. But there is a subtle yet perceptible threat to Tristan's message if he *doesn't* give us two minutes of his time, and it's not lost on our new buddy. "Where do we need to go?" he asks quietly, mostly containing the menace in his voice.

"The boiler room is always a likely place," Tristan says. "Why don't we start there?"

"Follow me."

He leads us to a door that says "Authorized Personnel Only," unlocks it with a key, and takes us down a flight of stairs into the nursing home's basement, which looks like it would be right at home in the bowels of a battleship in the 1940s. The only light is supplied by bare bulbs on dangling cords or in metal cages clamped to the walls. Large pipes and conduits span overhead, each bearing a warning that the world will probably end if the contents escape.

"I gotta tell ya," he says as we continue, "I don't smell anything."

"We'll be very pleased if there's no cause for actual concern," I reply pleasantly. "Always better to check these things out in person, though."

"I wish they'd come to me first. I don't understand why people don't just talk to me. I'm not hard to talk to, am I?"

The question comes out as threatening as a fully loaded knuckle sandwich, so we both opt to answer, "No, no. Not at all."

At the door to the boiler room, I smell it for the first time—gas. More to the point, since natural gas is odorless, the sulfur they add to it for just such an occasion. The look on Tony's face says that he smells it too—and that it is quite unexpected. I hear him utter a single syllable, more to himself than to us. "Huh."

He opens the door to the boiler room, and upon seeing what awaits us, I am unbelievably thankful that the light in that room is already on. If he'd had to flip a switch, the three of us and everyone else within a hundred feet would be dancing on a cloud right now.

The boiler itself is a monster—huge and old, resembling a doomsday device ready to go off, which, at the moment, is an incredibly apt comparison. A half-inch gas line feeds it from the side, and the three of us fixate immediately on the pipe. Somehow, there is an actual bubble of gas, easily a foot in diameter, protruding from a hole in the pipe. I've never seen anything like it, and from Tony's reaction, neither has he.

"Holy fuck!" he shouts, quickly but gently shutting the boiler room door. Without another word to us, he runs down the hall to a master control room and frantically shuts off the gas to the boiler and to the nursing home at large. He then picks up a phone and dials a four-digit extension. "It's Tony. I'm downstairs, and ... we just averted a crisis, maybe a disaster. We've got a serious gas leak to the boiler, but I managed to get it shut down in time. I'm going to call the gas company here in a second, but in the meantime, it's likely to get cold in here. We need to break out space heaters, and let the kitchen staff know that they won't have access to the stove or hot water until this thing is fixed. I'll let you know what happens."

He hangs up, presumably from a call to the director, and turns to face us. "Looks like I owe you fellas an apology. I doubted you, and if you hadn't shown up, I don't even wanna think about what could've happened."

"Not a problem," Tristan says. "Just doing our job."

"That just leaves the question of who you really are," Tony says.

"What do you mean?" I ask.

"When I said upstairs that I've never heard of Safe-Air Industries, I was giving you a chance to tell me what I already know: there's no such thing. It's my job to know these things. Renee at the desk doesn't know that, but it's not her responsibility; it's mine."

"If you knew we were making it up," Tristan begins, "why did you take us down here?"

"There had to be a reason. You don't act like terrorists, so I figured you knew something was wrong before I did. Doesn't happen often, I'll say that. But you saw what was in there. That's not something you see every day. Or any day, for that matter."

"What exactly was that in that room?" Tristan asks.

"A gas bubble. Line to the boiler must have cracked, and it was letting out enough gas to form a bubble. The gas company'll be able to work with me to keep it from happening again. Wouldn't have taken much to set off an explosion. It would've taken out the whole building, I think."

"Well, fortunately, that didn't happen."

"Still doesn't answer my question," Tony adds as we turn to leave. "About who you are and how you knew about this. Nobody comes down to the basement except me and my staff, and I promise you, any of my people who smelled gas down here would either go get me or take care of it themselves. So, what does that leave? Angels? Psychics? Time travelers? I've read a lot of books. I can believe a lot of explanations."

Tristan does his best to field this one. "None of the above. We just know sometimes when something bad is going to happen, and we do our best to keep it from happening."

"I'll be damned. I didn't think that sort of thing really happened."

"Neither did I."

"How do you—"

Before he can finish, I say to him, "I think it's more important that you call the gas company and get them over here. It's going to be cold tonight, and I expect people will want their dinner."

"Yeah, yeah, right," he says, almost as if he'd forgotten the potential crisis at hand.

"We'll show ourselves out."

We leave Tony to his phone call and move swiftly to the stairs. Even with the gas turned off, I want plenty of space between us and that boiler. Safely back on the ground floor, Tristan asks me, "So what happens now?"

"We head home."

"That's it? No follow-up, no aftermath?"

"That's the good part about working for celestial forces: a sublime lack of paperwork. The mission successfully completed, we collect our thanks—or lack thereof—and get out of here."

He eyes a corner of the lobby. "I think I'll avail myself of the restroom before we go. Bit of a drive ahead of us."

"I'll be outside in the parking lot. I'll meet you there."

Outside, I find an unoccupied corner of the parking lot and take out my phone. The number I need is neither memorized nor programmed in, but I have it on a slip of paper in my wallet. I dial the number and proceed in a voice that is all business. "Don't talk, just listen. I think you know who this is. I have information that may interest you. Tristan Shays is alive and recovering from his injuries. I also happen to know that he's back in the business of delivering messages. I can lead you to him, but it has to be on my terms. You have to prove to me that you're worthy of this gift. I will call you periodically, and I'll also be watching you. If you demonstrate to me that you've earned it, I will bring him to you myself. You've disappointed me gravely in the past. Don't disappoint me this time."

Chapter 3

Thursday, October 4, 2007

Tristan

The following morning, I'm still gently dazed by the whole concept of these missions. By all accounts, yesterday was a success. We warned the people, we seemed to avert a disaster, and no one caused us any trouble. I should be delighted at the way things turned out, and yet ...

And yet what's obvious to me is how incapable I felt while all of this was going on. It was like being on my first mission again. Fortunately, this time I had Ephraim to rely on. His help yesterday made all the difference, and I'm feeling much better about him than I felt before. I know I won't always have him with me, so I have to make the most of the time that he is here. Which means today is dedicated to training. We begin at the dining room table.

"You have to think of your job in terms of one word," Ephraim begins. "Specificity. For example, you're there to stop *one* particular person from walking into a building that's going to collapse. You're not there to stop everyone; you're not there to stop the building from collapsing. And you're not there to put the fire out or help people once it does. That said, you're certainly welcome to help other people out of the goodness of your heart, if your heart is feeling goodness that day. But it all starts and ends with the specifics of your mission. Pay close attention to the details. Names, faces, locations, times. It all matters."

"What if it's not clear when the details arrive?" I ask.

"Then you need to clear your mind and try to focus on whatever's missing. If you have no distractions, you should be able to pick up the details better."

"What about the pain?" I ask him. "Why does it hurt so much when these assignments come in?"

His face tells me he was anticipating that question and that he doesn't have a good answer. "All I can tell you is that some messengers are stricken with pain until they accept their mission. It's a motivator, to make sure we put this ahead of everything else. I'm sorry you have to endure it."

"I wish I could explain to you what that felt like."

"You don't have to," he says. "I've felt it. Early on, when I received assignments, they came with pain. And later, for other reasons, I experienced the pain again. So please believe me when I tell you that I know what you're going through."

"Is there a way to prevent it?"

"The brain injury you sustained, the medical procedure that nearly killed you, was done in the pursuit of stopping that pain, so any attempts to stop it again are dangerous and should be avoided. Some of us find ways to embrace the mission, which makes the pain stop. Others will always suffer it. The best thing you can do is focus through the pain, acknowledge the mission, and start on it as quickly as possible."

"Then there's the whole issue of my competence—or lack thereof."

"You know how to do this, Tristan. You just don't have access to the memories that prove it. So we'll work on it. Stand up." I stand, and he does as well, facing me. "Role-playing time. I'm Mr. Wallace Wilson of Albuquerque, New Mexico, and you've received an assignment to warn me that at 7:15 tonight, my house is going to catch fire because of something I left burning on the stove. Now come to my door and warn me."

I feel stupid. I don't want to sound ungrateful, but I wish there was a way I could express this to Ephraim without hurting his feelings.

"I feel stupid," I say to him.

"I can live with that," he replies. "You can feel stupid in private here with me, so you don't feel stupid out there, in the field. Come on. Approach my door."

Swallowing the feelings of embarrassment, I knock on the table. Though he is standing inches away from me, Ephraim looks away and doesn't answer. I knock again, louder. Still no answer.

"I'm knocking," I tell him.

"It's a big house. I can't hear you. Ring the bell."

Jesus Christ.

I put out my middle finger (a deliberate choice) and push. "Ding-dong."

He mimes opening a door and looks at me suspiciously. "Yes?"

"Mr. Wilson? Wallace Wilson?"

"That's right," he says. "Who are you?"

"My name is Tristan Shays."

"Nope," he says, breaking character. "Don't give them your real name. Too much room for trouble. Make something up long before you see them, and make sure you remember it well. Don't change names in midstream. And don't give the same alias to different people. Let's try this again: That's right. Who are you?"

"My name is … John Smith." He shakes his head. "Duncan … Donuts?" Another shake of the head. "Charles Astor." That gets a nod.

"I don't know anyone named Charles Astor. Why are you here?"

"I'm here because you're in danger …"

"Good," he says, again as himself, "but a little quick. Lead with the apologetic intro."

"And that would be …?"

"Remember, you're here as an agent of forces that are close to unexplainable. You want to lead with something that says 'this sounds impossible, but …'; something that says you don't know quite how this happened, but you've been given privileged information. Tell them that you mean them no harm; quite the opposite, you're here to help them. And most importantly, you don't want anything from them. Then talk about the specifics of the danger." He sees the self-doubt wallpapered all over my face. "You're doing fine. It'll come back to you." He gets back into the persona of Wallace Wilson. "I don't know any Charles Astor. Why are you here?"

Okay, here goes. "Mr. Wilson, what I'm about to tell you will sound strange, and honestly, I'm not quite sure myself how I know this information. But sometimes I get visions, I guess you could call them. Warnings that someone is in danger. And I get those warnings in time to go and tell the person, so they can prevent the danger from happening. I got a vision of you, Mr. Wilson, a vision that told me that at 7:15 tonight, you'll accidentally leave something burning on the stove, and it will start a fire that will consume your house. I don't want that to happen, so I hope you'll do whatever's necessary to prevent it."

"That's crazy," he says. "There's no way you could know that."

"And yet I do."

"Are you a neighbor of mine? Are you spying on me?"

"No, sir. In fact, I live in Maryland."

"Maryland?" he interrupts. "For God's sake, if you knew so much about me, why didn't you just pick up the phone and spare yourself the trip?"

It's a very good question, one I feel like I should know the answer to. Because I don't, I give Ephraim an inquisitive look, and he tells me, "You know why. It's like we discussed. Find the logical reason."

As if opening the drawer in my mind in which the answer is kept, I tell him, "I could have called you, but it's so important that you believe me, I traveled all the way across the country to tell you in person. I don't want anything from you, and you don't ever have to see me again, but please, for your own safety, be cautious with the stove tonight."

"I will. I think you should go now."

"Yes, sir. I'll go. Be well, Mr. Wilson."

He mimes closing the door and offers a slight smile. "How did I do?" I ask hopefully.

"For the words, A. For the presentation, C."

"C? What went wrong?"

"It's in the delivery, Tristan. If you ring somebody's doorbell and tell them the pizza they've ordered is there, it's no big deal. You're holding the pizza; they can smell it. Ring somebody's doorbell and tell them they're going to burn to death tonight if they don't heed the warning you've brought them straight from God, and it's another story. There's no pizza for them to smell."

"At least the religious fanatics will believe me, right?"

"They're some of the worst. They get very pissy when they think God is talking to you and not them."

"Great."

"You have to make up for the missing details with your attitude and your presentation," he says. "Lead with the apologetic intro, yes, but even as you do, show 100 percent belief in the reality of your message. Let your every word, facial expression, gesture, and action tell this person unquestionably that you are the only thing in the universe that can save their life."

"Can I do that?"

"I've seen you do it. You just have to do what you do already: believe in the reality of what you're telling them. If you saw that somebody was about to step in front of a speeding car, you'd warn them without even hesitating. Same principle applies. You can simply see the speeding car long before they can."

"This is hard," I mutter, sounding a bit more like an eight-year-old with math homework than I'm comfortable admitting.

"Then we practice until you feel like it's easier. Switch places this time. You're Mr. Peter Schmidt of Dover, Delaware, and I'm coming to warn you that you're going to be attacked by a dangerous dog."

Friday, October 12, 2007

The week that follows is peaceful. Despite two days of training and practice, I receive no assignments to put them to the test. With my luck, I won't receive any more, and all the training will have been for nothing. It has been a time of healing, though, and for this I am grateful. I can feel myself getting stronger, not tired all the time like I was just a week or two ago. I thought it was going to feel strange having Ephraim around so much of the time, but I'm getting used to it. Sometimes he'll disappear for a couple of hours and not say where he's going, but he really isn't obligated to tell me. Hell, he's not obligated to even be here taking care of me, so I don't ask about his whereabouts. He's a big boy.

Curiously, though, that expectation is not reciprocated. Anytime I tell him I'm going out somewhere by myself, he wants to know where I'm going and when I'll be back. When I jokingly remind him that I don't have a curfew, he quite humorlessly reminds me that I'm still recuperating, and as my primary caregiver, he needs to know where I'll be. The idea doesn't delight me, but there's a certain degree of sense to it. So I carry a cell phone when I go out, and he checks in on me periodically. And I keep my annoyance to myself, in the interest of good family relations.

Memories are starting to come back to me. Not the big, important ones, unfortunately. Primarily little ones. I'll taste something, presuming it's for the first time, and then remember that I've enjoyed it for years. I'll start to read a book from my shelves and, just a few pages in, realize that I know the entire story. It feels odd and a bit disconcerting, but I have to believe it's a good sign and that with enough time to recuperate, I'll have access once again to all the aspects of my life that are currently closed off to me.

It is a brisk Friday morning, only about fifty degrees outside, but I'm on the beach behind my home. The ocean is unspeakably beautiful, and it beckons me like a loving mother to her child. Some days I can stand or sit out here for hours, alone and silent, without a care in the world, watching the waves roll to shore. Today is one such day.

To millions of American workers, Friday is like the steps to the sacred shrine known as the weekend. They show up for their jobs, half-distracted all day with the plans for upcoming recreation. To me, in my new circumstances, Friday is just another day. I have no job to report to, and my unofficial position could just as easily summon me at 2:30 on a Saturday morning as at 9:00 a.m. on a Monday.

But even that hasn't been an issue for more than a week. God and his little angels are giving Tristan Shays a break to heal up, and it's appreciated. Sure, the excursion to the nursing home was exciting, and it felt great knowing we were saving people from a horrible fate, but I can't imagine having to do that every day. It would be exhausting, mentally and physically. Hell, coming up with a new alias alone would be taxing. So if I'm on a mini-sabbatical, I accept.

Quite without warning, I learn that the world has other plans for me. Beginning with my arms and traveling quickly to the rest of my body, my skin feels like it is on fire. Not like a sunburn or anything reasonable and explainable. Instead, I feel like someone has slathered kerosene on me like massage oil and then struck a match. In response, I do the thoughtful, analytical thing and begin screaming my goddamn head off.

In less than a minute, I am aware of Ephraim rushing to my side. I'm also aware that he's holding a pen and a pad of paper. I am running back and forth down the beach, as if I could somehow run far enough away from myself that it won't hurt.

"Where?" he asks.

"Everywhere!" I reply, not slowing down in my travels.

"No, not where does it hurt. Where do you have to go?"

This stops me from running, if not from hurting. "You mean this is—?"

"Unless you're prone to sudden attacks of random agony in other circumstances. Do what we talked about: try to forget the pain long enough to focus on the mission. Speak the pictures that come into your mind, and I'll take them down."

Despite the all-encompassing pain, I try my hardest to find a place of Zen, where I can communicate the details that accompanied this unprovoked attack on me. Images begin to form, and with them, words, as if written on paper for me to read. "Ohio," I verbalize. "Pressman,

Ohio. The campus of Pressman College. Tonight at 9:32, a nineteen-year-old student named Benjamin Holloway is going to die doing something called a … a keg stand? What the hell is that?" Ephraim takes this all down, and before he can answer, I see a vision of this student, standing on his hands, upside down on top of a beer keg, drinking from it. He loses his balance and falls to his death. "Now I see it. How fucking reckless and stupid." The images fade, but the pain doesn't, until I shout out, "All right, all right, I'll take the assignment!" In seconds, I begin to feel relief.

"Let's get you inside," Ephraim says. As we're walking back to the house, with him supporting me just a bit, he correctly points out, "Ohio is a long way away, particularly if we're driving. We need to leave very soon if we're going to make it there in time."

Once inside, he deposits me on the living room sofa and disappears to the kitchen long enough to get a cool, wet dish towel, which he then places over my forehead and eyes. "Does that feel better?" he asks.

"Actually, it does."

"I'll take the first driving shift, until the pain you're feeling subsides a bit more. Then we can trade off."

"What if we … don't go?"

"Excuse me?" He heard me; I know he did. His question is one of disbelief.

"What if we don't go and prevent this? What will happen to me?"

"You'll spend the next twelve hours in increasingly terrible agony, and a young man will die who could otherwise be saved. Why are you asking me this?"

"It seems so stupid. Why should we drive across three states to save some goddamn college kid from killing himself during a drinking game?"

"Because you were sent to. Presumably by someone who has a very good reason. We're just not allowed to know what it is."

"Yeah?" I reply, not convinced. "Well, maybe Darwin was right."

Inexplicably, I am doubled over with a different kind of pain. Where the pain of the new assignment was attacking my skin, this hits my head, my brain, my soul itself, like the words are some kind of trigger against me.

"Those words hurt you, didn't they?" Ephraim asks. There's something in his tone, a confusing air of self-satisfaction, almost like he's glad I'm hurting.

"What's happening to me?" I ask, in too much agony to even open my eyes.

"Your nature is at war with itself. Your questioning of this assignment has started a battle in your mind. It's linked to memories you can't yet access because you're not ready. But you're getting close, and you've picked at something that hasn't healed yet. Trust me: this is a wound you don't want to re-open. Take the assignment, Tristan. Save the stupid college boy from doing something stupid. And trust that the one who sends you is sending you for a reason. Repeat it over and over in your thoughts: *I accept my mission.* I'll go get the car ready. We need to leave in the next fifteen minutes."

He walks away, and I let my thoughts repeat: *I accept my mission.* What caused that pain? *I accept my mission.* Was it the doubt? *I accept my mission.* The defiance of my assignment? *I accept my mission.* What is it about the words "maybe Darwin was right" that turned everything so … dark?

I'm in the car, and this is jarring. I have no memory of leaving the house and getting in the car, yet here I am. And not just sitting in a parked car in my driveway. When things come into focus, I realize that I have no idea where we are. I look over at Ephraim, who is calmly driving. The sudden motion from my side of the car prompts him to greet me. "Welcome back," he says cordially.

"Wh- where are we?"

"Virginia. They say it's for lovers. Odd choice, given the whole 'virgin' thing, but who am I to question a state slogan?"

"How did we get here?" I ask, still feeling very disoriented.

With his hands at ten and two on the steering wheel, and with a little smile, he makes drivey-drivey motions with the wheel. We wobble gently in the lane.

"Yes, yes, I realize that. What I mean is, the last thing I remember, I was accepting my mission on the couch, and now, seemingly seconds later, we're in Virginia."

"That was three hours ago, sport. You needed rest, so I let you rest."

"So you're telling me I, what, sleepwalked to the car and got in?"

"For lack of a tidier explanation, yes. I told you these assignments will still kick your ass for a while. I'm fine driving for now, so if you want to go back to sleep, you're welcome to. We still have at least eight hours until we get there."

"Eight? Doesn't Jesus have a nationwide network of people who could come from someplace closer?"

He laughs a little at my question. "You're closer to the truth than you realize. But sometimes it's about more than just geography. Our employer knows exactly who is available for every circumstance, where they are, and what they're doing. Take into account how many situations are happening around the country on any given day. Then factor in how relatively few of us there are, and it's not always a matter of picking the poor sap who's in the next town over. He might be seventy-two years old, have questionable hygiene, and give people the creeps immediately upon meeting them. Not exactly who you want to send to a college campus to earn the victim's trust."

"So, how many of us are there?" I ask. "You said there's relatively few. Does that mean a dozen? A hundred? A thousand?"

"That's a good question. Your thought processes are strong; I'm pleased to hear it. And I wish I could give you an answer. Honestly, I don't know. If I had to guess, here in the States I'd say hundreds who know about it and a couple thousand who don't. They get the messages and dismiss them, disregard them, think they're losing their minds. A few even take their own lives because they don't know what to do with this ability."

"Devin Larimer." The words come out quietly, subconsciously.

"Who?"

"Back when I first started getting these visions, I searched for anyone who was going through what I was going through. I remember now that I found an article about someone named Devin Larimer, who had similar circumstances. But it was too much for him, and he killed himself. I had forgotten that, but now I remember it."

"That's good."

"And it makes me wonder if I'll do the same thing someday."

"That's not so good. For what it's worth, Tristan, I never met this Devin Larimer, but I suspect you're a great deal stronger than he was mentally. Before your injury, you had dedicated yourself to this life. You were prepared to spend whatever it took—time, money, energy—to help strangers, without promise of compensation or even an explanation as to why."

"That sounds noble," I reply. "It doesn't sound like me."

"Meaning you don't think of yourself as noble?"

"Meaning precisely that. All my life, I've done the things I've done because it brings me something—money, status, recognition, respect. I'm sorry if that sounds shallow, but it's how I was brought up. My parents were power players, and they taught me—directly and indirectly—that there's no profit margin in nobility, certainly none in altruism." He says nothing in response to this. "Hope I haven't shattered your illusions of me."

"Not irreparably. I've known *of* you for several years; *known* you considerably less. In that time, I've built up a certain set of qualities that I perceive in you. It's a bit jarring to hear you contradict them this way. If it gets to be too disruptive, I can always ascribe it to humility and continue to admire you quietly."

I shake my head at this. "You're a strange man, Shays."

He smiles just a little. "You have no idea, Shays."

After another hour of driving, I take over behind the wheel, giving Ephraim a chance for some much-needed rest. We don't talk much while I'm driving. Occasionally, I'll look over at him and see that he's dozing off. It's fine; I don't need small talk at present anyway.

About an hour and a half later, I see a sign at the side of the highway advertising Dinah's Diner at the next exit in two miles. I know nothing about the place, but it sounds really good. "Are you hungry?" I ask my traveling companion.

"I could eat, I suppose."

"Do we have time to?"

He looks at his watch. "If we don't do three courses of fondue, then yes, we have time for something beyond grab-and-go. The diner at the next exit?"

"That's what I'm thinking. Is that acceptable?"

"Let's give it a shot."

I get off at the exit and follow the signs north for a quarter mile, straight to the parking lot of Dinah's Diner. It lacks elegance, but what it does have is a good number of cars in the parking lot, most with in-state license plates. That's good enough for me. "Shall we?" I ask.

"Onward."

We get out of the car and lock it up, heading to the entrance. Before we can enter, we are intercepted by a man in well-worn clothing and an old overcoat. He is old, probably in his seventies, barely groomed, and in need of a shave. He smells vaguely of grass and potatoes. In one hand, he holds a bible, its pages curled from use, its cover starting to deteriorate. A few feet from the entrance to the building, he puts his free hand on my shoulder and looks me in the eyes. "God is smiling down on you today," he says, quite unasked.

"That's good to know," I answer, cordially but without inviting further conversation, because—dude, seriously.

"You do his work, and you have his blessing."

"Thank you," I reply, not knowing what else to say to such a statement. He's not asking for money or anything else.

He next pats me on the shoulder twice and says, "Don't fall in love."

Before I can even figure out what he means by this, Ephraim says to him, "Uhh, no, no. Too soon."

"Hmm?" he says. "Oh, sorry. Bye-bye, then!"

And with that, the strange man walks away, out of the parking lot and down the road, as if this were the most natural conversation in the world. Ephraim leads the way back toward the door, but I have to ask, "What was that about?"

"That? Nothing. Just a well-wisher."

"A well-wisher who comes up to us and us alone, speaks about God blessing us as we do his work, and then mysteriously warns me not to fall in love, for some reason."

Opening the door for us, Ephraim says, "The elderly. You never know what they'll say."

I follow him in. "That's a lovely explanation, except that you left out the part about your reply."

"Did I?" he asks nonchalantly. He tells the hostess, "Two, please. A booth in the nonsmoking section, if one's available."

As we follow her back to a corner of the diner, I continue. "Yes. You told him it was too soon."

"Hmm. Imagine that."

"As if this man was supposed to give me that message, but not yet. So tell me, dear cousin, who am I not supposed to fall in love with, and when?"

A portrait of evasion, he holds up the menu and points to a picture. "The chocolate-and-peanut-butter pie. Enjoy it, but don't fall in love, because who knows if we'll ever come back to this diner."

I am, at least, impressed by the swiftness of this completely invented answer. "You're totally full of shit, aren't you?" I ask.

"How about we accept that as an answer for now, believing that another answer involving your future circumstances would only make your head hurt."

His suggestion makes a great deal of sense, but it still bothers me tremendously. "You know, don't you, that I hate it when you know more about my own life than I do."

"Order the pie. It'll help with that."

As we wait for our order—yes, including the pie—to arrive, I ask Ephraim, "So, any words of wisdom for tonight?"

"Plenty. But you're going to give them to me, rather than the other way around. Use what we've gone through, and tell me how tonight will go down."

"No fair. I didn't know there was going to be a test."

"Yes you did," he replies pleasantly.

I gather my thoughts and engage the rational side of my brain. "Okay, college campus, Friday night, about midway through the fall term. Students everywhere. Classes are over for the week; it's time for the weekend. Time to study. By which I mean party their asses off. This is supposed to happen around 9:30 in the evening; still quite early by college student standards. Maybe there'll be fewer people out and about at that hour. Our boy is doing a keg stand. That's not something you do by yourself or with one or two friends. Keg stand means keg, which means lots of people drinking beer. A dorm party, or more likely, a fraternity party. We should try to find out if he belongs to a fraternity; if so, I bet that's where he'll be. How am I doing so far?"

"Spot on. What else?"

"Finding him is only half the battle. After that, we have to be admitted into wherever he is and then convince him that we're there to save his life. Plus, it's probably not a good idea to do that in a room full of his drunken friends. So we need to tear an intoxicated teenager away from his intoxicated friends, take him someplace private, and tell him that he's about to snuff it. All without looking like kidnappers or sexual deviants. Have I omitted anything?"

"Probably a few little details here and there, but the outline is quite thorough."

Our salads arrive, and we dig in.

"Any suggestions on how we *overcome* these little challenges?" I ask, hoping he won't counter by saying *You tell me.*

"You tell me."

Fuck.

"Okay, let's see. Obstacle one, finding him. Before we get to campus, we stop someplace with a computer terminal and Internet access, and we look him up. We see if he belongs to a fraternity, and if not, try to find out anything about him that will help us locate him once we get there. Failing that, we just search the campus for a keg party and hope like hell that we find him. These parties are sometimes pretty controlled about who gets in, especially if they don't know us, which—of course—they won't. We can't pose as campus security or the police; that's hardly a ticket in, and it's probably illegal impersonating them. So on this one, I'm stumped. I don't know how two adult men in business-casual clothing can get admitted into a college party on a campus we've never been to."

I look to him for the answer, and he just continues to look at me, wearing a knowing smile and a little cock of his head, until the relatively obvious answer comes to me. "No," I say.

"Or rather, yes," he answers.

"Can we do that?"

"Let me think. Yes."

"You're really thinking we should buy alcohol on the trip and bring it with us to the party?" I ask quietly.

"I was thinking marijuana, but alcohol's good too," he replies with less care for the volume of his voice.

"But isn't that illegal?"

"You're cute when you're law-abiding."

"Ephraim, be serious. If we get caught, we won't be there to make the appointment, and it could ruin everything."

"Okay, my one piece of advice for the day: Rule one—the secret to being *anywhere* is to look like you belong there. Bring these partygoers what they want, and we'll look like we belong there."

"Even though they've never seen us before, and we look like we belong at a frat party about as much as we look like we belong in a convent?"

"I've done convent," he says. "Easier to get in than you'd think."

"Okay, so by some minor miracle, we get in, bearing gifts. We find our guy, and he's about to do his beer-based acrobatics. Then what?"

He smiles at the question. "Oh, you know what that means."

"I do?"

"Role-playing time."

"What, here in a diner?"

"These people don't care. We're invisible to them."

"Literally?" I ask, realizing the stupidity of the question as it's being asked.

"No, not literally. In the more important figurative sense. Let's do this. You'll be you, and I'll be …?"

"Benjamin Holloway."

He jumps right into the scenario. "That's right. Who wants to know?"

"My name's Paul. This is my friend Jeff. We need to talk to you."

"Kinda busy, dude," he says, the words sounding quite strange coming out of his mouth. "Come back later."

"It's … it's about your mom. Is there someplace we can talk in private?"

"Ooh, nice," Ephraim replies as himself. "Didn't see that one coming. Good angle. I think that should work."

Further development of the plan is interrupted by the arrival of dinner. Mine is an open-faced roast beef sandwich, deluged by gravy and surrounded by mashed potatoes. Ephraim opts for the simple pleasures of Mediterranean chicken in a pita, adorned with a smear of hummus. *Damn, got the wrong entrée again. But there will be pie. Yes, there will be pie.*

Five minutes later, thoroughly enjoying his chicken, Ephraim glimpses me staring covetously at his dinner. "You want some of this, don't you?"

"Kind of, yes."

"Well, sorry. You can't have any." He continues eating.

"That's not very nice. In my family, we share."

"Sharing's bullshit," he says matter-of-factly. "An artificial custom of forced politeness that runs contrary to our basest human nature. Besides, if I let you have a bite of this delicious chicken dish, there are two possible outcomes, both of them bad. You could love it, forcing that awkward moment where you contemplate asking me if we can switch the remaining halves of our dinner, leaving me with that gravy-soaked abomination. Or you could hate it, leaving you disappointed in both my dinner and yours."

"You forgot option three: I love it and buy myself one of my own, and nobody ends up with the abomination."

"It's a sucker bet. Don't go for it. Learn from life's decisions, covet my chicken in peace from afar, and hold out for the promise of pie, which will make it all better."

"You seem to be pretty confident in the power of this pie," I respond. "Given that you've never been here before, that's an awfully bold assumption."

Before he can reply, a customer heads for the exit. As he passes us, he says, "Have a good day, Ephraim," earning an amazed stare of disbelief from me all the while.

"No one said I've never been here before," Ephraim says cryptically.

"Who are you really?" I ask him.

"It'll come back to you in time. For now, eat up. Depending on traffic, this may be the only meal stop before we hit campus."

He is, of course, right about the pie. But why shouldn't he be? Apparently, he's eaten here in the past—at a tiny local diner off a highway in an out-of-the-way corner of Virginia that I happened to choose randomly. No, that's not weird or anything.

Well-fed, we pay the cashier—whom he also knows by name—and get back on the road. Two hours later, when it's time to switch drivers again, we do so at a small grocery store that has a liquor department. At said store, we purchase a bottle of vodka, a bottle of tequila, and a bottle of scotch—all top-shelf. We also buy, curiously enough, a small box of zip-top sandwich bags and two bottles of dried oregano and bay leaves. The cashier—a fifty-something woman with unfortunate hair, whom I am pleased to say does *not* know Ephraim—gives us a look that says *I don't know what you boys are doing tonight, and I don't want to know.*

I'm not exactly sure what we're doing either, and I *do* want to know. He gets behind the wheel, as I take the passenger's seat. The booze goes in the back, and he hands me the herbs and a zip-top bag. "Fill this," he instructs, "with that."

"Taking up herbalism, are we? Or making spaghetti sauce, perhaps?"

He starts the car and patiently explains, "It's a prop. No one's going to smoke it. It just has to look authentic enough to get us in. This way, we don't have to search for actual marijuana, and you don't have to feel conflicted."

"Oh, I'm conflicted. But I accept. Just don't get pulled over, or we'll have some explaining to do."

In southern Ohio, we stop in a little Internet café around 7:00 p.m. and search for our boy. With a bit of diligence, we find a profile page for him. Benjamin Holloway, sophomore at Pressman College. Honors student. *Not tonight, however.* Comes from Dayton. High school track star. No apparent fraternity affiliation. In short, not terribly much to go on, unfortunately. Not voted "most likely to die in an embarrassing physical position." At least not if I have anything to say about it.

I look at his earnest, smiling face in his high school senior portrait, this seemingly bright, ambitious human, and I shiver at the knowledge that I am literally the only thing preventing the end of his life tonight. And for what? A moment of weakness. A lapse in judgment. Something that sounded like fun to an otherwise rational mind dulled by the power of too much alcohol. Is this the story of all of our lives? How many times have I sidestepped death by mere inches, blissfully unaware of it, simply by making a small, seemingly unimportant choice? Are we all too stupid to live but too lucky to die? Guess we'll find out tonight.

Time is short, so Ephraim is a bit heavy on the accelerator, as I keep a watchful eye for law enforcement. We're still a couple of hours from Pressman, and we're not likely to have much time to find him when we arrive.

By the time we pull through the gates onto the campus, it is 9:15 at night, a mere seventeen minutes before Benjamin Holloway changes his major for good. Ephraim finds a parking spot near the student union, and we get out, gathering the liquor and "herb" into a grocery bag.

"What do we do?" I ask.

"Working on it," he replies.

"Seventeen minutes," I remind him.

"Painfully aware of the time, thank you."

The campus is small, home to fewer than three thousand students, but it's still big enough that random searching isn't likely to get us what we need in time. We need a break.

"Excuse me ..." I say to a couple of passing students. No response. So much for respecting your elders.

All the while, I'm listening for loud music, telltale signs of a party. Trouble is, there's music coming from several spots, any one of which could be it. We walk east for about a block, and Ephraim asks a young woman, "Is there a party on campus tonight?"

"Fuck off, perv!" she replies unhelpfully, walking quickly away.

I can't help snickering a little at that. "Heh heh. Perv."

"Sixteen minutes," he retorts.

"I got this." I find a group of three male students, and I call out to them. "Hey, dude?" Perhaps the first time I've addressed someone that way in almost twenty years. But it works; they stop walking. "Yeah, we're with the band, and we're supposed to play a frat party tonight. I think it's a keg party. But they didn't tell us which frat house."

"Phi Delt, dude," one of them replies, pointing to the south. "One block that way."

"Solid. Thanks, man. Stop by later. We'll be there most of the night."

As we turn in the direction of the Phi Delt house, Ephraim looks at me with a half-smile. "Do I *know* you?"

"Worked, didn't it?"

We high-tail it across the campus, trying not to look out of place. My band story worked well enough, though we're not carrying anything even vaguely resembling instruments, and we're dressed more like accountants than musicians. That ruse only needed to get us directions. With said directions, it's time to move on to ruse number two.

The Phi Delt house is, I daresay, rockin', so we don't bother knockin'. Instead, we join the line of students waiting to get in the front door. There's a guy at the door, apparently in an official capacity, admitting people. He's not carding them or anything so formal, and I'm not exactly sure what his function is, as he seems to be letting everyone in. Until he gets to us, that is. Taking one look at us, he puts up a hand, which serves to block our way. "Whoa, hang on," he says. "This is a student party. No profs."

Ephraim and I look at each other and give a little "are you serious?" laugh. "We're not profs, bro," I reply, displaying the liquor bottles. "We're here with the beverages."

Ephraim discreetly unveils the bag of oregano. "And the salad, if you get my meaning." A euphemism made more accurate by the actual contents of the bag.

"Who ordered this stuff?" the doorman asks.

I reach for a plausible name. "Mike." Every fraternity has to have a Mike, doesn't it?

"Which Mike?"

Ephraim's clearly had enough of twenty questions. "Mike who had us chase all over town getting this shit, and who has our money for it, which we need to get. You gonna let us in, or you gonna pay the hundred and sixty-five bucks yourself?"

"Go on in."

As we make our way into the crowded main room of the frat house, over the far-too-loud music, I say into my cousin's ear, "You're brilliant."

"I have a BS in BS," he replies into my ear. "Come on, let's find the beer. We've got six minutes. When we find the keg, we'll find our boy."

I put the bottles of booze down on a convenient table, and like flies to feces, the students converge on them. Ephraim throws the oregano into a garbage can, and we continue to inch our way through the wall-to-wall bodies. *Did college students always look this young?* There's no time to ponder that at length or to engage any of them in social (or any other) intercourse. We have to find the keg; we have to find Benjamin Holloway.

We traverse three more rooms, each filled with students of varying drunkenness, until we find a particularly crowded room, in the center of which is a well-used beer keg. The music isn't as loud in this room, but the conversation is quite lively, and the twenty or more people gathered around mean we won't have anything resembling privacy.

It's 9:30, just two minutes until Benjamin Holloway will make the worst decision of his life. But which one is he? There are at least a dozen guys in here, and although I've seen his picture, I can't swear that I can find him here in this room. A chilling thought grips me—*What if there's more than one party on campus tonight?* It's not beyond the realm of possibility. The people I asked knew about this one, but what if there are two or three? What if, in some other building on campus, Benjamin Holloway is about to make his fatal move, and we're nowhere near?

Before I can give this possibility the level of panic it deserves, a voice from across the room announces, "Guys, watch this!" And there he is, our honors student. He steps up to the keg, and the assembled group begins chanting, "Stand! Stand! Stand! Stand! Stand!" It would be inspirational if they weren't unwittingly encouraging him to his death.

As he puts one hand on top of the keg, I call out a single word: "Wait!"

To my surprise, everyone in the room falls silent and looks at Ephraim and me. It is a crowning awkward moment, but I own it now, and it's time to go to work. "Benjamin Holloway?" I ask, 99 percent certain that the answer is obvious, but still obligated to confirm it.

"Yeah, that's right," he answers in a tone of slurred suspicion. "Who are you?"

"We need to speak with you in private," I tell him calmly.

"Are you cops?" he asks.

"No. We just have some information you need to hear."

"Well then, it can wait until later," he replies, putting both hands on the keg.

"It's about your mother," I continue, proceeding from the role-playing at the diner.

He turns to face us, a note of seriousness coming over his face. "My mother who died two years ago?" The seriousness turns to a mocking expression. "Nothing's happened to her, has it?"

Some of the partygoers laugh at this, and Ephraim's expression loses anything resembling humor. "I'm tired of fucking around," he announces. With that, he steps over to Benjamin Holloway, takes him by the arm, and begins to lead him away from the keg. "Five minutes," Ephraim says. "After that, if you still want to do your beer-based acrobatics, knock yourself out."

The two of us begin escorting Holloway from the room, but as we approach the door, a football-playing type stands directly in our way, blocking our exit. I'm convinced that we're already successful; 9:32 has come and gone, and Holloway is not doing his keg stand. My cousin, however, seems unconvinced. He calmly looks up at the towering human obstruction and quietly tells him, "You'll want to move."

The frat boy is unimpressed by his opponent, on whom he has eight inches of height and probably sixty pounds of steroid-fueled mass. "Man says he doesn't want to leave the party. I think *you're* the ones who should leave."

Ephraim doesn't even flinch. In that same emotionless monotone, he tells this guy, "You don't know me. That's why you get this one warning. I killed a man, eight years ago, using nothing but a dish towel and a teaspoon. Look at that. I can already see you working it out in your head. *That's easy,* you're thinking, *simple suffocation. Not so tough.* Except you're wrong. The cause of death was a broken neck. While you're standing there in your beer-soaked diminished capacity, trying to work out the physics of that maneuver, chew on one more piece of information: I liked him more than I like you."

A distressed murmur overtakes the crowd, and I can see the fear in some of their eyes. Ever tranquil, Ephraim adds, "My friend and I need to talk to Benjamin Holloway for five minutes, to give him some information that he needs to know. We're not going to hurt him or interfere with him in any way. When we're done, he's free to go back to the party or wherever he wants. All I need from you is to step … the fuck … aside."

The man-mound wordlessly steps aside, clearing the way for our exit. Still holding on to Holloway, we make our way through the other rooms of the fraternity house toward the exit. On passing through the main room, I'm amused to hear someone announce, "Dude, somebody threw out a whole bag of weed!"

At last, we are free of the crowds, the smoke, the smell, and the overpowering sound of the music that filled the place. Ephraim releases his grip on him as we lead him to a quiet area behind the house. Now sober by circumstance, he turns to us and demands, "What the hell is this? Who are you guys really?"

I take the lead this time; Ephraim's already had his fun. "Benjamin, I'm sorry to disturb your evening, but the two of us were sent here to give you a warning. We drove here all the way from Maryland to tell you this."

"So what's the warning?"

"The keg stand you were about to perform was going to kill you. If you got up there—if you get up there at any point tonight, you're going to fall off, break your neck, and die."

He takes a few moments to absorb this message before announcing, "Bullshit. I've done keg stands like a million times, and I've never had a problem. Besides, how the hell would you know, anyway?"

"That's a fair question," I answer. "And I don't have a good answer. All I can tell you is that I know. I get warnings when people are in danger, and I have to go and tell them. For whatever reason, you got picked to receive the warning. Somebody wants you to live through this night, and here we are. I don't want anything from you; I don't ever need to see you again. Hell, you don't even have to listen to what I'm telling you. But I'll tell you this: before you go in there again and balance your ass on top of that beer dispenser, you might want to give a lot of thought to why two people drove a hell of a long way just to tell you not to."

My words seem to have taken the edge out of him. His face suggests that what I'm saying—impossible as it sounds—might just be true. "So … are you … God?"

I laugh a bit at this. "No. I just work for him."

"What's he like?"

"I'll tell you if I ever meet him. He just tells me what to do and doesn't tell me why. Kinda like he didn't tell you why your mother had to die. Or mine, for that matter."

"Yeah," he says, defeated.

"We'll go now," I continue. "Sorry to bother you. Have a good night. Be safe."

He walks away, in the direction of the frat house. Not a thank-you, not another word. But there's something about him that tells me he's safe. Another close encounter with the supernatural, and a life is spared for some reason. Satisfied, I turn to my traveling companion. "Shall we?" I ask.

"Why not. But I don't think I have another eleven-hour drive in me tonight. I say we get a hotel somewhere and do the bulk of it tomorrow."

"Works for me." As we start walking back to the car, I have to ask. "That story you told back there, about killing a man with a spoon … that wasn't true, was it?"

He shakes his head a little. "Tristan, Tristan. You can't break someone's neck with a dish towel and a spoon."

That's a relief. "I didn't think so."

"It was suffocation."

I hate it when I can't tell if he's kidding.

As we get to within several yards of the car, we hesitate a moment at a curious sight. A man—who looks from a distance too old to be a college student—is standing next to my driver's-side door, working on opening the lock with a rather professional-looking tool. I'm prepared to spring into something resembling action, but Ephraim holds me back, indicating that he'll take the lead on this one.

"Having trouble?" he asks pleasantly as we approach.

The man startles but decides to play it cool. "Uhh, yeah. I locked my keys inside, and I'm trying to get back in."

"Yeah," Ephraim says, "it can be tough with these newer models. No lock button to snag with a coat hanger. I've found this tends to work well, though." He pulls out the key fob and presses the unlock button. The car obligingly gives its chwirp-chwirp tone, and our new friend appears to realize that he's boned.

He changes tactics. "Oh, is … is this your car? God, I'm so

embarrassed. I have the same car, and I … I must've gone to the wrong one. No wonder the key wouldn't work."

"I thought the keys were locked inside," I retort.

This isn't going well for him, and he knows it. "Uh, yeah, the main ones are."

"What kind of car is it?" Ephraim asks calmly. Always calmly.

"It's a Hon … dai … woo?"

"Lexus, actually," Ephraim corrects. "But hey, these days, so many models look alike. It's easy to get confused. The secret is to take a close look."

In a flash, Ephraim grabs the man by the back of the neck and slams his head ruthlessly against the roof of the vehicle—once, twice, a third time. The would-be thief staggers backward and falls unconscious to the pavement.

As casually as if he had swatted a fly, Ephraim opens the driver's door and tells me, "I'll take first shift," as he gets in the car.

I swear I am about to have a serious issue with this wanton display of controlled chaos, but the next thing I know, I'm losing consciousness too, ending up—I'm dimly aware—on the ground next to Ephraim's victim.

I wake up fuzzy-headed sometime later. It's significant to note that before this whole messenger thing came along, I had never in my life lost consciousness to anything other than a soft pillow and a comfy bed. So when I return to the world lying down in the back seat of my car, parked in an empty parking lot somewhere, with Ephraim standing just outside the open door, looking down on me, it is—to put it mildly—jarring.

"Did … did you hit me?" I ask. A reasonable question, given his recent actions.

"No," he answers gently. "I taught our little carjacker a lesson, and then you went night-night all on your own. I'm guessing you must like Ohio."

"Umm … why?"

"Because you've got another assignment at another college campus a few hours from now, a few hours away from here."

"I got an assignment in my sleep?"

"More like in your dazed semi-consciousness, but yes. You were quite the talker."

"I don't remember any of it," I tell him, sitting up slowly, as every fluid responsible for my sense of balance is swished around in the snow globe of my head. "Where are we going, and what are we doing?"

He tells me the same story I can't remember telling him. At 12:45 this morning, on the campus of the Ohio College of Liberal Arts, a nineteen-year-old woman named Megan Robinson will be at a party with a few friends. At that party, she will overdose on cocaine and go into cardiac arrest. Her friends, too drugged up and frightened to help her successfully, will decide in a moment of panic to hide her body. To cover their tracks, they will concoct a story that they were attacked and beaten, and Megan kidnapped by "three big black guys"—the exact words Ephraim says I recounted to him. But it doesn't end there. The community—largely white, conservative, and quick to anger—responds by demanding justice. The girl's family is left to agonize over her whereabouts, as a race war erupts in town, resulting in the arrest and mob killing of innocent men.

I'm astonished at the tale—first that it could be about to happen, second that I would get details stretching so far into the future events that will unfold, and third that I don't remember a thing about getting the message in the first place. I realize that I'm not in pain—unusual at this point in the process. Perhaps whoever delivered the message knew that I was already close, already practically committed to taking it, and chaperoned by Ephraim to boot. Maybe the pain wasn't needed this time.

"I'll get us there," Ephraim says. "After we deliver the message, I think we should sleep for the night. It's been a long day already, and something tells me this one could get hairy."

"I'll stay back here, if that's all right with you," I reply, referring to the back seat.

"Suit yourself," he says. "I'll try not to do any bootlegger U-turns or anything fancy."

With that, he closes the door, gets behind the wheel, and starts us on our journey to my second assignment of the night.

Chapter 4

Friday, October 12, 2007

Ephraim

Strange night, this. I've been in this game a long time, and I've never seen two assignments back to back. I don't know what they did to Tristan the second time, but the pain was obviously intense enough to make him lose consciousness right there in the street. And to wake up with no memory of the details he'd shared with me is distressing, especially given how touchy this one is going to be.

Another college student whose life is in jeopardy thanks to alcohol and drugs. It definitely is theme night, and I'm not enjoying the theme. Cocaine this time. I have a very bad feeling about this, but I don't want to share it with Tristan; he's been through enough, and it won't do anything to help his confidence or his concentration. For the moment, I know where to go and when to be there. That's enough.

I check the back seat and see that he is either asleep or resting; either is fine. He's still recuperating, and he's not yet used to the long hours and emotional demands of life as a messenger. He can sleep until we get there.

Something else is troubling me, and it takes me a few minutes before I realize what it is. When it hits me, it comes as a surprise. *I don't remember doing this.* My memories of future events are, at least I thought, quite thorough and complete. No, I don't remember every meal I'll ever eat or every movie I'll ever see, but the big stuff—life events of some meaning and impact—those are generally in there, right up until the day I die.

It's him. I glance back at Tristan again and realize that he's like a magnet held close to the compass of my memories, distorting everything and challenging my ability to find true north. He's such an anomaly. I know this is a strange thing to think about someone in such an unusual and elite group already, but even for a messenger, he's such an anomaly. To start so late in life and under such unusual circumstances. And imperfect as my memories are where he's concerned, I know what's coming. I know about the dancer, the road trip, the fisherman, the father. I know about the storm, the runaway, the Nine. Most of all, I know about the battle that awaits him and how important he is to the world.

I can't tell him, of course; none of it, the good or the bad. He has to wait two more years for it all to happen. The irony, of course, is that if he isn't there to fight that battle, it would be a real boon to SODARCOM's five-year plan. The global fallout that would take place would speed things along in all the right ways, without me and mine having to do a thing. All I'd have to do is divert Tristan from that path. *Or kill him.*

"Do you have any water?" comes a weak voice from the back seat.

I grab a bottle of water and hand it back to him.

"Thank you."

But, of course, I have to let my humanity trump my personal and professional aspirations. Aspirations I need to rethink anyway. I knew the risks when I joined a covert organization whose mission is the thinning of the American population. I knew I wasn't signing up to be stuffing technician at Build-a-Bear. I took the job because I could handle it. I *can* handle it. Unlike some of my colleagues, who think of the population as a series of changing nine-digit numbers, I know that each of those numbers is a human being, someone with parents and siblings, friends and children; people who wake up in the morning believing that their life means something, believing they can change the world. If they're right, they don't even have to know I exist. If they're wrong, I have a job to do.

"Do you want me to drive?" Tristan asks feebly. I can almost hear his thoughts repeating *please say no, please say no, please say no.*

"Sleepy drivers are statistically more dangerous than drunk ones," I reply. "You rest. I've got this."

"I'm sorry I'm not better conversation," he says.

"It's all right. I sometimes enjoy time alone with my thoughts."

He hesitates a moment before saying, "Thank you for taking care of the car thief."

I suppress a laugh at the words. *Pathetic* car thief would be more accurate. Still, the look on his face when I unlocked the doors was priceless. "You're welcome. I couldn't let us get stuck in Ohio, after all. We have work to do."

"Did you … did you kill him?"

"Not hardly. Attempted grand theft auto isn't a capital offense. I just gave him a headache he won't soon forget and left him to sleep it off on the curb."

"Still, that was pretty brutal, the way you attacked that guy."

"The world can be a brutal place, Tristan. I think you understand that better than some people. Strip away the finery, and we're animals."

"Who are?"

"We are. You, me; people. Sometimes animals fight over an object. He wanted my object, and I wanted it more, so I had to do the alpha male thing and put my opponent on the ground."

"It sounds better when *you* say it," he admits.

"Besides, we both know that there are individuals in the world who can stop bad things from happening to people. If he wasn't meant to get his clock cleaned, someone would have shown up at the last minute to warn him not to try to steal this car."

"You have an answer for everything, don't you?"

"No. Just some things. How are you feeling back there?"

"Dizzy," he says. "I didn't even get a chance to be excited about the success of the first mission before I hit the ground. Is this going to happen a lot, one right after the other like this?"

"I really don't know. The best I can tell you is I don't think so. It never happened to me like that. To give you two in one night suggests to me that this next one is going to be very important."

"I hope I have the strength to do what we have to do."

"I'll step up on this one," I tell him. "I know what you've been through, and I'm feeling fine. You can rely on me to do whatever you need me to do."

"Thank you, Ephraim."

"Try to get some sleep. We still have a couple of hours to go."

He doesn't utter another word, and that's fine too. I could hear the strain in his voice when he was talking. He's already worn out, and the night isn't even half over. I suppose it would be futile to question the reasoning of sending such a wounded man out on two crucial missions like this. If I had the answer, I'd be pope.

The hour grows later and later as we draw ever closer to the Ohio College of Liberal Arts, a place I've never even heard of. One of many hotbeds of progressive thought and social activism spread all over the country, no doubt. What would they think of me and my line of work, I wonder?

Five miles from our destination, it is time to awaken Tristan. He got the message, not me, so he knows exactly where we need to go. "Tristan."

He mumbles, somewhat the way children do when they don't want to get up for school. Time is short, and I'm not Mommy. "Tristan, wake up!"

He sits up abruptly with a start and a snort, looking dazed. His question is, "Where are we?" but his present state pushes it out more like "Wowee?"

"About five minutes from where we need to be, which means I need the exact details of where this is supposed to happen."

"Umm … okay," he says hesitantly.

"This is the point where you give them to me."

"I was out cold, remember? You told *me* where we're going."

"I told you only because you originally told me. But you stopped short of an exact address and things like names of the people we're looking for. I know they must have been given to you. Now would be a very good time to remember them."

"I can't," he replies. "I was so out of it when the assignment came in, I don't have the details."

"Think! You have to remember this, or we won't be able to do what we came here for."

"I'm thinking, but it's not in there."

In the back of my mind, I was afraid this might happen. Too much, too soon, and it overwhelmed him. Now we're minutes away from doing what we have to do, and we might as well be hours away. Without those details, we're dead in the water, and so is this girl—whoever she is.

An idea comes to me; it may be a long shot, but it's all we have. "Tristan, I need you to trust me and repeat after me. Fuck the mission. Let's go home."

"What?" he asks in disbelief.

"Trust me. Say it. As loud as you can."

In as elevated a voice as he can muster, Tristan shouts, "Fuck the mission. Let's go home!"

"Again."

"Fuck the mission. Let's go home!"

"Once more."

"Fuck the mission. Let's go—ow!"

"Ow?"

"Son of a bitch, ow! My head."

"It hurts?" I ask, hopeful but not trying to sound like a sadist.

"Yes. Terribly."

"They think you're rejecting the assignment. They'll resend the details. Pay attention now. Fight the pain, and focus on the details. Addresses, names, locations. We'll be there in just a few minutes."

He closes his eyes, and I see a look of concentration on his face mixed with what must be crushing agony. Seconds later he tells me. "Got it. Keep going straight."

"Thank them," I instruct.

"Thank who?"

"It doesn't matter. Whoever gave you this information. Thank them in your thoughts and tell them you're on your way."

He closes his eyes again, and I see the pain start to subside; it's evident from his expression. Tristan leans forward between the front seats and says, "I saw everything. All the details. Do you know how to save this girl if we don't convince her not to overdose?"

"I know CPR and basic first aid. I'm no EMT, but I think I've got a phone number for people who are. Let's get there first and figure out where we stand."

With Tristan's help, I navigate the unfamiliar streets of Peisker Heights, Ohio. We skirt the college campus, heading away from the dormitories. *Makes sense. Something like this isn't going to happen covertly in the heart of everything.* Past the school's perimeter are several blocks of old houses, row after row, converted into cheap apartments, run down over years of student use and abuse. Surprisingly few people are out and about at this hour on a Friday night. Either the student body is more focused than usual or everybody is already where they want to be for the night. Fewer people around can be good and bad for us; good because there aren't any witnesses if things go wrong, bad because there's nobody close by to help us.

"Left here," Tristan says. I make the turn. "Then take a right, and it's on this block." He points to an old two-story wood-frame house that was long ago converted to four student apartments. There's parking on the street out front, so I take a spot and shut off the engine.

"Okay, what's the strategy?" Tristan asks. "Do we have a plan?"

"We move our asses," I answer, getting out of the car. "We're way off the map on this one."

I follow him down to the door to the apartment on the lower right of the building. "You ready?" I ask him. He just nods. "Follow my lead."

Without a knock, without a warning, without an invitation, I open the door to apartment three, and it is precisely as bad as I thought it would be. For an instant, everything freezes—not actually, of course, because the world doesn't work that way. But in my mind, I capture the scene, the people we encounter in the positions where we find them. The front door opens into the apartment's living room. Against one wall is an old couch, ugly, sporting rips and stains and burn marks. Opposite is a television set, not terribly large or new; an older tube-style set, currently turned off. A few posters are stuck to the walls—rock groups, celebrity photos, movie posters. Off to the sides of the room are some mismatched chairs, nothing comfortable or expensive. Along the walls, plastic milk crates are turned to face out, and they hold books, DVDs, videotapes. There's a stale smokiness to the air that lingers on the furniture and in the fibers—those that remain—of the hideous calico carpeting. It is the carpeting that captures my attention in particular, because that's where the dead girl is lying.

We encounter six people in the living room; I would say *six souls,* but at a glance, I can see that one has already left the building. A girl, maybe eighteen years old, is on the ground, on her back. Her shirt has been ripped off of her, not in some clumsy attempt at sexual aggression, but in a deliberate attempt to gain access to her vital areas and save her life. A futile effort, clearly. There's no delicate way of saying this, but this girl is a goddamn mess. Her eyes are not just open but gaping wide and empty at the ceiling, as if she were terrified; I have no doubt that her final moments were terrifying. Blood is drying on her face where it streamed from her nose and mouth. Other substances have leaked from her mouth as well, most likely her last meal.

It takes the five living occupants of the room—three men and two women of college age—less than two seconds to react to us after our arrival. As we burst into the room, all eyes turn to us, bearing looks of fear and suspicion. The women are crying and don't stop when they see us. One of the men turns and runs into another room of the apartment; this I don't like. I want everyone where I can see them, but there's no time to pursue him. I have to make an effort, at least, to help this girl.

"What the fuck?" one of the men calls out. "Who are you?"

Utterly unconcerned about answering, I kneel at the girl's side and search for any evidence of life. No breath remains in her. I find no radial pulse, no carotid pulse, no temporal pulse. A hand on her chest confirms that her heart isn't even trying. If Tristan is right, and this was a cocaine OD, that organ went haywire and then quit.

"Anything?" Tristan asks.

"Nothing," I answer. I scrape away the various residues from around her mouth, silently wishing for a sheath or a dental dam, and then blow into the girl's mouth as I pinch her nose shut. Her chest rises, receiving the air I give her, but there is no further reaction. I blow again, with the same result. I locate the proper place on her chest and begin compressions, knowing full well that under ideal circumstances, CPR works in about 10 percent of cases, and this girl is far beyond ideal circumstances in many ways.

I continue CPR for only about three minutes before giving up and rising again. One of the men in the room demands, "Why did you stop?"

"It's over," I say, more to Tristan than to him.

"I don't understand," Tristan says, looking at his watch. "We're not late. We're almost ten minutes early. It doesn't make sense."

"Maybe it makes perfect sense. Maybe we just misunderstood the purpose of the mission."

Before he can ask me about it further, the first man speaks up again. I can smell the panic on him, literally and figuratively, but the pack dynamic calls for a pseudo-leader to assume the position of bravery, especially in the presence of two interlopers of unknown origin. "Will somebody *please* tell me who you are and what's happening here?"

At the moment, I need information more than he does. Rather than answer him, I ask him, "Is this your place?"

Crying girl speaks. "It's mine. Mine and hers." She points to the remains of her friend on the floor and starts sobbing afresh.

"Look at me," I tell her, "not at her. What's your name?"

"Don't answer him!" the faux leader cautions, earning my attention all over again.

I turn to look him straight in the eyes, and in my expression he sees how little I appreciate his intervention. "I'll talk to you when it's your turn." I turn back to crying girl. "What's your name?"

"Sandy," she says, interrupted by the hitch of a sob. "Sandra Rivera."

"Sandra, my name is Ephraim, and this is my partner, Tristan. I know everything is absolutely crazy right now, but I need you to keep as calm as you can—all of you—and trust us, because we're here to help you."

"Are you the police?" the second man asks quietly, with no apparent desire to make a fuss.

"No," I reply calmly, "we're not the police. I need to know where the other person who was in this room went."

"Right here." As I feared, the answer comes from outside of the room. The third man steps back into the living room, unsteadily leveling a .22-caliber pistol at the two of us. It looks tiny in his large hands. Tiny but still problematic. "Man asked you who you are and what's going on here. I'm here to repeat that question."

Fucked up as this night already is, the presence of a firearm does nothing to pull it back. "Marcus, don't!" Sandra Rivera cries out, her mood improved not at all by the latest development.

Tristan looks at me with deep concern on his face. It's adorable. He looks like this is the first time he's had a gun trained on him. If only he knew how many times I've had him at gunpoint myself. But we can reminisce later. First there's a troublemaker to disarm.

"You good with that thing, Marcus?" I ask him tranquilly but with an undercurrent of savagery in my voice.

"I do all right," he answers.

"Do you? So that's what, at the shootin' range? Paper target, maybe tin cans in the back yard during the summer? How good are you when it's a person at the end of that barrel? I'd wager, looking at you, that you've never killed a man before."

"First time for everything," he answers, much less flustered than I would prefer.

First gear's not working; time to shift to second. "You've got some courage. I respect that. And you've got the gun, so you've got my attention. Thing of it is—and here's the part I hope you'll listen to—what you don't have is reason to shoot us."

"You broke into this house," he answers, unflinching.

"Apartment, technically. And in point of fact, we opened an unlocked door. To *her* apartment, actually. Shouldn't you ask her if she thinks you should be pointing that at us?"

I watch as he casts a quick look at Miss Rivera. She tells him, "Marcus, put the gun away! Please?"

Looking none too thrilled at the emasculating effects of acquiescing, Marcus puts the gun down on a stack of milk crates—still close enough to reach, but less menacing than seconds ago.

Her tears now under control, Sandra Rivera speaks to me. "He did what you asked. Will you please tell us why you're here? What did the other man mean when he said you were early?"

Tristan breaks his silence. "We were sent here to stop this."

The second woman asks, "Stop what? Sent by who?"

"Stop what happened to your friend from happening. The second question is harder to answer."

The quietest of the three men asks, "Are you trying to tell us you knew what was going to happen here? That's why you came?"

"Can we all sit down, maybe," I suggest, "and talk about this rationally?"

"What about Megan?" Rivera asks. "Shouldn't we do something for her? Shouldn't we call somebody?"

"I'm afraid it's too late," I reply. "She's gone." This inspires additional tears, more controlled ones, from Sandra. "As for calling somebody, we'll figure that part out next. So for now, everybody please sit down."

Tristan and I each take a chair where we can see everybody. Three of them sit on the couch, while two pull up chairs from the makeshift dining room set. Sandra we've already met, and Marcus has made himself known to us. Going around the room, we learn that the faux leader is Bryan, the quiet guy is—amusingly enough—Guy, the second woman goes by Cheyenne, and our reason for being here, still on the floor like the world's most inappropriate throw rug, is the late Megan Robinson, who recently celebrated her nineteenth and final birthday. She's the proud owner of two incompatible things, unfortunately: a heart condition and a nose for blow. Thing one met thing two about half an hour ago, and even if we'd showed up here with a hospital strapped to our backs and cardiac paddles coming out of our asses, we couldn't have done thing-fucking-one to change that.

Before I can get into the metaphysical details, Tristan does that charmingly inconvenient thing he does, thinking out loud. "Half an hour ago? Ephraim, we weren't even scheduled to be here until after she'd been dead for fifteen minutes. I don't understand. I know I got the time right. I'm sure of it."

"Not now," I try to tell him discreetly, but the feline is out of the burlap.

"I want an explanation," Marcus says, and even with his pistol across the room, he still sounds like he means business.

"We're not with the police," I answer. "Or the FBI, the DEA, any of it. Like I said. We were sent here because he knew in his head that your friend was going to OD tonight."

All eyes turn to Tristan. "How?" Bryan asks.

"I don't know."

"Bullshit," Marcus tosses at him.

"It's true. I don't know how or why I know these things."

"So, you what?" Guy says. "You drive around Ohio, going to college campuses, waiting for someone to do something dangerous?"

"No," Tristan says. "Well, tonight kind of yes, but normally no. We came here from another campus. While we were there, we stopped a guy from doing a keg stand, I guess they call it, that would have killed him."

"So why didn't you save Megan?" Sandra says to him, trying hard to fight back her tears again.

"That's the part I don't know. The part that doesn't make sense. I know what time these things are going to happen. I know when and where, and who it's going to happen to. We got here in time, so I don't know why she was already dead."

"I do," I answer quietly.

He looks at me. "What?"

"I know the answer you don't. It won't be easy to hear, but you need to hear it—and so do they."

"What is it?"

"Tristan, we weren't sent here to save her. We were sent here to save them." I point to the five occupants of the room.

"To save *them?* But look at them. They're fine. They didn't even use the cocaine." He looks at their faces. "Did you?"

Bryan answers for the group. "No. Megan's into that shit. The rest of us aren't. She was already lit before we got here. What did he mean, you're here to save *us?*"

Tristan looks to me for an explanation. "Remember the details of the mission. The story."

A look of amazement comes over his face. "The story … I forgot about it when I blacked out. Then, when I was trying so hard to find this place, all I concentrated on were the particulars—the address, the way here. I didn't even remember the story. Ephraim, tell them. Please?"

So it falls to me. Fine. "On our way here, I believed, as Tristan did, that we had been summoned here to save your friend's life. But when we got here and I saw her, I knew that something else Tristan told me was relevant. It was made even more relevant by what I *didn't* see here, so I want someone to answer my next question, and if you lie to me—and I will know if you lie to me—I'll call the police myself. Why did no one call 911?"

The silence that sweeps through the room is like a wave of guilt and shame. Each of them looks to the others to be the one to answer me. Yet no answer is forthcoming, and I'm not enjoying it. "Tick-tock, children. Snow White here might have all night, but I don't."

"Fuck you!" Sandra spits the words at me. "Show some respect!"

"Then answer me. One of you, I don't care who, answer me."

"We were scared, all right?" Bryan manages at last. "Everything happened so fast. She was fine … and then she wasn't. And all that shit was coming out of her. We tried CPR; three of us. But it didn't work."

"So instead of calling in the professionals, you panicked and let your friend die."

"She was already dead!" Marcus shouts.

"Was she, Marcus?" I snarl, standing in a rush. "Is that your expert medical opinion? Or is that just what you're telling yourselves to rationalize away your very real contributions to her messy death?" They stare at me, wearing their guilt like the bloody stains that cover their friend. "So you sat here, not calling anyone, not continuing to try to help her. Not doing anything. But no. That's not quite right either. Is it, Tristan?"

"No, I don't think it is."

"What are you saying?" Cheyenne asks fearfully.

"You were talking to each other," I continue. "Working out a plan. An alibi, but not just an alibi. Was it? You were working out the details of what to tell people. You're planning to hide her body. Late tonight, you're going to put her in a car and drive her far away, hide her someplace no one will think to look for her."

They look at me in astonishment as I confess their plan for them. I'm not done. "But that's just the first part. You're working out a story. People don't just disappear, not without help. So one of you is concocting a kidnapping. What was the exact wording you saw, Tristan? 'Three big black guys,' wasn't that it?"

"Yeah," he says quietly, "that was it."

Sandra Rivera stands up. "That's impossible. We didn't even talk about that. We didn't say a word about that."

I step right over to her, right inside what would be any reasonable person's personal space, and give a little smile that contains not the tiniest measure of happiness. "But it's what *you* were thinking, Sandra. Your actions are as good as a confession. If we hadn't arrived, you would have proposed it to the others, and they would have gone with it. Sure, you would have hated yourselves for doing it, but let's face it—you're not troublemakers. Certainly never been in trouble with the law before. You've got plans after you get out of this school. Careers, families, fortunes to make. You can't risk going to jail because your friend got stupid and coked herself to death. Feel free to stop me if I've misspoken."

Nobody says a word.

"So you go to the police in the morning, and you tell them that sweet, innocent Megan was with you, and she got kidnapped by 'three big black guys.' Easy as can be. You didn't get a good look at them, but they sure weren't from around here. The police take your statement, they start an investigation; problem solved."

Tristan very graciously offers up a single word at this point. "Except."

Marcus takes the bait. "Except?"

My turn. "Except the world doesn't always behave. Ever play a little game called Jenga? Pretty simple, really. Stack up a bunch of blocks and start pulling them out oh-so-carefully. Thing is, Jenga's a lot like life. Pull out one tiny block, and shit starts falling all over you. Tristan saw the results of your plan as if you'd already done it. You go to the police with that story, and you're going to start a war in this lower-middle-class, white, conservative, Second Amendment-loving town. You think because you go to the gas station and the grocery store in good old Peisker Heights that you know the people of this community? Give them a reason to hate, and they'll devour it like they're starving. Spread this story, and they will find 'three big black guys.' Decent men who haven't done anything wrong. And the people of this town will lynch them like it's 1850. And all because of your lies, your cowardice, your moral bankruptcy. Now, if you'll excuse me for a minute, I'm going to use your bathroom while you sit here and ponder that."

I would love to be in that living room to watch them react to the future that was just laid out for them, but my dramatic exit really is motivated by a bladder that feels ready to explode. Tristan's with them; he can fill me in. In the less-than-pristine bathroom, I think about their reactions to my words, and I know I had it right. They were prepared to hide their friend's body and then scapegoat a convenient minority group. I think about the anguish the poor girl's family would go through, spending days—maybe months—not knowing if their daughter was alive, only to find the truth later, when some hiker or someone walking a dog stumbles upon her. Then, of course, there's the issue of the innocent men who would have been brutally slaughtered to satisfy a town's misguided need for blame and revenge. That just leaves the question of what to do to prevent it without sending five potentially well-meaning but overly self-protective teens to jail for a couple of decades each. Fortunately, the bathroom break I require is lengthy enough to allow me to formulate a plan that just might work.

The mood is understandably somber as I re-enter the living room. I'm pleased to see that someone has thought to close Megan Robinson's eyes. It doesn't make much of a difference, of course, but her unwavering stare was starting to get to me, and the others too, I'm sure.

"Tristan," I begin, "anything to report?"

"Just a lot of quiet introspection since you left."

I return to my seat and address the group. "What we said before is true: we will help you, but that comes with a requirement. I need to know that the five of you won't go through with the plan to blame someone else for this."

For many seconds, no one speaks. Finally, Sandra quietly asks, "If there's no one to blame, what's going to happen to us?"

"You'll be protected," I tell her, "but not until I hear it from each of you that you won't tell anyone your original plan. Say it. All of you."

"I won't tell anyone," Cheyenne says.

"I won't tell anyone," Guy agrees.

"I won't tell anyone," Bryan adds.

"I won't tell anyone," Marcus tells us.

"I won't tell anyone," Sandra Rivera finally says.

"All right then," I reply to them. "You've made a good choice; your first one of the evening, I might add. You might not realize it just yet, but you're all in shock over what's happened. It's what's letting you function at the moment, but soon—after we've left—you're going to feel this, and it's not going to feel good. Allow yourselves to feel what you're feeling, and when the time comes, use it to your advantage. Now listen carefully and follow my instructions completely. Everyone who doesn't live in this apartment needs to leave. You weren't here tonight, none of you. So get rid of anything that suggests you were. In about half an hour, Ms. Rivera, I want you to call 911. Tell them you were out of the apartment, and when you got back, you found her on the carpet like this. You tried CPR, but it was too late, so you're calling for an ambulance."

A couple of them look at me like this very elementary plan contains the meaning of life. *Students. Pathetically easy to impress.*

"The police will come," I continue. "They'll enter the apartment, and they'll find her body. With the information about her heart condition, they'll suspect that as the cause of death. They'll find evidence of the cocaine in her system, but you didn't know anything about that. This is the time for you to show your grief, but keep it sincere. Answer their questions, but don't volunteer anything. Most of all, don't tell them that she was with you tonight. Your freedom depends on the police believing that your friend Megan died alone in her apartment. You were nowhere near her, and you didn't even know she had a drug habit. It's called plausible deniability, my dears, and it's worth more than that diploma they'll throw at you if you don't fuck up too much in the time you've got left here. Questions?"

"We're going to lie to the police?"

"No flies on Bryan," I answer. "Yes, you're going to lie to the police. If that becomes a problem for you, and you develop a crisis of conscience, have the courtesy to make it a single. Don't confess for the rest of your friends. It's too late to save Megan, but it's not too late to prevent further chaos, and that includes preserving your futures."

"What about ..." Guy hesitates before finishing his question. "Repentance?"

Tristan and I both give him a strange look before I ask, "Repentance?"

"Yeah. I mean, I figure if you knew what was going to happen, and you came here to stop it, you must have been sent by God. We all sinned when we let Megan die, so I'm wondering what God needs us to do for repentance."

"Kid," I reply, trying unsuccessfully not to sound too condescending, "when you get out in the world a bit, you'll realize: you can work for someone and still think your boss is an asshole. You want to repent? That's between you and God. Just don't bring your friends down with you."

Tired as he is, Tristan agrees to drive us. I want to put a few hours between us and Peisker Heights, Ohio, and be nowhere close when the aftermath of this night goes down. Once we're far enough away, we can get a hotel for the rest of the night and much of the morning. Ten miles away from the campus, we've barely exchanged twenty words. He's sullen; that's clear. What's less clear is whether it's the circumstances of this night or something specific I've done. Only one way to find out.

"I fear you're disappointed in me," I offer gently.

Several seconds pass without an answer, but then he says, "Is it that obvious?"

"No, which is why I expressed it as a fear. May I know what I've done to earn this disappointment?"

"We committed a crime tonight, Ephraim."

"Strictly speaking, yes."

"Strictly speaking? It's not like we ran a red light when there was no traffic around. There was a death. We falsified information and disturbed a crime scene. We assisted five people in lying to the authorities about the circumstances surrounding that death. I think we've gone a bit beyond *strictly speaking*."

"You're right," I have to concede. "We did do that. Can I ask you a question?"

"I don't know. Is it one of those questions you ask that takes my perfectly valid statement, twists it around, and leaves me feeling stupid, even though I'm in the right?"

"Yes."

"Shit. Yeah, go ahead."

"Were those five people we met tonight directly responsible for that girl's death?"

His face shows that he dislikes the question, but he's already consented to being asked, so he can't exactly back out now. So the dance begins. "There are gray areas. Nuances of meaning and legality. Directly responsible? Well, strictl— to the letter of the law, probably not. I believe 'proximate cause' would be the argument made against them."

"If the police came to that apartment and we had left the crime scene undisturbed, the charges could have included possession of cocaine, failure to report a death, and quite possibly manslaughter. As a result, six lives would have been washed down the drain, rather than one."

"Possibly."

"We got them to agree not to scapegoat innocent people, and we know how that would have turned out. You saw it yourself. Three decent man, innocent of any wrongdoing, killed by an angry mob. We couldn't let that happen."

"True."

"Remember what I said about your missions and specificity. We can't always save all of them. But I believe we're always given the opportunity to do specifically what we were sent to do. In this case, that was preventing the spread of the story. Mission accomplished. You go home victorious."

"A hollow victory," he corrects.

"A victory nonetheless. Sometimes, Tristan, a small bad thing can prevent a big worse thing."

"Her face, Ephraim. I can't stop seeing her face."

"I know. It's going to stay with you for a long time. And I'm sorry about that."

"I just wanted to cry."

"You're mourning her," I explain. "You've never met her, but because of this mission, you're connected to her, and you feel the pain of her loss. It shows a very caring, compassionate side of you. But you have to remember that she made her choice. If her friends knew she had this heart condition, she knew it too, and I'm sure she knew what cocaine would do to her. She chose the drug, and it stole her life before it had a chance to begin."

"We saved Benjamin Holloway," he reminds me. "Saved him from doing something just as stupid. Why does he get a second chance and Megan Robinson doesn't?"

"That, my friend, is in the big book called 'Answers We're Not Allowed to Know.' I think the best you can do at this moment is content yourself in the knowledge that you succeeded in both of your missions tonight. It's been a very long day, and once we're a sufficient distance away, we'll find a hotel and get some proper sleep."

"I don't know if I can keep doing this," he says, the exhaustion evident in his voice.

"Don't give up. You're better at this than you realize."

Chapter 5

Sunday, October 28, 2007

Tristan

This shit is disgusting.

Four glasses into a bottle of scotch, that's all I can think. How in the hell do people drink this stuff? It tastes like turpentine smells, and the effects on the palate, I have to imagine, must be pretty similar. Still, I'm on a quest, so I'm going to persist.

My cousin walks into the dining room and gives me an inquisitive look. "What's with this?" he asks, pointing to the bottle.

"Whatshitooya?" I ask, non-drunkenly and more handsomely than usual.

"I've just never seen you drink before, so I wondered if there was a special occasion. But the sight of you drinking alone and the slurring of your words makes me think this might not be a joyful one."

"I'm noddrunk, if that's whatcher thinking."

"Wouldn't dream of it. Can I at least grab a glass and join you?"

I gesture an invitation; it may be a little bigger than I planned. "Knock yershelf out."

"Looks like you're well on the way," he repliesh. *Oh, Christ, I'm slurring my narrative too? That's not good.*

He sits at the dining room table with me and pours himself two fingers of scotch. After a satisfying drag on it, he says, "Twelve-year-old single-malt. Good stuff."

"Tastes like yak piss," I rebut.

"Which brings me back to my original question of why you're sitting alone on a Sunday afternoon in your dining room, drinking large quantities of a substance that you don't enjoy."

"People drink to remember," I answer.

"People drink to *forget,*" he corrects.

"When people get drunk," I continue, "they release their inim— Their imhib—"

"Inhibitions."

"Those. And they say things they wouldn't say otherwise."

"Still missing the connection here."

"My memories, Ephraim. It's been weeks, and I still don't have them available to me. I feel like I'm being inhibited, and I thought thishtuff would help."

"I scarcely think that alcohol poisoning is the key to mnemonic success. And for God's sake, if you're going to get plastered, at least drink something you enjoy."

"I don't own anything I enjoy. And besidesh, this ishn't about enjoyment. I have these … ghosts of memories that flit by me, but I can't grab on to them. And I know that you know thingsh that you're not telling me."

His expression confirms it. "I wish you could believe that it's for your protection."

I bring out the object that inspired this whole idea and hold it up for him to see. "What is this?" I ask him.

He takes it in his hand, inspects it, and answers, "It's a brass door knocker. Quite a nice one, actually. Looks like it's been engraved. It says 'Easily House, 2007.' What else?"

"I don't remember this. I've never bought a door knocker in my life.

I don't know any place called Easily House, and I've never called this place that. So what is it?"

"Maybe you bought it for someone else and never gave it to them."

"Maybe, except it was gift wrapped, and the card tag said 'Tristan.' I don't *think* I wrap presents to myself, so who gave it to me, why, and what does it mean?"

"Would it ease your mind if I told you it was a gift from me?"

"Probably. Is it?"

"No."

"Then it doesn't."

"Tristan, I don't know where the door knocker came from, and I don't know where your house got its comical nickname. But I do know that your memories will come back to you soon, probably sooner than you suspect, and it's going to be a difficult day—a very difficult and painful day. On that day, I want you to remember that I'm on your side. I'm here to help you and support you. Right now, the best thing I can do for you is to take this bottle away from you. You should go to your room and rest. There's nothing pressing today. Ease your mind and trust in things to happen when they will."

He's right, and even in the fog that four glasses of scotch created, I know it. I should thank him, but instead I mumble something like "Muh ne-mimph" and trudge up the stairs to my bed.

Monday, October 29, 2007

If sleep was a friend, following my ill-advised consumption, wakefulness is the playground bully sent to beat me up. I'll call my present state a hangover, though I've never had one before. The discomfort is not intense enough to make me believe I'm receiving a message. Rather, it's an all-over achiness, combined with some dizziness and a feeling like a water buffalo took a crap in my mouth. Now I remember why I don't drink.

Slowly I pull myself out of bed. I'm not sure initially what time it is;

not early, that's for sure. The sun started its day hours ago; the sun wasn't drunk off its ass. *What did I do yesterday? What did I say?* For someone with lasting memory issues, this shouldn't be distressing, but I feel like I may have embarrassed myself in front of Ephraim.

To my surprise, it is after 10:30 when my feet first touch the floor. I can't remember the last time I've slept this late; of course, I can't remember a lot of things lately. Maybe today is the day to do something about that. As I make my way through my morning routine, I am a bit relieved to see that Ephraim is not about. Though I doubt he would give me a hard time about yesterday's scotch-fueled misstep, it's better that I don't even give him the opportunity. As I ponder (read: brush my teeth), I realize how deeply I dislike having this much free time. I'm not used to it, and being in a state of either idleness or emergency day after day is disturbing any sense of equilibrium I'm hoping to establish.

I haven't lived my recent months in isolation; there are people beyond Ephraim who could help me find answers to what is missing. In fact, there's a big building with my name on it, and the last time I was there, the reception I got suggests that these people know me. Especially the one—*what was his name?* He was average height, dark complexion; Hispanic, I think. It seemed like he was in charge there now. He'll talk to me ... whoever he is.

Freshly determined, I power through the rest of my preparations and dress up a bit, just enough to look respectable walking into my former company. Still no sign of Ephraim as I leave the house and get into my car. That's fine; I don't answer to him anyway, despite his beliefs to the contrary. As I get on the highway from Ocean City to Salisbury, I realize that the route to this building is less certain than I would like. I don't remember the address or what streets I take once I get to town. The one time I've been there recently, Ephraim drove; so I'm relying on very shaky memory to guide me.

Maybe the secret is to think *less* about it. Don't overthink it; let instinct and habit take over. I've driven this route so many times, I could do it subconsciously, so that's what I'll do. Let the unconscious mind get me there, the reptile brain. *Reptile brain? What does that mean?*

Where have I heard that phrase before? A discussion, but with whom? And about what?

The reptiles clearly win, because when I distract myself from my thoughts, I realize that I am turning onto the road on which the Shays Diode building sits. Pleased at this, I park in visitor parking—which, under different circumstances I'm sure would feel strange—and make my way to the building lobby. Upon seeing me, the receptionist's face lights up with recognition, and she greets me warmly. "Good morning, Mr. Shays. It's good to see you. How are you feeling?"

"Getting better every day," I reply. "Thank you …" *Damn, why did I have to reach for the name?*

"Darcy," she offers without the slightest offense apparent. "I'm very glad to hear it. How can I help today?"

"Well, I didn't call ahead, but I was hoping to meet with my friend …" *And here we go again. Edward, Edgar, Escher, Aslan, Fester, Jester, Hester,* "Esteban. Is he available, by any chance?"

She checks her computer screen. "His phone status says he's in. Let me call up there to find out." Quickly dialing his extension, she says, "Mr. Padgett?"

Padgett, that's right. Esteban Padgett. I know this stuff. Where the hell did I get Fester?

"Mr. Shays is here, and he's wondering if you have time to speak with him? … Very good, I'll let him know." After ending the call, she says to me, "He'd be glad to see you. You can go on up." I can see the conflict in her eyes before she asks me the next question. "Do … do you remember the way there?"

I smile and nod a little, acknowledging the awkwardness of having to ask. "I think so, but I'm going to make myself remember. You've been helpful, and I thank you for that."

"It's my pleasure, sir."

I turn toward the elevators but then stop and linger at her desk for a minute more. "Darcy, this is going to sound like a strange question, but I want you to feel free to answer honestly. What do people here know about what happened to me?"

I know I've cranked up the awkwardness factor tenfold, but this day is about learning about myself, and this is an opportunity. She tries to keep a brave face as she says, "Well … we were told that you went in for a medical treatment for chronic pain … and something went wrong during the procedure. It left you in a coma for more than a week, and when you woke up, parts of your memory were … unavailable to you. Is that … close?"

I offer a pleasant smile. "Right on the money. Just wanted to make sure people didn't think I crashed a motorcycle doing extreme sports or anything like that. One more follow-up question, then I promise to let you get back to work: who told everybody about this?"

"Umm … it was that man who came here with you the last time you were here. Your cousin, I think it is?"

"Thanks, Darcy. I appreciate it."

With that, I make my way to the elevator and go to the eighth floor. I find that by not trying so hard to remember, instinct guides me in the correct direction. That didn't work quite as well in remembering my dear friend, Aslan Jester, but I'm working on it.

As I enter the CEO's office—*my office*—I'm greeted by an effervescent young woman. "Tristan!"

My mind is blank, my mind is blank. Say what you would always say to her. "Hello, Kayla, how are you?"

"Great, thanks. It's good to see you. You look good."

"Thank you. I don't think I've ever been this well-rested in my life, even without the coma."

She laughs politely. *Are coma jokes in poor taste if I'm the one who was in the coma?*

"I believe Mr. Padgett is expecting me."

"You're damn right he is," comes a male voice from the inner office, in a tone of playful scolding. Esteban steps out of his *(my)* office and greets me warmly. "Now that you're a man of leisure, I thought I would be seeing you more often."

I don't really have a good excuse, so a poor one will have to suffice. "You're a busy man. I didn't want to intrude. If memory serves, it's a lot of work running this place."

"It's good to see you. Come on in."

I follow him into his office, and he closes the door so we can speak privately. My efforts at looking around aren't lost on him. "Is it familiar to you?"

"It is and it isn't," I reply. "That's what's strange. I've been coming to this office every day for years, but my most recent memories of it—even the fact that I ran the company—are blocked from me. In a way, I wish I just lost all my memory. This bits-and-pieces stuff, it's … it's what I imagine Alzheimer's must feel like, and I have to tell you, if that's the case, I'm not looking forward to it."

"But it's temporary, isn't it? They expect that your memories will return as you heal?"

"So I'm told. I've been to the doctors a few times since it happened, and every time, they tell me that I'm in great shape, and I'm making great progress."

"That's good news."

"So why was it so hard for me to remember your name when I came here to see you today?"

He offers a gentle shrug. "Guess I'm just forgettable."

"I suspect not."

"Do you remember saving my life?" he asks.

It's a jarring question, one to which the obvious answer should be, *Yes, of course.* The best I can offer is, "I have flashes of memory. Visions of you in danger."

"That's how it all started, you know. This path your life took. You were here, running this company, just as ordinary as can be, and then one day, you told me that my wife was planning to kill me."

"I did?"

"Yes, you did."

"And was she?"

"Yes, and she would've succeeded, if it weren't for you. After that, everything changed. Suddenly, you'd be called away for days at a time. You'd be off saving someone else, a few states away. Eventually, you decided that it would be better if I ran the company, so you could dedicate your attention to this new calling. The last I heard, you were in Washington, DC, on some kind of extended mission."

Alien. It's all alien to me, like he's reading me the synopsis of a movie I've never seen. How can that be?

"Not ringing any bells, is it?" he asks.

"It's so strange. You tell me these things, and there's a part of my mind that feels like I should know them; feels like I *do* know them. But it's academic knowledge. I reach for images—memories of what these things sounded like, looked like, smelled like, and it's like 'file not found.' Or worse, 'password required for access.'"

"Have you tried '12345678' for a password? Sometimes people get lazy."

"I wish it was that simple. This one's locked behind wicked firewalls. And I can't get to them. The worst part is, I think Ephraim knows about all these things, but he won't tell me."

"The man who was here with you last time?"

"Yes. My cousin, Ephraim. Had you ever seen him before that day?"

"No. The better question is, had *you?*"

It's a fair question. "I admit, when I woke up in the hospital and saw him there with me, I didn't know who he was. But I didn't know much at that moment. The more time I spend with him, the more I believe he's been a part of my life before. Why? Do you think he's not who he says he is?"

"I'm not ready to say that," Esteban replies, "but if I were conspiracy-minded, I would admit it makes an intriguing scenario. Wealthy man has a life-threatening injury. He wakes up to find he's in the care of a relative he doesn't remember. Has he made a move for your money?"

"No, that's just it. He hasn't even asked for any."

"So what do you suppose he wants? Why spend all this time with you, away from his family, away from his work?"

"I don't know," I answer. "He doesn't seem to need money. He hasn't spoken of any family, and he seems to be on a leave of absence from his work."

"Hmm."

"There's one other thing you should know—he gets these messages too. At least he used to; I don't know if he still does."

"Runs in the family, then, huh?" he asks.

"I guess so."

He hesitates a moment before saying, "I don't know if I should say anything, and I'll add that I don't know if this means anything ... but before your injury, there was someone standing in the way of what you were trying to do."

"Standing in the way?" I repeat.

"All I know is what you told me at the time, and you didn't know much. But there was a man trying to stop you from helping people. I don't even know why. Now, I'm not going to sit here and say with any certainty that your cousin is that man. All I'll say is, until you're sure who your friends are and aren't, be careful who you trust."

"What scares me, Esteban, is that in my present condition, the person you're warning me about could just as easily be you, and I wouldn't know it."

"That's not an enviable position. I'll tell you right now, and I hope you trust me, that I've considered you a friend for many years, and I would never harm you."

"Thank you. That means a great deal to me."

After a silence of several uncomfortable seconds, he suggests, "Let's go have some lunch."

He takes me to a Thai restaurant that he says is one of our favorites, but for me there is no familiarity to the place. I choose dishes that Esteban says he's never seen me order before. What does that even say about the state of my mind and my memory? Even if I don't remember what I usually order, wouldn't I be drawn to the same things naturally anyway? The fact that I'm not is more upsetting than it should be. It makes me feel like I'm just renting my body, rather than owning it.

As we eat, Esteban gives me a history of my own company. I'm relieved to discover that I do remember things from the company's early years—although they come to me more as *oh yeah, that's right,* rather than knowledge that's deeply ingrained. But recent developments? They're terra incognita to me. We won a major contract with a huge developer in the past few months to supply his hotels and resorts with LED lighting, and I have no recollection of it. I handed the presidency over to Esteban, a man I've known and trusted for years, but you couldn't prove it by me.

I've read books and seen movies (I think) about people living with amnesia, and they always struck me as diverting but implausible. Until now, that is. Now I'm living the situation, and I wouldn't wish it on anybody. And now, the specter of doubt has crept into my mind about Ephraim himself. *Someone standing in the way of my efforts to help people? Who? And more importantly, why? What could someone possibly gain by stopping someone from saving another person's life?*

Despite my emphatic request to pay for lunch, Esteban insists, and I gratefully accept. I trust him. I *want* to trust him. But the same could be said about my feelings for Ephraim, and at the moment, I don't have full faith in my ability to do so.

Esteban drives us back to corporate headquarters, where I thank him again for his good company and return to my car. Lunch offered more food for thought than anything else. The drive back to Ocean City gives me the precious and dangerous commodity of time alone with myself, during which I have far too much opportunity to think. My thoughts remain fixed on Ephraim Shays. I go over everything that's happened between us since the moment I woke up in the hospital and found him there watching over me. I search fervently for anything remotely sinister, any hint of malice lurking in his words, his actions, his intentions. My efforts feel fruitless. His actions in recent weeks have felt overbearing at times, overprotective, guarded, and frequently secretive, but I can't think of a single instance in which he's tried to do anything that wasn't in my best interest.

Forty-five minutes later, I am back at home. Ephraim is home now, and he speaks to me as soon as I walk in the front door. "You went out," he correctly observes.

"Yes I did."

"Is everything all right?"

"I'm fine, thanks. I just went to have lunch with a friend."

"Who was it?" he asks.

His tone is making me uneasy. And it's doing nothing but bolstering the suspicion I've been trying to overcome, the doubts that Esteban unintentionally ignited in me. "No one you know," I reply in a firm tone. "Why the interrogation?"

"Concern for you. You don't have all your memories back yet, and I don't want anyone who might mean you harm to have access to you."

"That's a sentiment I share," I tell him, "but I need you have faith in my ability to read people and know who my friends are. I respect and appreciate your efforts to protect me, but I can't live my life with you by my side as a chaperone."

He stands silently for a moment, perhaps deciding what to say. He settles on, "You're right, of course. Please know that it's motivated by the best intentions. And if it's any comfort, the situation is only temporary. Very temporary." He's interrupted by the ringing of the doorbell, which evokes a curious reaction in him. He closes his eyes and gets a look of resolve, almost as if the sound happened right on cue. "You'll need to answer that," he says matter-of-factly.

It's a strange response, certainly, and one I want to ask him about, but I also need to see who's at my front door. I open it without asking or even looking—deliberately, to see if this breach of security brings a reaction from Ephraim; it does not. Standing there is a woman who appears to be in her late thirties. She is plainly dressed, not made up, and there is about her a pervasive air of sorrow, so powerful that it looks like someone wept her out of a nightmare. I don't recognize her as she stands there, but her facial expression upon seeing me tells me clearly that she recognizes me. The sight of my face turns her countenance from one of emptiness to one of barely contained rage.

What does one say in the face of this? Meeting someone you don't know who clearly despises you? Is she a former girlfriend? An old enemy? A business rival I ruined? I am in the embarrassing and vulnerable position of having to ask her. "Hello," I offer quietly. "Can I help you?"

She seems taken aback by the question. "Can you help me?" she repeats, clearly in disbelief. "That's what you have to say to me?"

"I'm—"

"I've spent the last six weeks debating whether I should come here. Whether I should face you, tell you all the things I've wanted to tell you. And you ask me if you can help me. Was that what the money was for? To 'help me'? Or to buy me off for what you did?"

"I'm sorry, but I don't …"

"Do you remember the last words I said to you before you went off on your fool's errand to Washington? Because I do. I said, 'Come home safe. Both of you.' And here you are, just you, home safe. Not her. I haven't done anything with the money you gave me. I'll give it to someone. I don't know who yet. Someone deserving. Some group that will use it to save lives. Like the life you didn't save."

None of this is familiar; none of it. I want to show this stranger some compassion, to help her through what she's feeling, but until I have a frame of reference, I can't do anything productive. All I can venture is my best guess. "I did everything I could."

Without warning, she hauls off and lands a surprisingly powerful open-handed slap to my jaw, which sends me reeling backward off balance. Owing to the pervasive effects of the brain injury, my balance has been a sometimes thing at best lately. I try to reach out, to break my fall with my arms, but I am disoriented and feel myself going further and further down, until the back of my head makes sharp, agonizing contact with the cold marble floor of my entryway. Seconds after contact, the woman spits words at me. "Is that what you told yourself when you let Genevieve die?"

In an instant, everything changes.

In a literal rush, memories flood my consciousness; it's as if every image that was shut off to me is instantaneously turned back on. I know the identity of my assailant, Allison Swan, and I know she is the sister of—

Genevieve.

Mercilessly, the cruelest moment of my life replays itself in brutally high definition, and the memory of the murder of the woman I love evokes a scream from inside of me that could have shaken the house from its foundation. Engulfed in these memories, I am barely aware of anything happening around me, but I see Ephraim rush over to her as she says, "What's happening to him?"

I hear him answer, "You assaulted a wounded man, that's what's happening! I'm very sorry for your loss, but you need to leave here right now, or I'll have you arrested for battery. Go!"

I think she leaves; she's no longer there, at least. My surroundings are barely registering at this moment, an amorphous haze in my consciousness, which is locked on the events of August 21. Somehow I realize that Ephraim has elevated my head and placed it on his lap for protection as he sits on the floor next to me. I'm trembling, gasping for breath, suffering spasms of muscle activity that correspond with each new horrific memory of what happened to me and to Genevieve Swan.

"What's happening to me?" I sob mournfully.

"What needed to happen," Ephraim answers gently. "I'm here. I'll keep you safe. Let the images return. Let yourself process them."

It's not as if I have a choice. Similar to the feelings I feel when getting an assignment, it's like a dam has burst, and every memory, image, and emotion held at bay behind it is pouring over me, threatening to drown me in its intensity. I see things in what appears to be reverse chronological order, starting with my surgery. *The Gnothautii—their orders to damage me irreparably. Genevieve trying to save me from them and losing her life in the process. Karolena, the horrible creature who orchestrated this whole thing.*

After the memories of that day, others rush in to take their place. I remember SODARCOM, Phillip Kean, Washington, the Swift Center, the pills, the unexplained death of my nurse, Cheryl. And through it all, I remember a figure in the background, pulling the strings. The figure of a man. My cousin, Ephraim Shays. *My enemy.*

With a dizzying, jerking motion, I pull myself away from him and crawl into the living room, over by the fireplace. Bracing myself on the rack of fireplace tools, I get unsteadily to my feet and decide to pick up an iron fireplace poker. Turning back to him, I brandish it indelicately as a makeshift weapon. "You!" The pronoun is an accusation. "You're behind all this. You who already know how my life will turn out."

He rises and approaches me slowly. "Tristan, you need to calm down. You're very emotional right now, and it's impeding your ability to think."

"Oh, I'm thinking clearly. For the first time in two months, I'm thinking clearly. You knew this day was coming. You knew I'd get my memories back. You didn't think I'd remember your part in everything that happened?"

"Do you remember the part where I rescued you from the Gnothautii? The part where I killed the men who hurt you?"

My answer is honest and not spiteful. "No. I don't. You told me that you did that, but I can't remember it. You know what I *can* remember? I can remember you shooting me with a dart and taking me out of Washington. I can remember you holding a gun on me at SODARCOM's offices, the offices of a company you worked for—probably *still* work for—that wants to kill 30 million Americans for the sake of natural resources. I watched you sabotage a plane full of children so that it would kill them all, just to prove a point. I watched you try to abduct a child from a museum field trip, just because I was there to protect him. So you'll have to forgive me, Ephraim, if I'm not leaping up to herald you as my salvation. Because I've seen the real you in action, and it makes me question the shit out of this whole setup. It makes me wonder who you really are and what you're really up to."

He stands his ground, and I stand mine, fireplace poker still in hand. His trademark calm—the stoicism I now remember from our every meeting—doesn't budge from his demeanor. He looks at me in silence for long seconds that feel longer than they actually are. "You just don't see the shades of gray, do you?" he asks at last. "It's all black or white to you, strictly good or strictly evil. No wonder they picked you. You spout the company mottos perfectly, and you don't even realize you're doing it. I'm all about the gray. Finding the good in evil, finding the evil in good. Part of having the clarity of vision that you now remember I have. Yes, Tristan, I knew this day was coming today, because I remember it. Like I remember every bit of my life, including the parts that haven't happened yet. There were times I envied you this memory loss of yours. Something that could wipe out this incredible, terrible prescience I endure. It's not the gift you think it is. You're about to ask me who I really am."

"Who are you, really?"

"I'm Jesus' unspoken anger for the crucifixion. I'm God's hidden self-loathing. I'm the flip of the coin that lands on the edge—not heads, not tails, but somewhere in between. I'm the song you whistle when you walk past the graveyard. The gun trained on the elephant in the room."

"Is that supposed to scare me?"

"Scaring you benefits me nothing. You asked who I am. That's how I see myself."

"Sounds exhausting," I retort.

"You have no idea."

"Do you want to kill me? Is that what this is all about?"

He looks surprised at the question. "Tristan, if you'll recall, I had nine days of coma during which I could have killed you quite easily and made it look like an accident. Not to mention six weeks of you and me alone in this empty, secluded house. Knowing what you know of me, do you really think I'm biding my time, waiting for the perfect moment to push you down the stairs?"

"What, then? The money? Is that what you want?"

"You've seen your accounts. Have I misappropriated even a dollar?"

"No."

"Given myself power of attorney or cosigner privileges on anything?"

"No."

"There you go."

"Then I'm running out of motives," I tell him.

"No, you're simply running out of *ulterior* motives. Search beneath the sinister, and a new layer of possibilities opens up."

"Are you really my cousin?" I ask point blank.

"Does that matter?"

"It shouldn't, but it does."

"Which answer would make you feel better?"

"Never mind. I couldn't prove it in either case, and the fluidity of your truth makes the question practically moot anyway. You're family; you're not family. In the end, you already know what's going to be. You're just waiting for me to catch up."

He takes this opportunity to walk over to me, slowly, without any menace, taking the poker gently from my hand and replacing it in the rack. Then, much to my surprise, he puts his arms around me and just holds on to me. It is awkward at first, particularly given our history. I don't feel motivated to hold on to him, but I don't feel compelled to pull away. Absent too many options, I decide to ride it out.

After a bit, he pulls back. "Words were failing to suffice," he explains.

I move to the sofa in the living room, and he sits in a chair opposite. "What happens now?" I ask, needing to break the silence.

"What do you mean?"

"This was the breakthrough, the return of my memories. I imagine this was the event you were waiting for. Now that it's happened, will you be moving on?"

"You speak as though your recovery is complete."

"You reply as if it isn't."

He gives a little shrug. "Complicated things, head injuries. Are you satisfied that I'm not your enemy?"

"Nemesis was the word that I used to use."

"I'm flattered," he says.

"It isn't a compliment."

"Not to you."

"You have to earn the right to be treated as an ally," I decide aloud. "So far, you've offered evidence that this is possible, but I still believe you could be playing the long game, especially because you're planning to stay here."

"The next few days are going to be very painful for you, Tristan. I know you've gotten used to the physical pain, but the unveiling of those memories will bring a level of emotional pain that you're not used to. I'm not prepared to leave you alone to face that. I'm very impressed that you're able to function right here, right now, remembering what you've just remembered."

"I'm not letting myself feel it," I admit quietly. "Not all of it. When the time comes, soon, I'll feel it. But right now, I need to be in control."

"Fair enough."

It takes me a minute to form the words of the next question. "Why did you do it, Ephraim? All the people who got hurt or killed. I've spent these weeks with you, and you take care of me, and you defend me. I don't think of you as evil. But then, I watched you with the guy who was breaking into my car, and the effortlessness you showed in attacking him—it scares me a little. Maybe more than a little. It makes me wonder if you could turn on me that way, be that ruthless with me. So I have to know—why did you do it? All of it?"

For many seconds, he looks at me, this man who knows my future. He looks at me like I'm superfluous to the conversation, and finally he says, "Tea."

"What?"

"You need tea. I know I do. You stay there and be comfortable, and I'll get some for us."

Chapter 6

Monday, October 29, 2007

Ephraim

I owe Tristan an explanation; I know this. It needs to be sincere, and it needs to be convincing, and to do that, I need a few minutes. Enough time to make a pot of tea. So instead of speaking with him right away, I go into the kitchen and get things ready, putting the kettle on the stove to boil. I weigh the merits of telling him the truth versus shielding him, and I realize that I've been shielding him long enough. After everything he's been through, he deserves to know.

After six minutes, I bring a tray out, fully loaded with tea the way he likes it. A simple Darjeeling; none of the silly, fruity stuff that passes for tea these days. I even find some shortbread wafers in the pantry and put them on the tray as well. As he takes his first cup, I begin my explanation. "We'll start with the obligatories. I mean you no harm. I rescued you from the Gnothautii because ..."

"I'm not interested in them right now. I'm more interested in you. In what you've done," he says. "Tell me about SODARCOM."

I take a sip from my own teacup, add a little more sugar. "You remember, don't you? Your encounter with Phillip Kean? The time you spent at Swift?"

"I remember it all. I know what happened. What I want to know is why. Why do they think killing 30 million Americans is the answer, and why were you so eager to help them?"

"I'm not here to make excuses for them. Apologies either. The reason you believe in our government, Tristan, is because you're not on the inside, watching them work. I know you think that the SDC is insidious. You have every reason to. It's about controlling the population. But the same is true of a lot of government agencies with names you know and respect. Above-board agencies you may have even supported with a monetary donation. We're just a little more ... *blatant* about the way we do things."

"But why you? Why help them? Does human life mean that little to you?"

"No, it means that much to me!" The answer comes out as an exclamation; louder than it needs to be. I let myself get offended, though I said I wouldn't. A few seconds of deep breathing allow me to compose myself again, so I can explain. "When I joined the agency, I admit it was for the wrong reasons. I had been a messenger for several years, and I was bitter. I wanted to take a job that would be a show of revenge against the God who moves me from place to place, doing his bidding. He wanted me to save lives; I wanted to help end them. And the money was good, absurdly good. Another reason why I haven't misappropriated any of your fortune—I didn't need to. But after I'd been with the agency for a while, I realized that *my* motivations were wrong, not the group's.

"The world is crowded, far too crowded with billions of humans, living day after day without making a single contribution to society. That's no way to run an ecosystem. It creates more of a parasitic situation. Human beings shouldn't be parasites. We should live symbiotically with each other and with this planet. So we turn to Darwin and his beliefs about natural selection. What's good for the deer and the turtles and the wolves is good for us as well. The SDC is not roaming the countryside with high-powered rifles, picking off the unemployed for sport. We're … testing mankind, if you will. Devising situations in which the fittest, the most intelligent, can survive certain natural and artificial dangers, and those who are least able to do so don't survive to propagate. Take away our cultural aversion to natural selection, and it doesn't sound so barbaric, does it?"

"What happens in 2012?" he asks. "I read something in their plans about 2012, some big event."

So he knows about that. Interesting. "Ah, yes—2012. The five-year plan. It's kind of a long shot, because it's so far off and so far from our control. Are you familiar with the Mayan calendar?"

He thinks a moment. "I know they had one. Something big, usually carved into stone."

"And quite long. Centuries, even. Well, as it happens, the current incarnation of the Mayan calendar is set to end on December 21, 2012. There's a growing wave of fear linked to this date. The less-knowledgeable have it in their heads that this date will mark the end of the world. They've invented earthquakes and firestorms and seas boiling away to nothingness, to go with their doomsday vision. It's kind of endearing in a stupid-people-say-the-cutest-things way. It's complete bullshit, of course. It's no more the end of the world than December 31, 2007 will be when the kitten calendar in your kitchen runs out."

"That was a gift," he says defensively.

"And it's adorable. But you see my point. This was a golden opportunity for the SDC to test its theories on the masses. Admit it: if someone came to your company to interview for a high-ranking position, and during the interview, he spouted off that he was certain the world was going to end in five years, you wouldn't hire him, would you?"

"I suppose not."

"As well you shouldn't."

"What is SODARCOM going to do in relation to this non-apocalypse?"

"Merely exploit the fear and superstition a bit. Rattle a few cages, shake the gullible down from the rafters."

His tone tells me he suspects there's more to it. "And?"

"There may be talk of encouraging a cultlike mass suicide on that date," I tell him, perhaps a bit too casually.

Tristan's response is one of disgust. "That's reprehensible!"

"Is it? Recall, dear cousin, your response upon receiving the assignment to go save young Benjamin Holloway from his keg stand. I believe your words were *maybe Darwin was right.*"

"That's out of context," he protests.

"*Au contraire,* that's exactly in context. You were hesitant to save him because you believe that some people might just be too stupid to live. Welcome to the Social Darwinism Commission, where we take that belief and use it to free up resources for those who *aren't* too stupid to live. The philosophy isn't that uncommon; people think they have a free pass to survival, but survival is meant to be a struggle, and there's a reason why the strongest and the smartest survive: because they're supposed to. But our technology rewards laziness, and that's ruining us as a people. Look at where our society is heading—the ones with the most kids win, and those aren't always the ones who will further society. Our culture is in decline, and you and I are tasked to save people. Are they the ones worth saving?"

"Your buddy, Phillip Kean, must have been."

"I guess he is. Still, it's hard to say what—"

I stop in mid-sentence, as I feel my thought processes commandeered out from under me, as if someone or something is carjacking my brain. It's a sensation I've felt before, but it's been a while, and I didn't expect to feel it again, quite honestly.

Tristan sees my sudden shift in expression and asks, "What is it? What's wrong?"

"Just a moment. Get me a pen and paper, please?"

He gets a pad and pen out of a nearby drawer and hands them to me. Quickly, I write down the details that are coming to me—names, places, times, everything I see and hear. When the vision is complete and I have full use of my thoughts again, I look down and see the particulars of my day.

Tristan looks in surprise at the sheet of paper. "Did you just get an assignment?" he asks.

"It appears I did."

"Are … are you okay? Are you in pain?"

I smile at his thoughtfulness. "No, my assignments don't come with pain. I'm simply surprised. I was foolish enough to think I'm off the roster. Apparently, someone has other plans for me."

"Why didn't I get the same assignment?" he asks. "Now that I can remember again, I seem to remember you and I being sent to the same places for the same missions. Why didn't that happen this time?"

I shrug and point to the ceiling. "Ask him. I've got places to be, I'm afraid."

He peers over, trying to see what I've written down. "Where are you going?"

Deliberately I hide the page from his view. "Can't tell you. Not this time."

"Oh, come on! I've got my memories back. You don't have to shield me anymore."

"This time I do, unfortunately. No time to explain either. I want you to rest up for the remainder of the day. The after-effects of getting your memory back are going to be painful for now. If you need anything, call my phone. Rest, I mean it!"

Without another word, I am out the front door and getting into my car. I have time, but not as much as I would like. Ocean City is lovely, but conveniently located to anywhere else it is not. Much as I tout the merits of driving to different missions, I have a long way to go, so travel will be by air, and it's going to have to be charter. This one's going to cost me.

Fortunately, Wicomico Airport is only forty minutes away. I push the speed limit a bit and get there in thirty-five, heading right for the charters desk. The man behind the desk is reading a newspaper as I approach. He sets it down and asks, "Help ya?"

"I need a fast plane to get me to Pensacola, Florida, leaving as quickly as possible. I'm the only one on the charter."

He checks his computer screen. "I've got a four-seater jet that could leave in the next twenty minutes, get you there by 9:00 tonight."

I check the sheet of paper with the details. It doesn't give me much time, but it'll work. "That's fine."

"Won't be cheap, though. You're looking at a cost of $3,255 for the one-way trip."

I pull a leather card case out of my pocket and open it up for him, displaying my identification card. "Any discount for federal government employees?" The card doesn't say Social Darwinism Commission, of course, but some sister agency I belong to, for purposes just like this one.

"Yeah, actually. For you it would be $2,120."

I present an American Express card. "Perfect. Ring it up."

Ah, private jets. Gratuitous, certainly. Absurdly expensive, without a doubt. But unbeatable for convenience, and fucking comfy, that's for damn sure. A fiscal conscience prevented me from using them all the time with the SDC, but sometimes they were necessary, and I've never had an unpleasant flight on one—unlike the game of Russian roulette that is commercial air travel. Aboard my little luxury jet for one, I have leg room, I have beverages and a decent dinner, and I have time alone undisturbed to think about what I have to do tonight.

Once again, I find myself approaching a situation that does not appear in my memories. I have recollection of the people involved, but I don't remember doing this—going to Florida to take this assignment. As before, it involves Tristan, so I suspect his presence has tweaked the memory for me.

Pensacola, Florida. Though I don't yet have the specific details of what's to come, I know who's waiting there for me. By rights, I should be scared. Terrified, even. There's an individual there with the power to tear me apart with his mind. A man I've never met, but what I know of him astonishes me. Even with all his strength, he is a prisoner. And that makes his captors even more dangerous than he. They're the ones I really need to fear. Fortunately, they don't know who I am. This alone might keep me alive during this mission. Because this man, this powerful creature, needs me to save him from his fate. And depending on how the evening goes, I just might do it.

Upon arrival at Pensacola, I dismiss the pilot. Though I could pay extra to keep him on for the return trip, I don't know when that will be—or, practically speaking, *if* that will be. I don't plan on dying tonight, but the universe has a twisted sense of humor.

As I get into the first taxi in line at the cab stand, it occurs to me that I've come on this mission completely unarmed—something I prefer not to do in situations far less tenuous than this one. But even with a chartered flight, there are FAA regulations about firearms, and to board the plane with no checked luggage, no carry-on bag, and a loaded weapon would just invite scrutiny. I don't have a single contact in or near Pensacola, so obtaining a gun here won't be possible either. Reflecting on my current assignment, I console myself in remembering that my adversaries won't use guns either. They'll just think me to death; that's much kinder.

I realize, upon looking up from my thoughts, that the cab driver is looking at me expectantly from the front seat, waiting. "Hmm?" I mutter.

"Where to?" he asks, sounding gently put out.

Of course. Reasonable question. I give him the address that was transmitted to me, not knowing if it will be an office building, a bar, a tanning salon, or a taco stand. He accepts the information, starts the meter, and the drive begins.

A curious sensation simmers within me, one I'm not used to: anxiety. I'm not immune to fear, where it's warranted; I've just learned to shut out its less-helpful aspects and use fear in situations where it gives me a physical advantage and produces an excess of body and brain chemicals I can use to my advantage.

One of the benefits of foreknowledge of my future is knowing how an upcoming situation will turn out. But this time, I'm flying blind. I have memories of events beyond this date, so I'm relatively certain that I'll survive tonight, but lately, things have been changing; events have become malleable, and that in itself is disturbing. So I'm feeling anxious about tonight, about being an outsider in this scenario, with no one to call an ally, no one to call for help if something goes wrong. I wish I could have invited Tristan along as backup, but not this time. These are people he'll have to face in his future, and it's crucial that they don't know about him yet. Not now; not until he's ready for them.

After about a half hour of driving, the cab pulls into the entryway of what is obviously a former hotel. Almost ten stories tall, it features a solid wall of balconies jutting out from sliding glass doors. Every room I can see is dark, and the signage that once identified the property is gone. "This is the place," the driver tells me, his first words to me since *Where to?* "It's not a hotel anymore, you know."

"Thank you," I reply. "I know. This is where I was asked to go. What do I owe you?"

"Forty-two fifty," he says.

I hand him fifty dollars. "Rest is yours," I tell him, a generous gesture, given his perfunctory level of customer service.

After exiting the cab, I close the door behind me, and he pulls away, leaving me as alone as I've felt in quite a long time. Uninviting as the place looks, I know this is where I'm supposed to be. I proceed slowly to the glass front doors and give a little pull; I'm completely unsurprised to find them locked. There is a key card reader on the wall for which I have no key card; beside it is an intercom button and speaker. I press the button, and a few seconds later, a voice says, "Yes?"

"I was told to come here."

"Name?"

Fortunately, I was given a name in with my mission, so I repeat it, hoping I'm not fucking up the pronunciation too severely. "Dr. Vyacheslav Zinovyovich." The details of this mission included information about the real Dr. Vyacheslav Zinovyovich, who was unexpectedly detained in Kiev. I know this is my only hope of entry, and I'm relieved when the name results in a buzzer sounding and the lock on the front door being released.

In the middle of the lobby, at what was likely once the concierge desk, sits a lone security guard, the one who buzzed me in. He presents a clipboard with a sheet of paper on it. "Sign in," he instructs. In scribbling something barely legible, I notice that there are only five names on the sign-in sheet for the day. I can't tell immediately if this is the latest of several sheets for today or if the place just doesn't get many visitors. From the looks of it, I'm more inclined to suspect the latter.

The guard points to a door on my left. "Go through that door and down the stairs to the basement. Follow the corridor, and you'll find the others."

"Thank you."

So far, so good. I make my way to the stairs with no further conversation. The guard is the easy part; what awaits me down below will be the true test. I'm counting on none of the others having met or seen Vyacheslav Zinovyovich. If any one of them has, it's over, and I've got shit for an exit strategy.

At the base of the stairs, a dimly lit corridor stretches in two directions. One leads to darkened rooms and closed doors. The other leads to an area of light, so that's my choice. Sincerely wishing I was armed, I make my way to a small room with light spilling out into the corridor. I weigh the merits of faking a Russian accent and decide against it, realizing that a bad accent would be harder to explain than no accent. As I pause in the doorway, the two people in the room stop their conversation to look at me.

Survey the scene. One man, one woman. He's in his forties, well-dressed, carries himself like he's got money and power; looks strong, mentally and physically, and something else. *Fuck. Probing me. Psychic. Time to put up the walls.* Fortunately, I'm sensitive to intrusions into my thoughts, and I can defend myself without looking like I'm defending myself. He's a psi, but he's not the psi I'm here for.

Then there's the woman. Considerably younger, maybe late twenties. Attractive, but more scientist attractive than supermodel attractive. She's not dressed to tease or captivate; she's dressed to work, so the beauty I pick up on is natural. It's just who she is. The way they're standing, they're not old friends, not colleagues. She is a visitor here, in his house; brought in as some kind of specialist. She respects him, fears him a little maybe. She's self-confident, so it's hard to tell for certain.

The man speaks first. "Are you Dr. Zinovyovich?"

Good, he doesn't know. "Yes, hello. Thank you for having me here."

"It's our pleasure, Doctor. Your reputation is excellent. And I'd like to thank you for obtaining the necessary visas to come here."

"I'm led to understand it is important."

"Forgive me. Where are my manners?" He extends his hand. "I'm Jordan Blaylock."

"A pleasure to meet you," I reply, grasping his hand. "And who is your colleague?"

The woman offers her own introduction. "Doctor Kelsey Adams," she says in a very pronounced Russian accent.

"Adams?" I reply in surprise. "Not the name I expected to go with that voice."

"It is my professional name," she explains. "Americans are less trusting of Ekaterena Dmitrieva."

I offer a polite little laugh of understanding. "Point well taken. Perhaps if I stay in this country, I could learn to answer to 'Steve.'" *Holy shit, am I flirting? Good, Ephraim. Way to focus.*

Jordan Blaylock takes control of the conversation again. "Can I get you anything? Food or drink?"

"Thank you, but no. There's work to do, as I understand it, so we should begin."

Dr. Adams tells me, "We've been working with the subject over the course of the past day and a half. He's remarkable. I would even say unique. I trust you've read the case file?"

"I have." I haven't, of course, but the forces that sent me here have acquainted me very well with who—and what—I am to face.

"Then you understand what we're dealing with," she continues. "In many ways, he is like a child, but don't let that give you a false sense of security. His strength is beyond measure, unlike anything I've ever encountered as a neuroscientist. He's in the room at the end of the corridor, in physical restraints, of course, but also wearing a cortical suppressor I designed just for him. It inhibits the areas of his brain that control his unique abilities. It's the only way we could get close to him."

Time for a bit more clarification. "So your wish for me is to …?"

"Understand him," Blaylock replies. "Catalog exactly what he is capable of doing. What his gifts are, what their limitations are. What his weaknesses are, if any. We need to know how to stop him if he becomes a liability. This is why we have called you here. Your work in psychic research and engineering is unparalleled. More than that, he doesn't know you, so he has no animosity toward you. He's already developed a level of antagonism toward Dr. Adams and me."

"What do I need to know, beyond what was in the file?" I ask. "What has happened in your interactions with him to cause this level of animosity?"

Blaylock and Adams look at each other in precisely the way two people do when they've both done something they're not proud of and neither wants to be the one to talk about it. Interestingly, it is our Miss Kelsey, nee Ekaterena, who comes clean. "Given the nature of our needs, it was necessary to … train him."

Curious euphemism. "Train him?"

She elaborates. "There was some conditioning involved in maximizing the effectiveness of his particular psychic abilities. He was not initially cooperative, so the conditioning techniques required some positive *and* negative reinforcement."

"Forgive the analogy," I reply, testing the waters, "but what you seem to be saying is that you created an attack dog, and now you fear it will bite you."

Blaylock answers me, the discomfort evident in his voice. "Your comparison is crude but not entirely inaccurate."

I choose this moment to give voice to the real reason I've come here. "I would like to confer with Karolena before I begin, if possible."

Blaylock and Adams look at each other once again. "I'm sorry," he says, "who did you say?"

"Karolena. I was told she oversees projects such as this one."

"It's not a name I'm familiar with," Adams says. "Did you have a last name for this person?"

"No, I'm afraid not." I do, of course, but I'm not going to tell them that, especially when I know that Karolena's got her creepy little hands in this. Turning psychics into weapons? There's no question in my mind. They're protecting her, keeping her away from me, when this is my one chance to get at her. *Fine. They want to fuck with me? Fine. These two might not be motivated to give her up, but I know someone who is.*

"Quite all right," I say pleasantly, all the while seething inside. "There is work to be done. If I may have the use of a pad of paper and a clipboard, I'll get started."

Jordan Blaylock obtains these objects for me and leads me to the door of the containment room at the end of the hall. "I must insist that I go in there alone," I tell him. "Much hinges on earning his trust, and to do that, he must not be aware of your presence."

"Agreed. There's a panic button near the table. If you have trouble and need help, press it, and I'll be in immediately."

"Thank you."

"Be careful," he warns me. "Your own safety is crucial, of course, but at all times be mindful of what a valuable asset he is. We worked very hard to cultivate him and bring him here. Do nothing that will risk harming him."

"Understood."

With that, Blaylock walks away, leaving me to face what's on the other side of that door. I open it and enter a room that was likely designed to be the former hotel's first aid center. Inside are cabinets now devoid of supplies, countertops that once held useful things, and in the center of the room, an operating table that almost certainly wasn't original equipment. Overhead is a powerful light, shining down on the table's occupant. The man—a word I use only in the strictest sense of its definition—is restrained at every possible point. Heavy leather straps hold his arms and legs down. Another strap immobilizes his head. Belts lash him across his chest and abdomen. Covering the top of his hairless head is a menacing-looking device that resembles a metal colander, hooked up to wires that lead to a nearby machine. Dr. Adams's cortical suppressor, no doubt.

As I look at all of these security methods, only one thing runs through my mind: *It's not going to be enough.*

All I can hope as I prepare for my encounter with this manifestation of energy in human form is that he's not yet developed the kind of strength he's going to have in a couple of years. *Time to find out.* I step over to the table so I am standing over him. Line of sight isn't important, as his eyes have never functioned. But he can hear me.

"Hello, Anatoly."

He seems gently startled by my appearance; the cortical suppressor must have impacted his ability to sense my presence. "Who … you?" he says in halting English.

"That depends on you. I could be your friend. I could be the person who has come here to help you, to rescue you. Or I could be the person who leaves you here—with them. You know who I mean, don't you?"

"Da."

"The people who hurt you."

"Da."

"I can save you from all that. Take you from here, bring you someplace where you can live your life in peace. Someplace where no one will hurt you ever again."

"Da, pozhalusta," he pleads.

"They want me to find out what you can do. What makes you special. But look at you; they put that mad scientist's spaghetti strainer on your big, bald head, chaining up that magnificent, unparalleled brain of yours. So I'm going to do something a bit risky, Anatoly. I'm going to take that thing off of you and see what's buzzing between those ears. I need you to be very good and not do anything to me while it's off, though."

Slowly and cautiously, I ease the cortical suppressor off of his head—not completely, just enough for me to sense what he's capable of doing. Just as I was able to sense Jordan Blaylock's probing of my thoughts, I can sense what this giant man has in his extrasensory and telekinetic repertoire.

As soon as the suppressor is on the table and away from his head,

I begin to feel a powerful sensation run through my body. It feels disturbingly similar to the sensation I felt at age six, when I discovered that the tip of a ball-point pen was exactly the same size and shape as the grounding hole of a three-pronged electrical outlet and decided to see what would happen. At present, I can't tell if this is an overt attack against me or just the unfortunate consequence of standing this close to him. I offer a quick warning. "*Nyet,* Anatoly!"

The energy surge subsides, not completely, but enough to let me see inside the mind of this force of nature. What I find there fascinates me. He is both a reader and a projector, capable of picking up the thoughts of those around him and implanting thoughts in their minds. Not just thoughts, but mental and physical sensations. With a single thought, he could instill in me a fear of snakes and simultaneously the belief that I was covered in hundreds of them. He could make me believe that I'd been shot or stabbed or suffocated without ever raising a weapon against me. He could throw me across the room with his mind, force me to kill myself in any way he found amusing, or erase every piece of information I possess about who I am.

No wonder they want you, big boy. You may just be the most dangerous man alive, an untraceable weapon for them to control.

I reach for the cortical suppressor and slide it back onto him. "I think we need you in your good-boy hat for this next part." With the device in place, the sensations I am experiencing subside, and I can think clearly again. "All right, Anatoly, listen well. I told you I have a choice for you to make, one that will decide your future path. Well, here it is. All I need from you is one thing, one piece of information, and I will get us out of here."

"Shto?"

"Where is Karolena?"

He hesitates before speaking. I see an expression cross his face. Despite the language barrier, the name Karolena registers with him, and I see a trace of fear in his features. It's a difficult question, so I give him a minute to answer, in case he wants to find the English words to tell me. But no words come out, so I repeat the question.

"Where is Karolena?"

"Ya ne znayu," he answers quickly.

"You *do* know," I correct him. "You know who she is, and you know where she is. She helped to make you what you are. And I know you don't like that, Anatoly. She hurt you, just like those people out there hurt you. Now the choice is yours. You can tell me where she is, tell me where she hides, and I'll make sure none of them ever hurt you again—or you can keep it to yourself, and I will leave you here. Leave you to the mean man and the pretty lady. And they will open up your brain and play with it like a toy. They will turn you into a weapon, Anatoly, and point you at their enemies. You'll hurt good people, people who never did anything to you. Just because the people who *did* hurt you told you to. But I can save you from that. I can give you the future you deserve. Right here, right now. All you have to do is answer my question. Where is Karolena?"

"Ya ne znayu."

"You've seen inside my mind. You know what I can do. You know I have knowledge of future events. I've seen you in those events. Seen you do unspeakable things to people; seen unspeakable things happen to you. Last chance, *tovarisch.* Where will I find Karolena?"

Without another word, he closes his unseeing eyes, resigning himself to his fate, a fate which—disturbing as it will be—is still less dangerous than betraying the woman I'm asking for.

"I'm sorry, my friend," I tell him quietly. "You may not believe me, but I truly am. I'm going to go now, leave you to your fate. But before I go, there's something I want you to know. Something to keep in the deepest recesses of your mind. Words you're going to hear again one day, and when you do, I want you to feel the deep, painful truth of them." I lean in close enough to whisper into his ear. *"Your mother would weep to know what you have become."*

Something catches my eye on a counter across from the operating table—a rack holding seven small vials of an iridescent blue liquid. "Is this what I think it is?" I ask aloud. A label on the rack confirms that I'm indeed holding something very valuable and very precious. I swiftly pocket two of the vials for later use.

Time to go. I haven't been in here nearly long enough to warrant heading back the way I came. Plus, I'm none too eager to share what I've learned about their guest with Blaylock and Adams. So an alternate means of egress is in order. I scan the room for the usual suspects and quickly find a conveniently large ventilation shaft in the ceiling. Fortunately, it's above a counter that's tall enough for me to climb up and slip inside.

Despite my storied past, I do not have a history of snaking my way through ventilation shafts. This experience is new for me, and it's not the most comfortable place to be. Though the shaft is big enough for a person to crawl through, I have no idea if it's meant to support my weight. As I move—as quietly as possible against the thin metal—I have visions of crashing through the shell and through the ceiling panels, dropping to the floor in front of Anatoly's captors as I concoct the mother of all good excuses.

Fortunately, I suffer no comical plummeting and actually manage to get myself far enough away that I can emerge in an unused store room at the other end of the hotel basement. From there, it is simply a matter of slipping quietly out of the room, up a flight of stairs, and out through a side door into the night air.

I allow myself to think briefly about the life I've consigned Anatoly to, but I soon dismiss the thought, knowing that guilt is not going to help anything right now. I need to put some serious distance between me and these people before they figure out that I'm not who I said I was. The former hotel is on a busy street, so it takes me only a few minutes to find an unoccupied cab and head back to the airport.

I could catch a commercial flight back to Baltimore, but who knows when the next one leaves? It could be late tomorrow. It'll have to be another charter flight, with the additional cost that goes along with it. But I don't care. It's worth it for the speed, the privacy, and most of all, the ability to get me out of this situation.

I won't get back to the house in Ocean City until the middle of the night, but that's not a problem. Tristan will be asleep, and I can enter quietly. He can never know how I've helped him tonight—or the fate I've subjected him to.

Chapter 7

Monday, October 29, 2007

Tristan

And just like that, he's gone. It's strange to see Ephraim as messenger, receiving an assignment, so enviably pain-free, and then rushing out of here without even telling me where he's going or what he's tasked to do.

But he's gone, and now it's just me and the memories I'm once again allowed to experience. I return to the living room sofa and sit, closing my eyes to help me get back in touch with what was so recently lost to me. The most powerful and prevalent thoughts relate to the period when I was receiving assignments. Esteban's friendship is now perfectly clear and very obvious; I'm embarrassed how easily I forgot about him. I remember saving him from his wife's plot to kill him. I remember every assignment that followed, right up to the undercover work at the Swift Medical Research Facility and my encounter with the Gnothautii.

My tranquility erodes as I allow myself to remember Genevieve. I begin with the good things—our first meeting at Virginia Beach, getting to know each other, the sound of her voice, the softness of her touch. And I let myself recapture the joy of those moments. Eyes closed, I let myself laugh and smile and hear her words, see her face. It is a doomed road, as I know all too well what is at the end of it. Before long, my reclaimed memories take me there, the operating room in Pennsylvania, where I lay strapped to a table. I relive every sight, every sound, every smell of that moment when Genevieve realized that this was all a trap, and she decided that she was my only chance at salvation. The last moments of her life, spent trying to save me.

Someone is responsible. Karolena, that's the name that was used, but who is she? I don't know a last name or even an exact spelling for the first name, so I can't track her down as I so desperately want to do. My rage needs a target. I'm not a violent man by nature, but if I found this woman, I would tear her beating heart out with my teeth and force her to watch me eat it. She would suffer more than anyone ever suffered, and I would be the one to bring that upon her.

My anger isn't enough to overcome my sorrow, and I feel myself begin to sob loudly for my loss. I never properly told Genevieve how much she meant to me. I was always so vague and so uncertain about my feelings that I left her wondering if she truly meant everything to me. What was I afraid of? What kept me from expressing the feelings that were so obvious to me? What brand of cowardice did I possess that let me keep this remarkable woman guessing whether I loved her?

The channeling. It hits me; a memory. Genevieve in a trancelike state, speaking the words of the long dead. Giving voice to them from beyond the grave. Surely if she could do this for those who had no special gifts, she herself could speak again, given the opportunity and someone to listen.

With that, every other thought flies out of my head. I have one purpose now, one goal—opening the door that stands between me and the woman I love. I stand up and pace around the room for a few seconds, realizing ultimately that a comfortable, seated position is most conducive to what I want to do. So I return to the couch, banish my tears and my emotional pain, and strive to concentrate on how to make this happen. I think back to everything Genevieve herself did when she channeled—the seated, relaxed position; the open mind; the focused intent. I place myself in the most relaxed position I can muster while staying seated, and I work very hard to drive every distraction out of my thoughts.

It takes several minutes before I feel like I'm ready, and when it happens, I close my eyes and begin to speak in a low monotone. "Genevieve Swan, I call to you beyond the reaches of this world. I invite your spirit to commune with me here today. I welcome you to pause your rest and visit me here now. Hear my words, know the anguish in my soul, and come to me, even briefly, so I can tell you all the things I should have told you in life."

My eyes remain tightly shut against the reality of my solitude. I hesitate, second after second, not even knowing what my success would sound like or look like. *Was it not enough? Should I say more?*

Before I can answer that, something strange happens. I hear a voice, sounding like it's in another room, but getting closer as it continues. Her voice. Genevieve's words. "Well done, my love." I open my eyes to see her step out of the hall around the corner and stand before me, healthy and unharmed. "I see so much anguish in your eyes, and I'm sorry I had to contribute to that. But the world had to believe I was dead, and that included you."

"You mean you're—?"

"When I saw that woman point the gun at me, I knew I was in terrible danger. My only hope was to let her believe she shot me. I let myself fall just right to convince her. Then it was just a matter of lying low until you were ready to know the truth."

It's unbelievable news, better than anything I could have hoped for. "Where have you been all this time?" I ask her.

"Staying out of sight, waiting for you to get your memory back. I couldn't risk letting you see me until your mind was all right again. Are you? Are you well again?"

"I'm getting better. Really I am. Now that I know you're alive and well, everything else comes second. We can start over. Do all the things we meant to do. You can live here with me."

She smiles. "I'd like that."

"I'm so sorry," I tell her. "I should never have dragged you into this. It's my fault; this didn't have to involve you, and I'm so sorry. Can you ever forgive me?"

"Far more important is to forgive yourself," she says gently. "You have a lot more living to do, and you can't thrive under the burden of guilt. Today is the day you decide to live and move forward. That's why I'm here."

"Oh, Genevieve, you're right. Of course you are. And you know something? I wouldn't even blame you if you never wanted to see me again."

"My love, the sorrow of never seeing you again is not my decision to make. In the deepest part of you, where truth and understanding live, you know this. And it's why you need to move forward with no grief, no hate, no self-loathing in you. Only the goodness of your heart and the strength of your will."

I want to shut my eyes against these words, but I discover—to my surprise and dismay—that they are already closed. They have been closed this entire time. When I do open them, I see that I am alone in the room. Genevieve isn't with me. She hasn't joined me from someplace beyond this life. Every word I heard her speak was born of that most damnable of liars, wishful thinking. She is truly gone, and despite my fervent desires to make it otherwise, I will never hear her voice again.

Quickly I rise and address the emptiness. "Nothing for me? Not a word of comfort? Not a single chance to apologize? After all those voices that spoke to me from somewhere else, I don't get to hear yours?" No one replies. I continue to speak anyway. "We were going to take a cruise. I remember that now. Alaska. We were going to see eagles and walk on glaciers. Without you, I don't even want to see it. I don't want to know it's there. Without you, who do I have? Without you, what is any of this for?"

There is no answer, but the words I imagined her saying are the ones I need to hear, to get me through this. Genevieve has died, never to return, and by any reasonable estimation of the circumstances, it is my fault, almost as if I'd pulled the trigger myself. But if I allow that knowledge to persist, it will cripple me, emotionally and physically. In a way, she *has* spoken to me today; she opened my thoughts to the painful reality that I have to find and embrace, instead of embracing her.

The hours of the day crawl by. I try to sleep, but my mind is too filled with memories leaping up to be the center of attention. The irony is more than I can take. For weeks, I've longed for this day, for the return of those areas of my life that were closed off to me. Now that they're back, I feel like I'd give anything to be rid of them again.

After 1:00 in the morning, I hear a car pull up outside. Moments later, the front door opens, and Ephraim enters, back from the assignment he received, whatever it was. Apathy has a firm hold of me as I sit in a wingback chair in the living room, staring at the unlit fireplace, not giving a fraction of a shit about anything.

He approaches me and hesitates a moment. I don't move an inch, which prompts him to bend down to get a better look at my face. Convinced that I'm awake and not in a vegetative state, he offers, "I'm back."

"I see that," I reply, moving nothing beyond my lips.

"You're up late. How was your day?"

"You know how my day was," I remind him, "just like you know a hundred things about me that hit me as a total surprise."

"True enough. Consider the question rhetorical, then." He starts for the kitchen. "Did you eat dinner? Are you hungry?"

"No and no. Have what you want, but you'll have to make it yourself."

As he begins to gather ingredients, he says, "I can't help feeling you're a bit cross with me."

"Gee, you think?" I retort unemotionally.

"I hope you don't think I'm responsible for your current situation."

His unwavering calm irritates me deeply. "My current situation? You mean ruining my life?"

"That's hardly my fault."

"You forget, I've got my memories back. And I can't help but recall you crossing my path on several occasions. Oh, and I seem to recall you trying to kill me on a few of those occasions."

"*Threatening* to kill you. Not trying. I had no intention of hurting you. I just couldn't let you know that back then."

"Oh, that makes it *so* much better."

"Consider it tough love. It's what you needed to hear at the time. I'm heating up the beef stew. Do you want some?"

"No. Yes. A little. I hate you."

"You don't really hate me," he says.

"A little."

"Don't you even want to know how my day went?"

"Not really."

"It was fascinating, actually. I can't tell you too much about it, but it was a real exercise in human nature for me. You know, sometimes it's a question of good versus evil, and that's an easy one. You do the expected thing and assist with the good, or you stir things up and give evil a fair shake. But this time … this time, Tristan, it was evil versus evil. A terrible person in the clutches of even more terrible people. Who do you root for? And there I was, given a prime opportunity to rescue this terrible person from a dreadful fate, from a life of misery, servitude, solitude."

"So what did you do?" I ask, trying not to sound too interested.

"I gave him a choice. I offered him a chance to demonstrate his humanity, to do something positive for me, and he wouldn't do it. He had something I needed, and he wouldn't give it to me."

"Wait, you *knew* this person?"

"Never met him before. Only knew *of* him. But the things I knew … I can't even speak of them. And he didn't know me. But he knew what I needed to know, and he wouldn't share it with me. So I left him there. Left him to his fate."

"You mean you rejected your assignment? What about the pain?"

He smiles and gestures up and down on his body. "Do I look like I'm in pain?"

"No."

"I went on the Boss's little assignment. I found my subject, and I gave him the chance to save himself. But it came with a condition. He knew that, and he rejected it. What happens after that is on his head. Probably quite literally."

"Are they going to kill him?"

Ephraim brings two bowls of beef stew over mashed potatoes to the dining room table and gestures for me to join him. Despite my continuing desire to sulk, I go and sit with him as he answers. "I can't say for sure, but I have good reason to believe that they won't. Though, mind you, I think he'll wish that they did. I know you think you've faced evil in this world, cousin, but let me tell you—there's evil out there that hasn't even made your acquaintance yet."

"I know evil," I rebut. "Evil is what tried to rip my mind out of my body. Evil is what killed Genevieve."

The spark leaves his voice, and he simply says, "Yes. It is."

I pound the tabletop, causing the spoon in my bowl to clank loudly as it hits the side. "God damn it, Ephraim! Who is she? You act like you know her. Tell me who she is!"

He hesitates a moment. I see on his face the decision process. At last he tells me, "Her name is Karolena Prizhen."

"Prison?" I ask, momentarily confused.

"Prizhen," he clarifies. "It's Ukrainian, I believe. She seldom uses the last name. For those who know her, the name Karolena alone is enough to inspire absolute terror and absolute loyalty. Those men in Pennsylvania, the ones who hurt you so badly, they did it because of her—because of the fear of what she'd do to them if they didn't."

"What, kill them?"

"Eventually. But not quickly. And not mercifully. Karolena has an intensity about her that people fear. She accepts nothing less than complete obedience, and there's no arguing with her. You're either in her clutches or you're her enemy. The doctors at Gnothautii were in a very delicate position."

"Until you killed them."

"That's right, I did."

"Care to tell me why?"

"Because they were seconds away from killing you, and they probably didn't know it. And ..."

"And?"

"And because they're the ones responsible for me being the way I am today. The Gnothautii Institute was where I went to develop my mental skills. Even then, Karolena was at the heart of it. She wanted to hurt me, and I didn't know why. I had never even met her, let alone gotten in her way. But she wanted to be rid of me, so she had them do their worst. None of them expected the results I ended up with. So when I saw you on that table, taking what was about to be your last breath, all that rage welled up in me, and I directed it at them."

"You killed them, Ephraim. You just ... killed them."

"I did, and I own that. It's on my hands and on my head for the rest of my life. You're lucky, Tristan; you've never had to kill anybody. We're messengers. We work for the ultimate owner of life and death, and sometimes, without any advance warning, he calls on us to deliver it for him. And it's the worst job in the world, every single time. But working with the Social Darwinism Commission taught me something very important: life is a privilege, not a right. Our constitution feeds us a line of bullshit, telling us life is a right. Tell that to the accident victim. Tell that to the stillborn child, never even given a chance to sin. Tell that to the baby blown up in an explosion somewhere. Talk to them about their right to life, and see what they say.

"When you wake up each morning, if you don't feel a powerful sense of gratitude, then you're taking something very important for granted. Because this life, fucked up as it may be, is an absolute privilege, one that can be revoked at any time, for any reason."

I'm finally able to taste the food he's prepared, and I get one bite of it in me before I realize how little I really wanted it in the first place. He uses the gap in the conversation to dig in to his.

"Why is Karolena untouchable?" I ask, diverting the discussion again.

"Some people in this world just are," he answers, "but she's not one of them. She likes to think she is, but she's just good at hiding—

letting others get their hands dirty. She's elusive, well-protected; seldom surfaces. I've been looking for her, but I haven't had any luck. I'm trying to draw her out into the open."

"When you do, I want to kill her," I tell him.

"You're not a killer."

"You just said ..."

"Never mind what I said. It's a line, a very distinct and difficult line to cross, and once you cross it, you're not the same person anymore. I need you to trust me."

"You want me to trust you, Ephraim? Fine. There's one thing you need to do, one way to prove your loyalty to me. Find Karolena Prizhen and kill her."

He drops his head for several seconds of silence. "I can't promise you that."

"Will you be leaving, now that I've got my memories back?" I ask directly.

"No. Not yet."

"Why not?"

"Because things will be better for you if I'm here. The day will come when it's time for me to leave, but it's not today. You know me; you know the things I'm capable of knowing. I need you to have faith in me when I tell you that I can and will help you."

I rise from the table. "I'm going to bed. Thank you for making dinner."

Wednesday, November 7, 2007

The next week passes uneventfully, which is a blessing and a curse. It's good to be able to rest up and finish my recuperation. Finally, I feel like myself again. I have control of my memories, and the lingering pain from my undesired medical procedure is gone. But I feel unbearably idle. My memories include all my days as CEO of my company, and I miss it. I miss the feeling of control, the vitality that responsibility gave me. Now I've given that away, so I have time to take on these assignments, and I haven't had one in almost two weeks.

Ephraim and I don't talk much. Our relationship is tentative at best, and I have come to value my solitude. I spend hours sitting and looking at the ocean, still more hours documenting what I've been through over the past weeks. I don't think I'm writing my memoirs or anything dramatic like that. I just want a record of what I've done. What I've endured. What I've lost. In case somebody wants to take me from myself again.

Mid-morning, Ephraim finds me in the kitchen, about to scarf a Fig Newton, and he initiates a needed conversation. "So what'll it take to call a truce?"

"Truce?" I ask.

"A cessation of hostilities. I feel like I'm the enemy, and I don't know how to change that. If I had a white flag, I'd wave it. I have a handkerchief, but it's allergy season, so I don't think you want me waving it around."

"There are no hostilities. There's just me and you. What you see is me stripped of everything I identify with who I am. I was a CEO; that's gone. I was someone's lover; that's gone. Now I'm some kind of celestial errand boy, and even that's drying up. I know you care, and I know you mean well, but your presence here is a lingering reminder of how much everything has changed. You've agreed to be my caretaker, but I don't need a caretaker."

"Caretaker is a harsh word," he counters. "If you prefer personal assistant, I can wear that title."

"I'm good on that front too. You can wear the title of cousin. *Distant* cousin is preferable. Because, as you can see, I'm fine. I don't need a helper, because I don't need help."

I pop the Newton into my mouth, and in an instant, the sensation of burning overtakes me. It feels like I've taken a bite of the most potent chili pepper known to man. I can breathe, but the feeling of fire goes all the way through my digestive system. Instinctively, I look to Ephraim, who looks like he is trying not to gloat. I manage to choke out the words, "What's … happening?"

"You look like you need help. Do you need help?"

I shake my head vigorously to protest my independence and not prove him right, but at the same time, I find myself painfully uttering the word "Burning."

Literally a single second later, Ephraim hands me a very large glass of milk—which I swear he must have conjured, as I didn't see him obtain it from anywhere. Without too much contemplation, I down it in one stomach-enraging gulp and find that the fires of Vesuvius are settling down within my digestive tract, long enough for me to start speaking. "Bayonne, New Jersey."

Ephraim now holds a pen and paper in his hands, and as I speak, he begins taking it all down.

"Elizabeth Senn, age forty-six. She's … how is this possible? She's a freelance terrorist hunter. Today at 4:30 p.m., she's going to Newark International Airport to intercept three militant extremists who are targeting a plane full of passengers for destruction, unless I can stop her."

Ephraim finishes writing as I pant furiously to catch my breath. He offers me a second glass of milk and warns, "Drink it slowly. Too quick and you'll bring it all back up again, and that won't be pleasant."

"You knew this was going to happen, didn't you?"

"Well, I don't like to … but yeah. A bit."

"That's why you insisted on staying, isn't it? Because of this mission."

"Partly," he answers.

"Another airport. I trust we won't have a repeat of last time?"

"Last time was different. This time I'm here to help you."

"We're driving, I assume?" I ask him.

"Let me put it this way: you've just been told that terrorists are targeting a plane connected with Newark Airport. Do you *really* want to fly into Newark?"

"I'll get my car keys."

Mercifully, the burning sensation subsides as we are preparing to leave. I've never been a huge fan of spicy food, and this little mishap reminds me all over again precisely why. What still burns within me, however, is the annoyance at Ephraim's smugness. I have to keep reminding myself that somehow, he knows things about his own future, including things that intersect with mine. And while I understand why he can't just give me a recitation about what's going to happen to me, it still chaps my proverbial ass when he toys with me this way.

It will be a drive of more than four hours to get to New Jersey, followed by what could be a very tense scene, so it behooves me to play nice with my clairvoyant cousin as we proceed north to the Garden State. Nothing would please me more than to just ask him, "So, how does this turn out? You can tell me." But being the relatively intelligent boy that I am, it occurs to me that if there were a tactical advantage to the foreknowledge, he would tell me about it. So I have to sit back and experience events in the correct order, like a barbarian.

"Penny for your thoughts," Ephraim says to me as I drive us up Highway 1 through Delaware.

"You mean you don't already know them?" I ask in a tone of playful indignation.

"Cut me a little slack. Just because I know certain things about the future doesn't mean I know every little thing you're thinking."

"True enough," I counter, "but don't your memories include us having this conversation?"

"Well played. And correct. But consider this: when the Gnothautii's experiment on me went wrong, my mind was filled with so much information, it physically injured me. To store tiny details of every conversation I ever had and ever will have in my life would be agonizing. So, as I healed, I purged the smaller bits of information, in favor of the larger, more important topics. Ergo, I recall that on this drive to New Jersey, you and I talk, but what we talk about is lost to me. Hence the proffered penny for your thoughts. Are you selling?"

"Who hunts terrorists?" I ask, bypassing the direct question.

"Besides the CIA, Homeland Security, Navy SEALs, and our Miss Elizabeth Senn, no one I know of."

"Doesn't it seem like ... I don't know ... an *oddish* thing to do? Not to mention more than a little dangerous?"

"To the average person, sure," he says. "But what did you learn about your recipient?"

"Only that she has an adult daughter who lives with her."

"Nothing about her past? No military service, no government employment? For all we know, this could be her job, rather than her hobby."

"Hadn't thought about that, but it makes sense. But wait, if she's skilled and trained in this and it's her job, why would I be sent to stop her from attempting it?"

He smiles at this. "Good. You're asking the difficult questions. That's one of the benefits of driving to your assignments: it gives you time alone with your thoughts to weigh all the angles, all the possibilities, all the eventualities. Always drive there, any chance you get. Trust me on this."

"One other thing," I continue. "I'm going to stop her from confronting these terrorists. If I succeed, there'll be no one to stop them. Should I call someone? Warn them?"

"Unfortunately, your incident at the airport in Washington put you on a list of watched individuals. So soon afterward, to be at the center of an incident like this would be a bad idea."

"And I have *you* to thank for the first incident," I remind him.

"I'd apologize, if I thought it would make a difference."

"What about the terrorists? If they're going to bring down a plane, someone needs to know about it. And please don't start in with the Social Darwinism shit. I'm in no mood for it today."

"Wouldn't dream of it," he replies. "Would it help you to know that if you're being sent to stop the terrorist hunter, someone else is almost certainly being sent to stop the terrorists?"

"Yes, it would help. Do you know this for a fact, or are you speculating?"

"Let's just say I have it on good authority."

"Then that just leaves the question of how to stop this woman from dealing with these terrorists without looking like terrorists ourselves. If she's taking them on by herself, odds are good that she has some badass in her. I don't relish the thought of a skirmish with a woman who may be armed and dangerous."

"That wasn't really the tactic I was contemplating," Ephraim replies. "No offense, but you're not exactly a warrior. Not yet, anyway."

"Not much offense taken. And I'll let that last cryptic bit slide for now, so I can get to the part about what's plan B."

"Two choices: reason or deception. The reason approach presents us as the only ones who can convince her that she's walking into her own brutal murder. She has a daughter; we appeal to that. Tell her she doesn't want to leave her daughter without a mother. Maybe we can talk some sense into her."

"And the deception approach?"

"We convince her that the threat is over. We're with the government. Otherwise, how would we know about her plans? She doesn't have to go to the airport, because ten of our best men are already there, and the hostiles are in custody. Always call them *hostiles;* it sounds very governmental."

"Which plan should we use?" I ask.

"Don't know yet. It all depends on what will work best. But you have to go in with a backup plan in case the first one doesn't work. That's why you didn't succeed at the airport in Washington. You hadn't thought it through. Your first story fell flat, and then you got sloppy and panicked. Got yourself arrested and interrogated, leading to the crash of that plane."

"Which, of course, was thanks to *you.*"

"How long are you going to hold that grudge?" he asks, sounding disappointed in me.

"Maybe I could let it go if you weren't so cavalier about it, if you felt something for those lives ..."

"For Christ's sake, Tristan, I didn't crash that plane."

About a mile of open road passes beneath us in the silence that follows his announcement. But I don't buy it. "I was there. And you were there. I know it went down, and you even told me you did it."

"Did I?" he asks pointedly. "Think back. At any point, did I tell you that I caused that airplane to crash?" I search my thoughts, but he continues before I find anything. "You accused me of it—several times, in fact—but not once did I admit to doing it. The fact of the matter is, an equipment failure caused that airplane to go down. An equipment failure that had nothing to do with me. Did I know about it ahead of time? Yes, just as you did. Could I have stopped it? Maybe; I don't know. *You* certainly didn't have much luck. For me, it was an opportunity to test many things at once."

"What things?"

"My dedication to the SDC's beliefs, even in the face of an unspeakable tragedy, for one. If I could cling to the precept that human life can be taken away so senselessly and yet some greater good can come from it, then I knew their cause was just. Secondly, it was a test of our employer's ingenuity. He sent both of us on this mission, with the knowledge that I might work against plan. And he let me, Tristan, without even inflicting the kind of pain on me that you suffer all the time. What does that tell you? I'm not even sure what it means, but it's as intriguing as hell. Finally, it was a test of you. I was still learning about you at that point, and that day was the master's-level course."

"So you *didn't* kill those children?"

"No, of course not. And when that day was over, I wept for each one of them who died so needlessly."

"Then why did you go on letting me believe you were responsible?"

"Because I needed to know if you could work with me, even if you thought I was capable of unspeakable things. I wasn't honest with you, and I'm sorry."

For many seconds, I am speechless. I don't know whether to feel relieved or furious. "God damn it, Ephraim. You want me to trust you, and … and it's like you're messing with me, experimenting with me. You realize how that undercuts what I have to do?"

"Yes."

"Then why are you doing it? Why not just cut through the bullshit, tell me nothing but the truth, and be someone I can rely on without question and without fail every single time?"

"Have you ever met *anyone* who meets those criteria? You're being groomed for events yet to come, and I, for better or worse, am part of that grooming. One of the vital lessons to learn is that sometimes a friend appears to be an enemy, and sometimes an enemy appears to be a friend. Your task, often without help from anyone else, is to spot the difference and act accordingly."

"You could've told me. You could've said, from the very start, what was going on, and let me learn these things from you in a normal way, instead of letting me think you were trying to kill me for the last few months."

He hesitates a few moments and says, "It's complicated."

"I hate those words."

"I know. They've become a cliché for every indecisive asshole who can't commit to something. But in this case, they're very true and very meaningful. This is the part where people say, 'It's not you, it's me.' But not this time. It is you, Tristan. All of it, everything that's happened; everything that's going to happen. You are at the center of something so big, so meaningful, it will change everything."

"Tell me what it is!"

"I can't. You know that. Telling you what I know could jeopardize everything and put your life in danger. I shouldn't even have told you this much, but it's so important that you understand that you were truly selected for something crucial."

"How can I prepare if I don't know what to prepare for?"

"All I can tell you is this: there's a war coming. Not like anything you see on CNN, with armies of fresh-faced young volunteers trekking through the desert to hunt down people with different pigmentation and different ideologies. This is going to be a very quiet war; almost no one in the world will even know it's happening. But you will be on the front lines, my friend, and the outcome has global implications."

What does one say in the face of this information? "Do … do I win?"

He cocks his head a little. "Always in motion is the future."

"Come on, quit with the Yoda shit. If you know this is going to happen, you know how it's going to end. You can tell me."

"I only know the parts I'm there for," he says. "And I'm sorry to say, I'm not there when it all shakes out."

"I'm scared."

"You should be. Keeps you sharp."

"Will I be on the right side?"

"I believe you will, but you know the kind of company I've kept. I'm not sure I should be your moral barometer."

"Is there nothing else you can tell me?"

After a few seconds of silence, he says, "You won't be alone."

I continue driving all the way to Bayonne, New Jersey. Ephraim offers to take over at the halfway point, but I decline. I need to concentrate on the road; alone with nothing but my thoughts, it would be overwhelming.

So I follow the route in my mind to an unassuming house in an ordinary neighborhood and park on the street out front. I shut off the ignition and prepare to exit the car, but Ephraim stops me. "Whoa, not so fast. This isn't just 'Don't let your cat go near that tree.' We're about to confront a terrorist hunter, someone used to dealing with the most dangerous individuals in the world. Read the scene."

"Read the scene? You mean there's a script?"

"No, not the scene—the *scene.* The surroundings. What do they tell you?"

I look at the house and see a house. There's no signs of movement, nobody hiding in the bushes that I can tell. I don't see any booby traps or surveillance cam— "Wait, there are surveillance cameras under the first-floor eaves, panning the front of the house."

"Good. What else?"

"There's a car in the driveway, so I think someone's home."

"But …?" he prompts.

"But there's one car in a driveway wide enough for two, and it's parked to the far left side of the driveway, suggesting that it's a two-car family, and one of the cars is gone."

"Good. Anything else?"

I look again, but nothing else of significance occurs to me. "Nothing I can see. Did I miss anything?"

"A couple of things we'll need, to avoid getting killed, but you did good. Come on, let's go see who's home."

He gets out of the car, and I scramble to keep up, as we make our way up the driveway to the front door. The two cameras follow us like attentive dogs, and before we can knock, the front door opens just enough for us to be greeted by the barrel of what looks to be a very large handgun.

Anything resembling a plan or a strategy flies out the window for me at the sight of that weapon, which hangs there without a sign of anyone holding it. "Whoa," I say, "whoa, whoa! Don't shoot. Don't shoot!"

"I know how to use this," a woman's voice warns from behind the door.

"I have no doubt," Ephraim says calmly, not even moving to step out of the way. I, in the meantime, am trying to see if there's room for me under the welcome mat.

"Put your weapons down on the ground and show me your hands," the voice instructs.

Ephraim continues to engage her unemotionally. "We have no weapons, but you can see our hands through the peephole." He makes a grand gesture of displaying his empty hands and encourages me to do the same.

"Who are you, then? You don't look like Al-Qaeda."

"No, we're sure not Al-Qaeda."

"CIA? Homeland Security? If you've got badges, drop them on the ground and kick them over here."

I finally build up the courage to talk. "We have a message for Elizabeth Senn. We have reason to believe she's in danger, and we want to help keep her safe. Are you Elizabeth?"

The door opens, and a woman in her mid-twenties stands there, still holding the gun—just not holding it on us, which makes a nice change. "I'm her daughter, Anneke."

"It's nice to meet you, Anneke," I reply gently. "My name is Tristan." Ephraim gives me a disapproving look, but I'll have none of it at the moment. "Save it, Ephraim. I think we could all do with a little honesty right now. This is my cousin, Ephraim. Could we talk somewhere with more chairs and fewer guns?"

I watch her decide to trust me. It takes several seconds, but she says, "Come inside."

She allows us inside, and I scan the interior, looking for anything interesting or out of the ordinary. All I see is someone's home. It's no mansion, but there are signs that they have enough money to live comfortably. No pets come to greet us. I do notice that the dining room table is piled high with manila folders, bulging with papers. I don't get close enough to snoop, though I am curious.

"What do you want with my mother?" Anneke asks, dispensing with pleasantries.

"I assure you," Ephraim answers, "we mean her no harm. Quite the contrary. We have reliable intelligence that suggests that she's in great danger today if she carries out her plans. We came here to talk her out of them."

A bit of fear creeps into the young woman's voice. "What kind of danger? And how do you know?"

I pick up the story from here. "We're part of a private domestic security organization, and we've been monitoring chatter …" *I think that's what they call it, anyway.* "… regarding potential terrorist activity at Newark Airport today. Your mother's name came up as a private individual who may be planning a counterstrike against the terrorists."

Ephraim gives me an impressed look, and I take it in stride. Two can play at this game. I continue. "Anneke, is the chatter accurate? Is your mother planning a counteroffensive at the airport today?"

She tries to keep her composure as she answers, "Yes. She left for the airport twenty minutes ago."

"Tell us what you know," Ephraim invites.

"I'll tell you everything I know in the car," she says.

"Car?" I repeat.

"What car?" Ephraim asks.

"Yours or mine, whichever you want," she says. "You're going to stop her, and I'm going with you."

"That's a very bad idea," Ephraim tells her. "This situation could get dangerous, and I don't want you to risk being injured or worse."

She strides right up to him until her face is inches from his. "Okay, then. You're going to find her at a crowded airport? Great. What does she look like?"

He opens his mouth a bit, but no answer emerges. He looks to me for help, but I've got nothing, and a shake of my head confirms it.

"I thought so," Anneke says. "You need me there. I don't give a damn about the danger. I'm going along."

"My car," I respond. "I'll drive."

She brings her handgun along. I remind her that the airport probably isn't the best place for it, and she says she'll keep it in the car. We all get in, and I start us on our hasty trip to Newark Liberty International Airport.

"If she left twenty minutes ago," Ephraim says, "odds are good she's there already. Tristan, take I-78 to US-9. That should be the quickest." He turns back to Anneke. "Now's the time to share anything you know."

"My mother found out about a group of Saudi extremists who have been in a prolonged dispute with an American oil company—I don't know the name of either group. But the American company has been trying to tap a new reserve in North America, which could potentially put the Saudi group out of business. Only thing is, I think the reserve can't be drilled legally, but the American company is trying to go around that somehow. The Saudis tried every legal means they knew to fight this, but nothing worked. So a splinter group made plans to disgrace the American company by targeting a US flight for destruction. That's what they're going to do today, and that's what she's going there to stop. After they blow up the plane, they're going to broadcast the reason why they did it—blaming the greed and corruption of the American oil company."

"But you don't know that company's name?" I ask. "If you knew it, we could contact them and ask them to do something—anything—to meet with the Saudis and prevent this violence."

"I don't know it, I'm sorry. I think it might have the word Offshore in its name. But even if we knew it, even if we contacted them, I don't think it would do any good. Everything my mother tells me about them says that they're just as evil as the terrorists."

I bring up an unpleasant reality. "Anneke, if we're successful in protecting your mother, that may mean that the terrorists will succeed in their plans. We have to know now: if it comes down to that choice, what do you want us to do?"

She sits silently for a few seconds before answering. "Save her. I know that sounds horrible, but she's my mother. She's all I have now. It's awful that innocent people would have to die, but sometimes that just happens, and there's reasons for it we can't know."

In the rearview mirror, I catch a slight smile of agreement on Ephraim's face, one Anneke cannot see. She continues. "Besides, if she survives today, she can do more in the future, save other people. I know this shouldn't be my choice to make, but you asked, and that's what I feel."

"It's perfectly all right," Ephraim consoles her. "It's an impossible decision, and you gave a very reasonable answer. We're going to do everything we can to keep her safe. Part of that is keeping you safe as well. When we get there, stay back and let us work."

"So, you're professionals?" she asks.

"In a manner of speaking," I answer.

"All right," Ephraim says, "let's focus. We'll be there in a few minutes."

"How are we going to get to the gate area without a ticket?" I ask.

"Any ticket would get us there," he says. "But remember Washington. Too many civilians at the gate area. Lots of security, and we've got no luggage. Besides, if I'm right, the people we're looking for may not even be posing as passengers. They know how much security is there, and it's nearly impossible to smuggle an explosive of any size onto a plane. More likely, they'll be posing as baggage handlers, giving them access directly to the cargo area of the flight they want. That's where we'll find them."

He has his moments; I'll give him that.

"That's brilliant," I tell him. "I would never have thought of that, and yet you sound so certain. How could you possibly know?"

In the mirror, I see him smile once more. "I'll tell you later, after we win."

Chapter 8

Wednesday, November 7, 2007

Ephraim

With each passing mile, we draw ever nearer to Liberty Airport, Tristan navigating the city traffic effectively. I'm sure he's nervous about this assignment, particularly after our last visit to an airport ended so badly for him. But he's not showing it, which is good. The last thing our little tagalong needs now is to know that her "professionals" really aren't. Yet another piece of information I get to keep to myself for now.

Tristan must think me a master strategist after what I demonstrated in the car, my knowledge of where to look for the terrorists and their tracker. What I can't tell him—not yet, anyway—is that I have this information because at the same time he got his assignment, I got one of my own. *I* am the one being sent to stop the terrorists, just as Tristan is supposed to save Elizabeth Senn from them. *Won't this be fun.*

It is advantageous, however, since I do know for a fact that these individuals will be in the baggage-handling area. Once we get in there, it'll save us a lot of time we would otherwise have spent looking for them.

More than that, I know precisely who the oil company is—Consolidated Offshore—and Anneke is right in feeling animosity toward them. Between the oil company and the terrorists, I prefer the terrorists; at least *they* listen to reason. This proves something I've wondered about for a while now, that Tristan was involved with this whole Consolidated situation two full years before he realizes. For him, it'll start in 2009, in Key West, Florida. But here and now, we're in the middle of it. My trip to Pensacola—that was Consolidated as well. Karolena's involvement; this assignment to New Jersey. Ever since I first became aware of Tristan, I've suspected that he was at the heart of something much bigger than him. Now, with each successive mission that relates to it, I realize even more how specially he was chosen.

We park in the airport's short-term parking lot, and the three of us get out of the car. I see Anneke pick up her weapon with the intention of bringing it in. "We agreed," I remind her, "unarmed."

"The terrorists will be armed," she counters.

"Then we have to behave better than they do. Will your mother be armed?"

"Yes."

"That's enough guns for this equation. Our task will be to make sure nobody uses them. In an airport full of civilians, more guns could lead to innocent people getting killed."

Tristan chooses this moment to inject some sarcasm. "That attitude is a nice change for you."

"Let it go," I reply, my tone infused with a warning.

Anneke Senn looks at us and asks, "What's going on?"

In unison, we reply, "Nothing."

She places herself between us and says, "I don't believe you. Listen to me: I don't know what's going on here or what history you two have, but I'll remind you that you brought me into this, and I'm counting on you to work together with me to save my mother."

The girl has a point. "Come on," I say, "let's go. I fear we've lost too much time already."

I lead the way into the terminal, the other two close at my heels.

This time, I have the advantage; I know exactly where to look for my quarry, whereas Tristan only knows that Elizabeth Senn is somewhere inside the airport terminal.

To the casual observer, everything around us looks fine. It's another day at a busy airport, and people are where they should be. A few are hurrying to make it to their gate; others are standing in long lines. Some are complaining about fees, while others are grumbling about security measures they must endure. Any day at any American airport. The hundreds of travelers here have no idea that not far away, very dangerous men are working to bring death and destruction with callous disregard for human life, all in the name of making a statement.

"Where do we go?" Tristan asks.

I seek out the sign I need: Baggage Claim. "This way. Downstairs."

It's not the best way to get where I'm going. In fact, the room I'm looking for is by the gates, in the area where handlers load the planes. Trouble is, that's airside, and we can't get to it without going through security—and we can't go through security without tickets. All thanks to the efforts of terrorists like the ones we're seeking right now. So our alternative is to go to the baggage-handling area through baggage claim and work our way backward until we find them.

Quickly we take the stairs down to the lower level, scoot past the luggage carousels, and go to a door marked Authorized Personnel Only. As with all secure areas in the airport, the door has a ten-button number keypad. Tristan tries the knob and quickly announces, "It's locked."

That might be the end of it, were it not for the information that came to me with this assignment. I punch in the number 7-0-5-4, listen for the click, and turn the knob. The heavy metallic door pops open, and we hastily enter.

"How could you possibly know that number?" Tristan asks.

"It was an inspired guess. You can marvel later; for now, we have to move. We have a lot of ground to cover."

I soon realize how accurate my statement is. The baggage claim area is huge, and it is just the beginning. I realize there's one more thing we need, so I stop inside an employee office and find just what I'm looking for: a stack of ID cards for new hires—just where the details of the assignment said they'd be. I find three that are close enough to what we look like and distribute them. "Hold on to them," I instruct the others, "but avoid showing the picture if you can help it. Flash it long enough to get where you need to be."

Another door takes us out onto the tarmac, where the newly obtained IDs get us through the secure area, across the field, and over to the gate area. I aim for a door with a number of baggage trucks parked outside; this is the place we need to be. The code for this door is 2-8-1-7, and in seconds, we are sprinting through more corridors, past fewer employees than I expected. No one stops us or asks us why we're running. Timetables are tight, and employees are used to seeing their colleagues in a big hurry. And we are in one motherfucker of a hurry.

This part of the airport is at least as big as the baggage-distribution area in the main terminal. Corridors meet and diverge, branching out and ending in huge rooms with conveyor belts and sorting machinery. As we proceed deeper and deeper, a sound begins to rise above the others: shouting. Not the shouting of workers trying to be heard above the din of their environment, but the angry shouting of a woman and three men. This may be the place. As we get closer, I get the confirmation I need, when Anneke cocks her head for a moment and quietly says, "Mom."

Good enough for me.

I follow the sound to one of the myriad sorting rooms, and immediately upon bursting into the room, we find three high-powered automatic weapons and a very large handgun pointed at us. For the second time in two assignments—the second time in recent memory—I feel fear. In the second and a half I'm given to survey my surroundings, I take in as much as I can. We've clearly broken in on a very tense, heavily armed standoff between a woman I have to assume is Elizabeth Senn and three dark-skinned men, possibly of Middle Eastern descent. I hate to generalize, but given that I don't have time to brew some tea and truly get to know them, I have to lean on Anneke's description of them as Saudi nationals until proven otherwise.

Before turning, Elizabeth had her back to the door and to us, while the three men were already facing us. They're wearing the uniforms of one of the airlines, which makes sense, given the places they needed to be, but I'm certain they're not airline employees. Nor are they any too thrilled about seeing us.

Upon staring down the barrel of her mother's weapon, Anneke cries out, "Mom!"

A look of surprise and dismay visits her mother's face, and she quickly trains her pistol on her original adversaries, who are apparently having a pickle of a time deciding which of us to shoot first. At least I assume that's the gist of their discussion, since they are bellowing rapidly in a language I do not speak at all. They continue during the heartwarming family reunion that follows.

"Anneke, what the fuck are you doing here?" Elizabeth demands.

"I'm here to help you. To stop you. To help … stop … you."

"And who are they?"

"Counterterrorism agents," she says, rather impressively embellishing the story we gave her. These words register with the armed trio, inspiring very anxious chatter I also can't understand.

"Did you do a background check?"

"Jesus, Mom, there wasn't time!"

"You know the rules, Anneke. You stay out of active ops."

"Mrs. Senn …" Tristan says.

"It's *Ms.*," she corrects.

"Ms. Senn, we have reason to believe you're in very grave danger."

"Gee, you think?"

She's a charmer. I'll give her that.

"For that reason, we've come here to remove you from this situation," he continues.

"If you know that I'm in danger, then you know why. You see those?" She points quickly with her gun to three cardboard boxes on the floor in front of the three men, each large enough to hold a bowling ball. "Each one contains an explosive device, and these assholes are getting ready to put them on an airplane full of innocent people. You can 'remove me from the situation' when these three are disarmed or dead."

Not surprisingly, this last statement whips the trio into a frenzy of what I'm guessing are Arabic profanities and threats. They refocus their weapons on Elizabeth, who shows no indication whatsoever of backing down. I'm starting to wonder if Anneke has a father or if her mother just had balls enough to make the baby on her own.

As the conveyor belts slow to a stop, the sounds of shouting build frantically, with Anneke screaming for her mother to do the right thing, Elizabeth giving orders to put the goddamn guns down or she'll goddamn kill them, goddamn it—or words to that effect—and the three terrorist suspects growling words that probably translate to "Death to everyone in this room who isn't us!"

I am gently surprised to see that the next person who makes a move in this rather uncomfortable stalemate is my dear cousin. He steps between the warring factions, puts his hands forward, and loudly says, "Time out!"

This actually halts the shouting match, as everyone looks genuinely confused. The lead man looks at him and repeats, "Time … out?"

"I might remind you, Tristan," I offer, "that in the arena of international relations, 'time out' is not known for its staying power. If you have a follow-up statement, now is the time to make it."

Clearly making this up as he goes along, he looks at Elizabeth and tells her, "We're not counterterrorism agents." Her expression is filled with annoyance but not much surprise. "We were sent here to stop you."

"Sent by who?" she asks.

"That's classified. But we have it on good authority that you won't survive the encounter with these men without our help."

"Then help."

"The way we help you is to get you out of this alive. Come with us."

"Out of the question!" she answers. "I leave now, and they get to complete their mission. They blow up that plane, and hundreds of people die."

"Look, I understand the importance of what you're here to do, but I have to ask you—why you? Why are you risking your life to do this?" he asks. "You're one person, taking on agents of a foreign extremist group, men who would think nothing of killing you. Why take them on by yourself?"

She hesitates before speaking; clearly this isn't part of how she envisioned this would go down. "I was a real estate agent. Living a normal life with my family. On September 11, my husband was on the eighty-eighth floor of the North Tower of the World Trade Center. In a meeting, a business meeting. He wasn't involved in politics or the military or anything the least bit complicated. He was just doing his work. When I lost him, I found my new purpose in life. I've dedicated every day to tracking down enemies of this country and telling the right people about what I found. I told them about this, about what would happen here today."

"Who? Who did you tell?"

"All of them," she answers. "FBI, NSA, Homeland Security. None of them took it as a credible threat. No evidence to substantiate it, they said. They wouldn't even send anyone to check it out. So I came to stop it myself. Because the government wouldn't help me."

"Look around you, Ms. Senn," Tristan says. "You're outgunned. This is a no-win situation if you stay. They will kill you, and then they'll do what they came here to do anyway."

"Listen to him, Mom. Please."

"No. I can't let them do this. I can't let them win. The government made its choice. Now this is my fight. If you want to help me, then help me. If you don't, then let me do what I came here to do."

When she stands her ground, I know I can't keep silent any longer. I have to play my hand. Calmly, I step forward, facing the hostiles, who keep their guns primed, ready for any sign of trickery on my part. *And I've got a trick, all right.* "Yousef, Suleiman, Khalid, please—lower your weapons."

Their expressions tell the story; I believe I even said the correct name as I looked at each man.

"What is this?" their leader, Yousef, asks me. "Who are you?"

"I am Efrayim ben Hosea, and I am sent by Allah to speak to you on his behalf."

"Blasphemy!" he retorts angrily. "You are American. Allah would not pollute his words by passing them through the filth of your tongue."

"Do not question me, Yousef Ibn-Saud!" I order, allowing a tiny dramatic flair into my voice, to show that I mean business. "I am a scion of the Koran. Allah offers you his love, but he has sent me to correct you."

"Ours is a glorious mission," he answers. Clearly, he has either the best English skills of the three or a little bit of a power trip. Either way, it's all good. "What we do today, we do in his name. *Allah akbar!*"

"Allah akbar!" the other two men reply just as enthusiastically.

"This is a false jihad," I explain to them, "rooted in the evil that is money. Your leaders are using you as pawns, expendable foot soldiers to stand up to a corrupt American corporation. Allah sees this and cannot bless your task. I have seen into the future, by his mercy, seen the results that will occur if you do this thing today. The three of you will be captured, subjected to interrogation that is a thin veil and a polite euphemism for brutal torture. The American government will look upon this as an act of war—not by your group, but by your country—and they will retaliate."

"You don't frighten us," Yousef says boldly. "We welcome the prospect of war with America."

"You welcome victory, but I have seen the seeds that will grow, and they include inglorious defeat for your people. Your oilfields and refineries will be spared, taken and exploited by your enemy; but your villages, your citizens will be destroyed utterly. Tens of thousands of lives lost because of what you're about to do. Your wife and daughter, Yousef. Marwah. Five years old. She burns to death as your wife watches. It's the very last thing Badriyah sees in her life. Suleiman, your mother and grandfather die slowly of starvation, cut off for days from needed supplies. And Khalid, the warrior, with no family to lose. Allah has shown me a vision of your beloved dogs, all seven of them, ripped to pieces and eaten alive by nomadic scavengers. All of this will come to pass if you allow those bombs onto that airplane."

I'm pleased as silence falls over the crowd. For the first time since our arrival, the room is hushed. The Senn women are looking at me in puzzled amazement; Tristan's expression shows that he's figured out my big secret. And the three armed men share a look of fear that they wish was actually disbelief. Trouble is, I know too many details. The child, the wife, the mother and grandfather. And the crowning touch, the dogs. Nobody gets that level of intel without divine help. And my willingness to drop Allah's name without fear has made believers out of them. They may not know who I am or how I came here, but they know the voice of God when they hear it, and today, I'm his answering service.

Curiously, it is Suleiman who speaks next. "What must we do to earn Allah's forgiveness?"

"Walk away," I tell them. "All of you. Give me the weapons and the airline uniforms. Disarm the explosives, and leave this place. Never come near an airport again."

"We cannot disarm the explosives," Khalid says. "They are on a timer, and we have no way to stop them."

"Then give them to me," I order. "Quickly. Do what I tell you, and don't report back to your superiors. Find a way to disappear, and find other ways to serve Allah that don't involve the slaughter of the innocent. Only then will you earn his forgiveness."

I contain my satisfaction as one by one, each man hands me a rifle and a boxed bomb before getting out of their airline coveralls and making their way to the exit door.

"You're letting them go?" Elizabeth Senn asks me in disbelief.

"Yes."

She raises her pistol and points it at the third man in line to leave.

"And so are you," I add. "Theirs isn't the only future I can see." It's a bluff, of course, as she is Tristan's assignment, not mine. But I sell it convincingly enough to make her lower her weapon and allow the men to leave quietly.

Once they're gone, I open each box enough to lift the lid, and—just as he said—inside each is a homemade chemical explosive, each bearing a digital timer set to detonate in one hour, six minutes, and twenty-five seconds, twenty-four seconds, twenty-three seconds …

Each device is small enough that, on its own, it might not do extensive damage, but all three of them triggering at once in the cargo hold of an aircraft would be plenty strong enough to bring the plane down.

"Somebody owes me a goddamn explanation," Elizabeth demands.

"Almost certainly," I reply, "and if I didn't have to get these bombs out of this airport, I'd be glad to do the honors. Tristan, if you would accompany our new friends to Ms. Senn's car and provide them with a satisfactory explanation, I'd be grateful."

"What about you?" he asks. "You're not going to … I don't know, throw yourself on those things, are you?"

"Oh, good heavens, no. Even if I were the type to throw myself on an explosive device to save others, I scarcely think my body would be sufficient to prevent any of the destructive force. I'd be happy to go into the physics of it with you later, but I really should be going. Elizabeth, Anneke, a pleasure to meet you both. Please stay safe. Tristan, wait for me at the car."

With that, I stack all three boxes, which are heavier than their small size would suggest, and make my way toward the airport exit by the least-populated route I can find. While, to an onlooker, I simply appear to be a man carrying supplies, I don't want to invite discussion or inspection of the parcels. Nor do I want to drop the damn things, which I'm fairly certain would make the whole countdown timer issue a moot point.

As I make my way down empty corridors toward the exit, I become increasingly aware that I don't have a good plan for what to do with them once I'm clear. Not knowing their strength, I can't tell if I can discard them in an empty field or a garbage dumpster, or if I should be looking for a concrete wall behind which to stash them. It's the one tiny detail that my buddy Allah didn't share with me, and I'd like to have a word with him about that.

Mercifully, I manage to avoid most human contact as I work my way from the gate area back to the check-in area and out the doors of the

Departures section, into the light of day. Once there, the problem is far from solved. Hundreds of people are milling about, and police on foot and in cars are a constant presence. There are no bins, no empty areas, not even a large enough and remote enough trash receptacle in which to deposit them. I briefly contemplate placing the boxes in the trunk of an empty taxi in the far lane of traffic, but there's still too much room for chaos. My day will take a decided downturn if I have to throw myself on these stupid things after all.

Just as I'm about to consider allowing a little bit of panic in, I look across the road and see a familiar face. Not a close friend, not an associate, but someone I've seen before. He's old, as they so often are, dressed simply, and sporting Semitic features—if you'll pardon the racial profiling. I certainly didn't expect to see him here, but I'm very glad I do. His attention is fixed on me, just as mine is fixed on him. I walk toward him casually, and he shows no sign of concern.

"Hello, Ephraim," he says, his voice warm and kind.

"Hello, Ruben," I reply, attempting to match the warmth, despite my nerves.

He gives a little smile and a gently scolding shake of a finger. "Now now, you know that professionally, I go by my designation."

"Forgive me—Ehad. How are things in the New York chapter?"

"Busy," he says, "but this is nothing new." He gestures with his head toward the packages I carry. "Are those what I think they are?"

"I imagine they are. Three of them, identical. Synchronous timers, set to go off in about fifty-five minutes. I've looked at them, and I don't see any obvious disarming protocols. I came out here looking for a safe disposal site. That's when I saw you."

"May I see them?" he asks calmly.

I hand him the packages, which he places on a high counter designed for travelers to rest their luggage as they await their shuttle bus. He pulls one of the devices out as casually as if it were a clock-radio, turns it over, and removes a ten-prong chip from the printed-circuit board on the bottom of the device. The timer stops, and the display goes out. My face displays my simultaneous astonishment and admiration.

Ehad shrugs a little. "Eh. You learn some things." He then disarms the other two devices and returns them to their cardboard boxes. "I'll take these with me. You did the hard part."

"I take it, then, you knew I would be here."

"We got word that a messenger had been sent—two, in fact—but we didn't know it was you. I came in case assistance was needed. Did the other messenger come?"

"He did."

"Is it ... *him?*"

"It is."

"The Chicago branch has been looking for him. They want to speak with him about joining. They've lost a member, and now they are incomplete."

"He's not ready," I reply. "Won't be for some time."

"Ephraim, you of all people should know that we can accelerate his readiness. He's very special to us. You've seen the ancient writings."

"I've seen more than that. I've seen *him,* and I know that when the time comes, he'll find the Chicago branch. Until then, he has things to do."

"And what about you?" he asks. "We've been watching you."

"You'll forgive me if I don't find that comforting."

"You've made some troubling decisions of late," he says. "Things that belie who you are, where you come from. You should be taking the proper path and encouraging Tristan to do likewise. You should join the group."

"Last time I checked, you had a full contingent of nine. Or did someone abdicate?"

"We can find a place for you. Arizona. Europe if you'd like. I'd have to pull some strings, but I could even get you a position in the Holy Land. It's a high honor."

"Flattered, but no. You know me well enough to know that I've never played well with others."

"You have such a gift; if only you would use it for the right reasons."

For the first time, his words touch a nerve; it's not a subject I wish to pursue. "My reasons are my own. Thank you, Ehad."

I turn to leave, but he's not done. "You also know what's coming—the war that's building. The enemy is calling upon the forces of Yenne Velt."

Against my better judgment, I remain in the discussion. "Yenne Velt?" I manage a laugh of gentle derision. He's actually invoking ancient legends of the next world? "Ruben, you're really reaching with that one. Absurd Hebraic mythology."

"There is a world beyond ours, and those with access to it have a terrible force at their disposal. You have encountered the Ukrainian?"

"A pitiable byproduct of too much exposure to ordinary earthly radiation. He's no more from the world beyond than you are."

"Or than you are?" he retorts, clearly inviting me to take the bait.

"Don't you wish you knew?"

"I cannot guide your path, Ephraim, but I can tell you this: be careful if you decide to interfere. Perils await, unlike anything you've ever known. I think that inside you is a good man. I wouldn't want him to get hurt."

Just to prove that the good man isn't the only one inside of me, I turn and start to walk away. As I pass a security officer, I call out to Ehad in a voice louder than it needs to be, "Thanks for taking care of the bombs, Farook."

Wish I could stay for the awkward scene that follows.

Ten minutes later, I am back at the car. Tristan stands beside it, looking as patient as he can in light of the circumstances. When I don't offer an opening statement, he takes the reins. "So?"

"Done," I reply.

"I didn't hear an explosion."

"You didn't hear *three* explosions, more accurately. Not that you would have just yet. There's still almost forty minutes before they're supposed to go off."

"You didn't just, I don't know, whip them into an empty taxi, did you?"

"Oh, now, would I do that?"

Damn, he's good.

"I would hope not, but one never knows."

"As it so happens, I ran into an old friend with skill in bomb disposal. He disarmed them and got rid of the offending devices."

He looks at me for a moment, trying—I'm sure—to determine if I'm joking. Once he's convinced that I'm not, he says, "Don't you think that's an amazing coincidence?"

I smile in reply. "You are positively adorable, still believing in coincidence after all we've been through. Shall we go home? And maybe pick up some dinner along the way? I'm about ready to eat."

He gets behind the wheel, as I slide into the passenger's seat. "What did you tell our Ms. Senn?" I ask as we leave the parking garage.

"Boilerplate. We get warnings; we don't know why. But we're given a chance to save people from making a mistake. Which brings up a not-unrelated topic. You could have told me you got the complementary assignment to mine."

"Need-to-know basis," I offer, the words sounding as feeble as I thought they might.

"Oh, horse shit," he answers, quite rightly. "If *anyone* had a need to know, it was me. When will you just admit that you're the world's biggest control freak?"

"Not the *biggest.* There's a man in Georgia, I think."

"My point is, I could have felt a lot better about this assignment, knowing that the enormous X factor—three armed terrorists with bombs—was under your control."

"My dear Tristan, you don't do your best work when you feel better about your assignment. You do your best work when you're under the pressure of fear and uncertainty. When you believe you're the only thing standing between the world and disaster. So I didn't say anything, and I might add, you did excellent work."

This inspires a few seconds of silence. "You really think so?" he asks.

"I do. Don't you?"

"I guess so. Elizabeth Senn didn't get killed, and the terrorists didn't carry out their mission. Brilliant work on your part, by the way. Where'd you get the whole 'voice of Allah' thing?"

"Born of necessity," I answer. "They wouldn't listen to an American, but I hoped they would listen to a more divine source. I made a judgment call, and it paid off."

"If it didn't, they could easily have killed us."

"True, but I also had a fallback plan that involved grabbing Elizabeth Senn's weapon, taking out their leader, and then overpowering the other two in the confusion."

He looks gently impressed but changes the subject. "So, the whole 'saving the lives of the innocent' thing doesn't go against your agency's mission?"

"It's not about random killing. It's about extensive study, rigorous planning, and population control based on the needs of the larger subset. These men were looking to make a statement because of what an oil company was doing to them. The people on that plane had nothing to do with it, no part to play in this international struggle. Their deaths would have been senseless, and the war this would have started would've been even worse."

"Those passengers have no idea how close they came to dying, do they?" he asks.

"No. And it's for the best. Far more important is that we prevented it."

"I was surprised to see you let the terrorists go."

"Capturing them wasn't part of the assignment."

"What do you think will happen to them?"

"Depends on how well they can hide," I answer. "Elizabeth Senn might go after them herself. If she doesn't, and their government finds them, they'll almost certainly be killed for failing their mission."

"Even if they explain that Allah told them not to do it?"

"Probably."

He offers a small sigh of disappointment. "So we didn't save everybody after all."

"We very rarely can."

Chapter 9

Sunday, November 11, 2007

Tristan

Mercifully, the days following our trip to Newark are peaceful. It troubled me for a bit that Ephraim received an assignment that complemented mine and he didn't tell me ahead of time. Still, I try to keep in mind that he has the foreknowledge that he has, and his actions are with my best interests in mind—so he says.

The airport mission was a success. We stopped Elizabeth Senn, and we stopped the people she was hunting, and nobody got hurt. I call that a win. I was fairly certain that was the assignment Ephraim was staying around for, but here we are, four days later, and he seems quite content to remain. Late Sunday morning finds us at the dining room table, playing a game of chess. As I contemplate my next move, I ask, "You don't already know how this game will turn out, do you?"

"I swear I should never have told you about my precognition. It's made you all paranoid. If I knew how the game was going to end, there'd be no fun in playing. So you can't use that as an excuse if you lose. Which, if my calculations are right, should be in about eight moves."

"Aha! You see? Sorcery!"

"No, seven years of competitive play. That and your flagrant overconfidence in the Perenyi Attack. Your move."

"I'm thinking."

Or rather, I was. Without warning, I'm overwhelmed by a powerful pain that surges through my head. I bring my hands to my temples, looking up to see—to my astonishment—Ephraim is doing the exact same thing.

Simultaneously, we both say, "What the fuck?" and look up at each other. The synchronized speaking continues as we ask each other, "Are you seeing this too?" Without answering, we both know the truth—we're receiving the same assignment simultaneously, and to my amazement and his, Ephraim shares the pain I'm experiencing. We ride it out until the details we need are done, at which point we look at each other in disbelief.

"You felt what I felt, didn't you?" I ask him.

"Yes."

"The same images, the same assignment—and the pain in your head that you're still feeling now."

"Yes."

"But there's more to it, isn't there?" I ask. "What I see on your face now is beyond physical pain. It's surprise. You didn't know this was coming."

"No, I didn't."

"That's significant; it has to be significant. You've been staying here in anticipation of helping me, and reason dictates that it was because of this mission. But if you didn't see this coming …"

"I knew *something* was coming, and I knew it involved a higher degree of danger. But what I just saw … what *we* just saw? That wasn't in my memories."

"Is it even possible?" I ask.

"It must be."

"But how? I mean, how could such a thing even exist? You know what we saw."

"I know," he says.

"Zombies."

"You need to avoid that word. It'll psych you out, and that's not what we're dealing with here."

"No? Then what would you call ambling, vacant-eyed creatures with their flesh partially torn off of them, hunting down innocent people and trying to eat them?"

"Victims," Ephraim says simply. "Unfortunate victims whose minds are not under their control. *Zombies* suggests re-animated corpses, and that is *not* what we're dealing with. It's not possible."

"In Haiti," I remind him, "decades ago ..."

"The zombies of Haiti were not dead; they were drugged with a very powerful combination of substances, and I think that's what we're dealing with here. Different substances, but same principle. Believe me, Tristan, I almost wish it were the undead. In a way, that would be easier. They'd go down relatively quickly, and they'd already be dead to start with. We're dealing with living people, under the influence of something I barely understand, and I'm afraid we may have to kill some of them. Come on, time is short, and it's a six-hour drive to Raleigh-Durham. You get the car ready, and I'll stockpile weapons. We can compare notes as we drive."

After the preparations are made, we get in the car, and Ephraim takes the first shift driving. Something about this is bothering me, and I waste no time asking him about it. "I need to know something. When you got this assignment, you were caught off guard. You didn't know what was coming, didn't know the nature of it until the details arrived simultaneously for both of us. And yet now, when you talk about it, it's like you know what we're facing. You know what to expect out there. I need to know how and why."

"Let me be clear," he replies. "I may have an idea of what we're going to face, but I truly don't know what to expect. This will very likely be the most dangerous assignment we've ever had, which is why I suspect we were both chosen for it. I think our employer is starting to trust me again, but he sent the little dose of pain as a reminder that I'm supposed to behave myself. As for the situation in North Carolina, once I got the details, it stirred a memory for me. A project that I had heard about but wasn't working on for the SDC."

"Oh, Jesus ..."

"Hear me out. This is information you'll need to know. There's a recreational drug that's gaining popularity in America. It's called methylene dioxypyrovalerone, but for obvious reasons, it's better known by the abbreviation MDPV. It popped up in Europe first, but pretty soon it was appearing here. We're still not sure exactly what it does, but it's a strong hallucinogen. An unfortunate side effect can be violent behavior—sometimes exceedingly violent."

"Charming."

"Well, the SDC found out about this, and as you already know, drug abusers are one of their targeted populations. Their research scientists were intrigued by this new drug, but they wanted to see how it would interact with other drugs."

"Oh, this just gets better and better."

"So they got a small group of test subjects, and they combined the MDPV with another drug called ketamine. Do you know it?"

"Can't say that I do. What is it?"

"A different hallucinogen, one used by native populations for centuries to induce visions. In some users, it can have a dissociative effect, removing the individual from his own personality and sense of self. Put the two together, they figured, and you've got a creature that's perfectly happy to tear itself apart, limb from limb. Problem solved. Drug abusers committing suicide in droves, sending a message to society that drugs are bad, and nothing to tie the deaths to our little society."

"But?" I ask. "I'm waiting for the other shoe to drop."

"That's just it," he says. "There was no other shoe. It was working beautifully. All the double-dosers, as the research team so colorfully named them, did exactly what they were supposed to. They took both drugs, reacted in textbook ways, and snuffed out their own lives, smiling and content as they did so. Fade to black."

"And yet, you and I are driving to intercept cannibals in North Carolina, and your brain immediately suspected SDC involvement. I can't wait to hear the reason why."

"David Ivorson."

"And who is David Ivorson?"

"A researcher on the team. He put forth a theory that was soundly ignored by everyone else involved. He postulated that each drug individually would have a controlled effect on the target population, but when combined, there was an increased chance of extreme reaction in as much as 10 percent of the population."

"Extreme reaction?"

"Exactly the kind of thing we saw in the details of our assignment. A violent outburst not against self but against others. There would be dissociation from one's own identity, so a person who would never hurt anyone else under ordinary circumstances is now divorced from that restraint. Add to that two very unpleasant side effects: blinding rage and uncontrolled hunger."

"Shit."

"Precisely. Ivorson tried to warn the team. 'But we haven't seen even a single instance of that,' they rebutted. To which Ivorson reminded them that they had far too small a sample for any kind of accurate prediction. But, as so often happens by those too eager to prove a point, they dismissed the naysayer's objections and called their experiment a rousing victory."

"Until today."

"If I'm right. This could also be something unrelated."

"Why North Carolina?" I ask. "That's nowhere near SDC headquarters."

"Washington is just one office. We have another in Raleigh-Durham and others all over the country. My guess is, the latest experiment was taking place there. But I need to confirm." He gets his phone and dials while driving. "This is Z7. Connect me with David Ivorson, please." I'd love to ask him about the Z7 thing, but he's connected too quickly. "David, are you in a secure location?" Satisfied with the answer, he continues, "I have an important question. Later today, in Raleigh, there's going to be an incident. From what I know, it sounds like the results of the scenario you postulated on case 224MKI. Are they testing the case on a larger population there today?" As Ephraim hears the answer, his face falls a bit. "How large? … Damn it. How did they get that many to agree to it? … Of course. That makes sense. It would take that long to get that large a group hooked on it. David, I have it on good authority that things are going to go very wrong down there. It hasn't happened yet, and there's a chance we can stop it before it does. Where's Kean? … Okay, that might work in our favor. I want you to get on the phone to him right away. Tell him to call off the experiment. … It can't come from me; I'm on leave from the group, but you're in the thick of it. Make up a story, and make it a good one. Give him a convincing reason that this can't go forward. Because if I'm right, then your worst fears were accurate. Call me back at this number when you know more."

He puts the phone down but is not immediately forthcoming with further information until I prod him. "So?"

"Kean is in the Raleigh office today. They've found more than five hundred test subjects for case 224MKI, the double-dosing of MDPV and ketamine, and they've spent the last month alternating the two drugs with them, getting them hooked on both. As far as Ivorson knows, today is the day they're going to dose the subjects with both drugs."

"Why isn't he there in Raleigh with them?"

"He's the dissenting voice, remember. When you're eager to push something forward, you don't invite the person who's trying to hold you back. Truth of the matter is, that decision may just save his life. Kean and everyone related to this study may be in mortal danger."

"So I saved Kean's life, just to let him unleash this shit on the world?"

"Don't look at it that way. I may not understand everything about the assignments we're given, but one constant seems to be the necessity of doing them. If somebody wanted Kean dead, you wouldn't have been sent to save him. This happened for a reason."

"What are we up against, Ephraim?"

"If Ivorson can't prevent the test, we're facing a group of up to fifty young men, strung out on two powerful hallucinogens that make them feel impervious to pain in a traditional sense. It will give them an unnatural feeling of physical strength and a distorted audio and visual perception. Meaning if you tell them to stop, they won't be able to process the words. You call to them by name, and they won't know who they are. Another human being could look to them like a giant hamburger, and yes, they will be extremely hungry. Ketamine is a sedative, but the effects of the MDPV will counteract it, so they'll be energetic. And any euphoric effects of the drugs won't be exhibited by this subset of the population. Odds are good, it's because they have a pre-existing chemical imbalance in the brain that predisposes them to violent outbursts and fits of rage."

"Is there any *good* news?" I ask.

"I've got lots of guns."

"That's not much comfort. I don't think I could shoot somebody."

"If that somebody is a drugged-out motherfucker coming to chew on your head, you'd be surprised how quickly conscientious objection yields to survival."

Over the next hour, our conversation doesn't offer much in the way of good ideas. For the first time since I've met him, Ephraim looks like he's not in control of the situation, and I can see the anxiety lurking below, which he's trying very hard not to let me see. I don't make a big deal out of it, but in a perverse way, it's good to know. It's a glimpse of his humanity, his vulnerability. Until now, I've only seen the unwavering self-confidence, the almost maddening aplomb that's his trademark. Today, he and I are on a level, going to fight this thing—whatever it is—side by side. No unfair advantages, no special skills. I'm still glad he's with me, but I think that for the first time, he's glad I'm with him as well.

The ringing of his phone breaks me out of this thought pattern. He answers quickly. "Yes?"

"Is it Ivorson?" I ask him in a whisper.

He nods and continues talking. "Did you reach him? … What did he say? … And what did you say? … Did you explain that it … I see. … I see. … I know you did your best. Well, this is unconventional, but I may have to call him myself, and … When? How long ago? … I see. If there's anyone in the Raleigh office you care about, tell them to lock themselves into the safe room now and not come out until they're sure there's no danger. … Thank you, David."

As he ends the call, I interject, "I take it that's not the answer you were looking for."

"Far from it. Kean wouldn't listen to the warning, and the experiment has already started. They have more than five hundred people down there right now, double-dosing on these drugs, and we have almost five more hours of driving."

"I can take us to the nearest airport and get us on a flight down there," I suggest.

"And I would very readily take you up on that, were it not for the fact that the only luggage we have with us is a trunk full of weapons. Even if by some miracle, they allowed us to check them, we'd have an awful lot of explaining to do."

"Shit. I hadn't thought about the weapons. Couldn't we fly there, leave our current arsenal in the car, and get other guns once we get there?"

"Unless we want to paintball them or spray them with BBs, we're a little out of luck on that front, Tristan. I don't know anybody in Raleigh who could arm us."

"So what do we do?" I ask.

"We drive. At the next truck stop, pull in. I'll buy a radar detector, and every second it's not going off, we'll drive as fast as conditions will allow."

"Is there any estimate of what's likely to happen?"

"With a group of five hundred, the guess was that fifty of them would kill themselves. I'll guess another seventy-five will kill each other. And then there's the civilian population. Who knows how many of them will be in danger?"

"Jesus, this is … I don't know, Ephraim. I've got no frame of reference for this. I mean, my very first assignment involved a woman with a gun, but this—this is the stuff of nightmares. If these people are as drugged-out and dangerous as you think they'll be, there's no reasoning with them, no restraining them. I'm afraid violence is going to be the only answer."

"I hope that's not the case, but if it is, I have to know: what are you prepared to do?"

I think about it for a minute and then give the honest answer: "I don't know. I really won't know until I'm there, in the heat of it. I've never killed anybody, God knows, and I've only ever fired a gun at a practice range, during one of those rich-guy-self-preservation courses. We need to think practically. We're not the police or anything remotely like it. If we kill a stranger, couldn't we be charged with murder?"

He lets out a breath that tells me he's frustrated but also says he knows I'm right. "You're like the tiny, good version of myself, sitting on my own shoulder. You're right, of course. Orders from on high will hardly stand up in court if some poor victim's family decides we had no right to shoot their son. Which leaves us two choices: avoid using deadly force or make ourselves look like we *can* use it."

"Which one do we choose?"

He gives a little smile. "Which one do you think?" Without hesitation, he dials his phone and says into it, "Cornell, it's Ephraim. I need a favor. I'm going to be in Norfolk in a couple of hours, and I need a few props. It'll be a rental; I can get them back to you when I'm done. I need two jackets with FBI lettering on the back, and two Bureau photo IDs. I'll send you the photos for them in a minute. Use whatever names you want. … Great, thank you. How much to rent them for a day? … More than reasonable. I'll see you later this afternoon."

After he ends the call, I watch him fiddle with his phone for a minute, presumably finding and sending the photos for the fake IDs. I want to ask him where he got a head shot of me to use, but I suspect the answer will disturb me, so I skip the question for now and proceed to the more distressing matter. "So, impersonating federal agents *and* using deadly force. This gets better and better."

A hint of annoyance sneaks through as he tells me, "Tristan, obviously if we can accomplish our mission without the use of violence, that's the ideal scenario. But if it comes down to it—and it very well might—I don't want you hesitating because you have to wonder if there will be legal ramifications to your actions. Despite everything you may think of me, my main consideration is getting you and me out of there safely. If we have to pretend to be G-men to fight off the bad guys, then so be it. Trust me, by the end of this day, I suspect that impersonating a fed will be the least of our sins."

My next question is crucial but almost impossible to ask politely. It takes me many minutes of silence to find the words and the courage to voice them. "How do you do it? How do you … kill somebody? How do you get your mind to the place where you can look at that person and say to yourself, 'He forfeits the right to live'?"

It takes him a moment to answer. At first, I'm afraid I've offended him, but when he does answer, I realize that he was just crafting an intelligent response. "It usually involves less thinking than that. Usually, the only thought you have time for is 'If I don't kill him, he's going to kill me.' In that instant of realization, you'd be amazed at what you're capable of doing. Morals, ethics, cultural restraints—these all tend to fly away in that moment when you realize that you alone are able to prevent your own death. Later, after it's all over, of course, you have time to overthink and to punish yourself; but in that moment, when it's literally you or them, your mind doesn't let you think 'It's all right for this person to kill me.' Survival instinct; one of the most powerful innate forces in any species. It's one of the subjects I studied intently while I was with the Social Darwinism Commission. I find it fascinating. Later today, you and I will get the master class in it."

"I'm scared," I confess to him, not even knowing where the confession comes from.

"You should be. It'll serve you well. And believe me when I tell you that I will do everything in my power to protect you, so you don't have to hurt anyone. But if things go south and it comes down to you or them, I need you to steel yourself to the fact that the answer is *you walk away from this, and they don't.*"

"Thank you. And thank you for your honesty in the face of some difficult questions."

"You've asked me many times why I stayed with you after your recovery period was over. I knew something was coming, something big. I didn't know exactly what it was, but I knew I had to be there for it. This is the day. I only hope that I can make a difference by being there."

"You and me both, cousin. You and me both."

A few miles down the road, we find a high-end radar detector for sale in a large truck stop, and I buy it, placing it discreetly on the dashboard of my car. I also pick up a Diet Coke and a bag of Funyuns, as I'm fairly certain that dinner isn't in the plans for this evening. Ephraim eyes my purchase with an expression of confusion and distaste. "What the hell are those?" he asks.

"What, the Funyuns? These are great." I open the bag and hold it out to him. "Try one before you judge."

He sniffs the contents and decides, "I'll pass, thank you."

"Suit yourself. More for me."

"I didn't think you were the junk food type."

"I try to eat properly, but every now and then, I need to feed my inner six-year-old. Funyuns just happen to be my favorite indulgence." He merely shrugs. "Okay, now that we've got the magic box, what would you recommend for our cruising speed on the Interstate? Seventy-five?"

"How do you feel about ninety?" he asks.

Ninety feels mighty comfy after the first couple of white-knuckle miles. Before long, we're passing traffic and making excellent time. Every ten or fifteen minutes, the device gives a little squeal, and we slow down to law-abiding speed for a couple of minutes before resuming our death-defying velocity.

Sooner than originally expected, we pull into Norfolk, Virginia, to meet the man Ephraim phoned, the man called Cornell. Though the encounter is brief, he seems like a stand-up guy. Except for the whole selling of fake FBI IDs, of course. But hey, supply and demand. I'm heartened when Cornell asks Ephraim if his plans for the goods are unsavory in any way. Ephraim assures him that he's on the side of goodness and virtue, hands over the two hundred dollars, and we are again on our way.

The closer we get to Raleigh, the more my intestines curl themselves into a Gordian knot. Courtesy of the vision that accompanied this assignment, I got a cinematic preview of the horror to come, but it's very difficult to process images that your brain is used to seeing only in movies. *Zombies.* Though Ephraim was quick to discount the description of them as such, it's the word that keeps coming back to me. I see their faces, and there's no presence there, none of the deliberate action that comes from cognitive processes. They move by will and instinct, not slow and shuffling like in horror films, but with speed and urgency. And as horrible as the vision is, I know that the reality will be infinitely worse.

With our increased speed, we arrive in Raleigh at 4:35 in the afternoon. I know where to go, thanks to the details of the assignment, but I do not want to be there. When I was a child, one of my favorite picture books featured a *Sesame Street* character warning his young readers on every page that they had to be careful, because there was a monster at the end of the book. As the child turned each page, the warnings grew more and more emphatic. *Don't go any further! You don't want to see that monster.* Of course, what child could resist? The pages turned, our narrator grew more frightened and more desperate to dissuade, until finally one more page turn remained. When it flipped, there appeared only the lovable Muppet, who realized to his surprise and delight that *he* was the very monster he had been so afraid of.

As mile follows mile, the pages of this day turn, and there is most definitely a monster at the end of this book. True to form, and to my uncontrollable fear, I am relatively certain that when I get there and take firearm in hand, I will learn that the monster is indeed me.

I turn onto the street where I am supposed to go, but I see no immediate evidence of chaos. "How do I know we're in the right place?" I ask Ephraim.

As if in answer, a woman's scream passes right through the car's closed windows, assailing our ears. "I think that's your answer," he says. "Find a place to park. It's time."

I find a spot in the parking lot of a large city park, away from onlookers, and we go to the trunk. Inside, Ephraim has placed the FBI jackets, which we don, the federal identification cards in their leather display cases, which we grab, and a stack of automatic and semi-automatic weapons, which scare the shit out of me. Ephraim sets aside three for himself, putting one in his waistband and one in a shoulder holster, and hands me a killing tool, introducing it to me like we're new friends. "Browning Hi-Power nine-millimeter semi-automatic. Handle with care." He spends a minute or so showing me the basics of how to use it, which I think to myself is woefully insufficient for such a big gun. But time is short; I get that.

"Follow my lead," he says, grabbing his third weapon and closing the trunk. "Be watchful all around you, 360 degrees. Use deadly force only if you're directly threatened and only if you're unlikely to hit a bystander. You ready?"

"No."

He smiles just a little. "Me neither. Let's go."

Jackets on, guns held discreetly, we make our way through the section of the park nearest the parking lot. A dense stand of trees gives us good cover but also blocks our view of what awaits us. In the distance—though not nearly distant enough—I can hear the sounds of panic: shouting, screams, possible gunshots. It's a symphony of everything I want nothing to do with, and yet we press on.

Within a few steps, we are met by a wave of people running in our direction, trying to get away from the scene we're approaching. A woman pauses long enough to say to me, "You have to do something!" Clearly, the FBI disguise is working, but she doesn't stay long enough to be of any help.

"Stay sharp," Ephraim says authoritatively yet completely needlessly. Terrified as I am, if I were any sharper, you could slice tomatoes on my shoulders.

When the trees clear and the crowds part, I get my first look at the horror that awaits us. Though I have seen glimpses of it in the vision that accompanied the assignment, my brain doesn't have a frame of reference with which to process what my eyes see. Roughly twenty test subjects are spread out in a central open area of the park. What drew them to this place I don't know. Perhaps it's near the SODARCOM facility; maybe they're just hungry and the park looks like a buffet.

Zombies. Again the word fills my mind. I may be using it as a defense mechanism. It's easier to shoot a zombie than to shoot, I don't know, a college student or a cashier or a pizza-delivery guy. It helps not at all that their appearance bears an uncanny resemblance to the movie monsters. The test subjects are pale and unkempt. Some have blood on them; whether it is their own or someone else's I can't tell. A few of them are missing some or all of their clothing. They move with speed and purpose, bearing down on people who thought it would be good to spend an afternoon in the park. And to my shock—that special, deeply penetrating disgust that will fill my nightmares for months to come, I'm sure—I see clearly and graphically that the zom—*fuck,* that the *test subjects* are biting their victims. Not just biting, but gnawing on them and eating what they tear free. Flesh from arms, legs, even faces.

There's a difference, I learned in a college composition course, between horror and terror. Horror is the feeling of fear and unease you get when you see someone in danger or distress. Terror is the feeling you get when the person in danger or distress is you. To see the scene currently unfolding before me on a movie screen would evoke a feeling of horror. Knowing that I am about to immerse myself in it floods my entire body with blood-freezing terror. "Ephraim …"

"I know."

"Chewing …"

"I see it."

"What do we do?"

"Whatever we have to," he says, which is almost helpful.

In seconds, we are met by two officers of the Raleigh Police Department. Ephraim produces his "badge" and displays it for them. "Special Agent Matheson," he says, and then gesturing to me, he adds, "and this is Special Agent Finney. We got word that you might need some help."

"You are a sight for sore fuckin' eyes," one officer tells us, clearly comfortable in his choice of words, if nowhere else. "I can't even begin to explain what this is, but it's the most horrible thing I've ever seen."

The other officer explains, "They don't stop. They don't listen. They're not slowed down by loud noises or threats of arrest or even violence. They're just … chasing people and—eating on them."

"It's a drug overdose," Ephraim says calmly. "A mixing of two hallucinogens. It makes them very strong, ravenously hungry, and dissociated from the world."

"Yeah, no shit there," the first officer says. "When the calls came in, people were talking about zombies in the park. By the time we realized something was actually going down, they had a real foothold here."

"Casualties?" Ephraim asks.

"No fatalities … yet. More than a dozen civilians with some pretty severe injuries. These … *things* attack them and won't let go; won't leave 'em alone so we can get medical help to them. That's why I'm so glad you boys are here."

"Do you have permission to use deadly force against them?"

"We're strongly encouraged against it, because of all the civilians right there with them. We'll take any help you can offer."

"Let's go then," I reply, wondering where the sentiment came from.

Weapons drawn, we enter the fray. God's truth, it's like nothing I've ever encountered before. If a cheese sandwich walked up to me and started talking about Kafka in Portuguese, *that* would make more sense than what I'm seeing and hearing. The drugged-out test subjects have each chosen a target. Some are clutching their victim menacingly and sobbing for no apparent reason. Others are pummeling the person with closed-fisted blows indiscriminately. It troubles me further to see that some of their victims are women and even children. Still others have begun biting and tearing into the person they've chosen, while the helpless individual screams and cries in unprecedented anguish.

A half dozen local police officers try to tear the predators from their prey, but each time they approach a perpetrator, they are literally thrown clear, and the attacker then resumes his previous assault. Ephraim steps up with a different approach. He fires one of his collection of handguns into the air three times, but unfortunately, it does nothing to dissuade the overmedicated. It does, however, help to throw their movable feast even deeper into a panic, if such a thing is possible. And I believe one of the falling bullets even manages to kill a squirrel, though I can't confirm this, given everything that's going on at the moment.

"Well, *that* didn't work," Ephraim says calmly, confirming the obvious.

"Is there a plan B?" I ask.

"I don't know. I'm kind of making this up as I go." He chooses one of the walking not-dead and spins the man away from his human entrée and around to face him. The aggressor, clearly not concerned about sticking with the same food source, focuses all his attention on Ephraim now. I notice, to my mounting dismay, that another … another … ah, fuck it, I'm running out of polite euphemisms for *zombie.* Another zombie has turned his gaze toward me and is approaching.

"Ephraim, I shouldn't let them bite me, right?" I ask, fearing that this is the likely outcome.

"That's right," he calls back to me, backing away from his own problem.

"What'll happen if they do?"

"It'll really fucking hurt," he says.

"Oh yeah. Right. That makes sense. I know this isn't the best time, but do you have any pithy advice about the one coming toward me?"

"You could try this," he replies, and in a flash, he strikes his aggressor behind the knees, bringing the man swiftly down on his back. Before the once-upstanding citizen can mount a counteroffensive, Ephraim takes his head and bounces it against the grassy ground twice, rendering the attacker motionless.

"Is he dead?" I ask, still watching my own personal conflict move swiftly toward me.

"I'm not a doctor, but I think he's just going to sleep off a very bad headache for a while. I suggest you introduce a similar level of pain to your new friend here."

And with that, my dance partner leaps toward me, making rather disgusting sounds of slurping and drooling, none of which I particularly want anywhere near me. He has his hands on my shoulders, and I have my hands on his shoulders, and I imagine it looks like a perverse wrestling match. Only in this case, if he wins, the trophy is my face. His own visage is no prize-winner at present. These drugs, whatever they are, have blown the blood vessels in his eyes, giving them a sickly red tinge. His tongue is swollen, and his cheeks have deep scratches and gouges of unknown origin. I shudder and try not to think about the amount and nature of this man's bodily fluids I'm being exposed to. At the moment, I'm trying very hard not to add digestive juices to the list.

Ephraim calls to me, "Sweep the legs! Bring him down."

I'm not exactly in the best position to do so, but I manage to spin my foe around and then go for that same area behind the knees. Unfortunately, my position in relation to his results in *both of us* going down together, giving him an advantageous position. Before I can offer a friendly warning on the dangers of eating while lying down, Ephraim charges in and delivers a very timely pistol-whipping in precisely the way I have no goddamn idea how to do.

"Thank you," I offer, pushing my now-unconscious assailant off of me.

Ephraim smiles and extends a hand to help me up. "You're getting too big for me to fight your battles for you, you know."

"I'll take the next one. I promise."

I notice that my feeble attempt at dry wit is lost on him, as his attention is focused on a man in a suit, entering the park—walking right into the heart of the impromptu war zone. Turning my attention in the same direction, I quickly realize it is someone I've seen before. A look of mute rage overtakes Ephraim's face, and he walks quickly toward the man, with me a few steps behind, struggling to keep up.

The new arrival is watching the scene before him with pale horror in his expression, so he doesn't see us until we are almost upon him. At the last second, he turns our way, and in a surprised tone, he manages to utter, "Ephraim …"

With grace and purpose, my cousin picks up Phillip Kean by the neck and carries him that way for about ten feet, slamming him up against the trunk of the nearest tree of suitable size. "What have you done?" he snarls in accusation.

Kean looks afraid for his life—appropriately so—but unlike everyone else in the park, he fears someone who's very much in control of his actions. "From your tone," he offers, struggling to keep his composure, "I'd say you know what I've done."

"You mixed the MDPV and the ketamine, didn't you? Contrary to my concerns and to Ivorson's findings."

Kean glances over at me with a look of concern. Ephraim dismisses it by saying, "Give it a rest, Phillip. What he knows is the least of your worries right now."

"It was working," Kean said, still braced against the tree by Ephraim's unrelenting grip. "We administered both substances, and the reaction was exactly what we were hoping for. They lashed out—against themselves, against each other. In a communal setting, with no one but the subjects around, it would be 100 percent successful. Not all of them had this extreme reaction, but those who didn't would be at the mercy of those who did."

"And *this?*" Ephraim asked, indicating the chaos all around us.

"A containment error. An unfortunate perimeter breach. We underestimated the strength it would give them. Next time …"

"Next time?" I interrupt.

"Of course. With proper containment, this could be entirely successful in future iterations."

"Look around you, Kean," I reply. "You see any success here?"

"Who, precisely, are you?" he asks.

"The guy who should've let you choke on your chicken."

A look of recognition comes to his face. But before he can even question my presence here, Ephraim says to him, "Why are you here? Why put yourself in the middle of all of this?"

"It's called personal responsibility," he says, a suggestion of umbrage in his voice. "I'm going to help contain this and get these people back to the facility, so we can ease them down from the drugs."

"Unbelievable. With all these cops around, you're risking that kind of exposure?"

"I stand by my work," Kean says. "What we're doing is for the betterment of the country and the world."

"Then by all means, don't let me keep you from it," Ephraim retorts, pulling Kean off the tree trunk and shoving him in the direction of several of his test subjects.

We watch as Kean draws attention to himself by calling out quite loudly, "Please give me your attention! You're having a reaction to the medication you were testing, but I can help you. I have a bus waiting at the edge of the park, and if you'll follow me, we can take you back safely. No one has to get hurt."

I look to my cousin with a heaping order of disbelief on my face. "They're going to eat him, aren't they?"

"Most likely, yes."

"Shouldn't we prevent that?"

"Do you have pain radiating through you, telling you to save Phillip Kean's life?"

I think about it for a moment. "No. No, I don't."

"Then fuck him."

Kean's words appear to be lost on the drug-addled crowd, but his presence has the positive effect of drawing the lurching horde away from innocent victims and toward him. As five of them converge on him, I have to turn away.

It's a good thing I do, too, because somehow, a stealthy cavalry has arrived from behind us. I grab Ephraim and pull us both out of the way seconds before a dozen men in flak jackets, shields, and visors charge in from the rear. Their vests bear the name "Raleigh PD—Critical Emergency Response Team." Good enough for me. We watch from a safe distance as the CERT officers draw weapons and proceed to fire at the aggressors, striking each in the neck or shoulder. I gasp at the sight, but Ephraim quickly reassures me, "It's all right. Those are tranquilizers. They're not killing them."

"Great," I reply, "just what they need … more drugs."

With swiftness and efficiency, the crisis is neutralized in a matter of minutes. The emergency responders carry the sleeping subjects out of the park, presumably for treatment, followed by the most unusual fact-finding mission they're likely to encounter. Once the unfriendlies are down, paramedics flock to the field to take care of the wounded—and there are plenty.

A thought occurs to me at this point, and I give voice to it. "Ephraim?"

"Yes?"

"We drove six hours to get here, presumably because we were needed to avert this crisis. And, not to sound ungrateful or anything, but we kinda didn't do shit in the crisis-averting department."

"I noticed that," he replies.

As I'm about to ask what that's about, the first Raleigh police officer we encountered earlier comes up to us. "I really want to thank you guys for coming to help us," he says.

I try not to sound too dumbfounded when I say, "Uhh, sure."

"When the call came in about zombies in the park attacking people, we were like, 'Yeah, right, sure.' We thought it was a hoax or some elaborate practical joke or video stunt. But when we got here and saw that the FBI had sent somebody, I called in the CERT team. How did you guys know this thing was legit?"

"It what we do, officer," Ephraim says heroically. I stifle a laugh. "It's what we do."

My attention is diverted by a sight behind Ephraim's back. Lying on the ground, bleeding from the face and arm, is Phillip Kean. A paramedic is seeing to his injuries, but I can see the look on his face, one of shock—physical and otherwise—and real fear. "Ephraim," I say quietly, pointing toward the injured man.

We walk over to Kean without urgency, standing over him. In a neutral tone, Ephraim asks his former employer, "Hurts, don't it?"

Kean answers with no wind remaining in his sails. "You … knew this would happen."

"Correction," Ephraim replies calmly, "I knew this *could* happen. As of this morning, yes, I knew it would. And if you search your selective memory, you'll recall that I warned you on several occasions about the potential effects of this study. You chose not to listen. Now the results, if you'll pardon the gallows humor, are written all over your face."

"Not so … loud," Kean mutters between moans of pain.

"Why? Because this paramedic will hear you? I have it on good authority that he didn't hear anything." In a movement too quick for me to track, a hundred dollars in cash appears in Ephraim's hand, held up toward the EMT. "Isn't that correct, sir?"

"I didn't hear shit," the medic says, swiftly pocketing the cash.

"So here's how it's going to be," Ephraim tells Kean. "You take a few days to rest up and recover. Once you're feeling better, I want a letter sent by you by registered mail to the board of directors, a copy to me by e-mail, tendering your resignation, effective immediately. You will nominate me as your successor, and you'll include a notarized non-disclosure agreement for good measure. And then you'll disappear."

A look of terror visits Kean's face.

"No, not *that* way, you pussy. I mean the good way. Mallorca or the South of France or the Caribbean. I've heard good things about Aruba. But I don't want to know where you are. Do we have an understanding?"

It takes Kean several seconds before a reply passes his chewed-up lips, whether the hesitation comes from pain or simple uncertainty. But at last he says, "Yes."

"Good." Ephraim puts a hand on the paramedic's shoulder. "Sir, thank you for your attention. Please get my friend here to a hospital as swiftly and safely as you can. He's had a very difficult day, as you can see."

"Yes, sir," the EMT says, in a tone that says he's aware of the dynamic but compensated well enough to let it pass. "Best care money can buy."

As we walk back toward the car, Ephraim stretches his arms high above his head. "I don't know about you, but I could go for some dinner. Have you ever had authentic North Carolina barbecue?"

He never fails to amaze me. "You've just witnessed a cannibalistic orgy of terror and mayhem, and you're hungry?"

"It's not like *I* ate anybody. If I'd had a few bites of innocent bystander, I might not be hungry, but as it stands, some brisket or a pulled-pork sandwich sounds quite good right about now. There's a little place called Mama Q's downtown; looks like the biggest dive ever, but the sauce … heaven."

"You're going back to SODARCOM," I reply, quite off topic. It's more of a surprised statement than a question.

"Soon. Yes."

"Do I have room to hope that you're going back to show them the error of their ways, and you're going to turn it into a charitable organization that helps the poor and downtrodden to thrive?"

He smiles a little. "Have I told you that I've long admired your unyielding optimism?"

"I'll take that as a no."

"Dear cousin, if you're looking for a savior, you're barking up a very incorrect tree with me. I fall somewhere in the middle, between the hero you'd like me to be and the demon you once thought I was. Right or wrong, I still believe in what the Social Darwinism Commission practices and believes. Under Phillip Kean, there was a certain … zealotry that disturbed me of late. With me in charge, I hope to curtail that and focus on a philosophy that ends suffering for those who truly have no hope."

"I might remind you," I say to him as we get into our car again, "that the group plans to target 30 million Americans in the next five years. I hardly think that one out of every ten people is truly without hope."

"The figure may require some adjustment," he replies, starting the car and backing out of the parking space. When I don't answer, he looks at me and says, "I've disappointed you."

"No. It's not that. I just have this naïve belief that every human life has value."

"Every human life has the *potential* for value," he corrects. "Far more humans than you would suspect do not live up to that potential. The SDC is not a power-mad genocidal organization. We simply have found a way to look at human life and human society in a way that emphasizes the greater good. You, my friend, are more typical of the average person than you may realize."

"Thanks ... I think."

"Yes, you're one of the smartest people I know, and I believe you have six dollars more than God, but when it comes to human emotion and empathy, you've taken the chairlift to the apex of the bell curve. You see a soul in turmoil, in the worst of need, and your instinct is to ask, 'How can I help?' The SDC looks at this individual and asks, 'What happens to this person five years after I help?' Think of all those aid concerts, with rock stars raising money to feed the starving in Africa. People look at that and they feel good. They donate ten dollars and they watch the concert on cable TV—for which they pay fifty dollars a month—and they say, 'I helped.' And they're right. A few thousand starving people can eat for a few days. But then what? When the stage is struck, and the rock star is again commanding a hundred dollars a ticket in a stadium named for a business that paid 100 million dollars for the vain privilege? Who feeds the starving then? Intelligent and sophisticated as we are as a species, Tristan, we are short-term creatures with limited attention spans. This isn't a criticism of you or anyone else, merely an observation of things as they now stand."

"It still sucks," I reply quietly, as non-judgmentally as I can.

"Unquestionably."

"Then why do it?"

"Because 999 men out of a thousand won't."

We park in front of a small restaurant that really does look as downtrodden as Ephraim described. For a long moment, we just sit there, looking at each other wordlessly. Other people would share an understanding hug at this point, but neither of us feels so inclined. Instead, he simply offers a quiet piece of advice. "Order the cornbread. It's out of this world."

Chapter 10

Monday, November 12, 2007

Ephraim

The next morning, it is at last time for me to leave my cousin's home and his life, so I'm up early, finishing packing my personal belongings. Much as I wish I had an extra day to decompress after the great North Carolina adventure, I know I have responsibilities. The SDC needs me, and in a perverse way, I need them. Taking care of Tristan in his hour of need has been rewarding, but that hour has passed, and he's ready to live his life on his own now.

"You're really leaving?" he asks, more than a hint of sorrow in his voice as he enters my room.

"I might remind you that you've been giving me the 'here's your hat, what's your hurry' speech for weeks. Now I've got my hat, and I do need to hurry."

"I know, but … I've gotten used to having you with me here for these weeks."

"You're not going to start singing 'I've Grown Accustomed to Your Face,' are you?"

"I think I can restrain myself," he answers.

We head downstairs and stand by the front door of the house for a moment. I watch as he reaches for the right words, settling on, "Thank you."

"Pleasure's mine," I reply honestly. "I'm glad I could help you."

"You did. You really did." He shakes my hand, and I watch in amusement as he decides whether it's appropriate to hug me. He looks hesitant, so I don't initiate anything in that direction. It doesn't happen. "What now for you?" he asks.

"Greener pastures. Back to the SDC; see what I can do there."

"Will I ..." He pauses a moment. "Will I see you again?"

I give him a little smile. "I think that can be arranged."

"Take care of yourself."

"You do the same, Tristan."

After closing the front door behind me, I move quickly to my car and head back to Washington, DC, to the offices of the Social Darwinism Commission—my offices. With my battlefield discharge of Phillip Kean, the place is mine to run now, for better or for worse. And while I believe in the mission of the organization, I also recognize that we've lost our way. Individuals have incorporated personal agendas into the structure of the agency, and it's led to unacceptable practices; profiling, targeting of groups. It could also lead to public scrutiny and risk of exposure if we're not careful.

I have to be mindful of the office politics. Some of the inner circle know me, but others don't. My role to date has been that of enforcer, rather than leader. The truth is, I've been ready to lead for more than a year now. I know what we do, and I know how we do it. I'm not naïve; I understand that because of our actions, people will die. Not because they're criminals, though some of them are criminals. Rather, because they are surplus to the sustainable population limitations for the ecosystem. Is it a rationalization, expressing it in such clinical terms? Maybe. But it lets me sleep at night. A lot easier than sorting through whose son or whose niece or whose grandfather has to die.

With a dim respect for the posted speed limit, I make it to

Washington in two and a half hours and proceed directly to the office building. Owing to the small size of the DC chapter and the need to keep a low profile, we rent a suite in a larger building, the lease held in the name Federal Division of Resource Management. As confident as I'm prepared to be, I walk up the stairs to room 306 and greet the receptionist at her desk. "Good morning, Maggie."

"Good morning, Mr. Shays," she says. "Welcome back."

"Thank you. The time away did me some good. How are things here?" She gives me an uneasy look instead of an answer. "You saw Phillip over the weekend, didn't you?" I ask.

"I was here on Saturday, and he came to clean out his desk. He wouldn't tell me what happened, but there's a copy of his letter of resignation in your e-mail. He said you'd be taking over."

"That's correct. Will you be able to work for me as faithfully as you worked for him? If the answer is no, there'll be no hard feelings, and I'll write you a very strong letter of recommendation."

"Oh no, nothing like that," she says. "It's just very sudden, and I don't know what happened."

I offer her a gentle smile. "Everything's all right. I can't say much, because of security clearances. I'll just say that a project Phillip was working on went wrong, and he chose to step down for the good of the agency."

"Yes, sir. Is there anything I can do for you?"

"Yes, please. Call a meeting of the officers one hour from now in the conference room. I'm going to go move my things from my old office to my new one. Until the meeting is over, please hold my calls, and if anyone calls for Phillip, please tell them he's unavailable, and give any messages to me."

"Yes, Mr. Shays."

"And I'll ask you to call me Ephraim. I understand that you're loyal to Phillip and that change can be disruptive, but I promise you I have the best interests of this agency and the country at heart."

"Yes, sir."

With that, I head to my former office.

Maggie. Her security clearance is quite a bit lower than mine, so I can't tell her any details of what happened in North Carolina, including why her erstwhile boss is now erstwhile. Still, she's worked here for the past ten years; she must know who we are, what we're about. Even if nobody told her outright, she's not stupid. She sees things; she hears things. Besides, I have it on good authority that she and Phillip Kean had a relationship that was more than just professional. No wonder she's so shaken up this morning. Still, she doesn't have to worry about me; I have no reason to get rid of her—unless she creates a problem. Then she has no one to blame but herself.

I'm on edge this morning; I can feel it. Maybe I've been away too long. Maybe I'm doubting myself, in anticipation of the executive team doing likewise in an hour. How many of them were part of Kean's drug-interaction project, I wonder? And if they were, is it an unpardonable sin? I came down hard on Kean in Raleigh, but in the light of day, what was his mistake, anyway? The containment breach, certainly. But beyond that? He had reason to believe that mixing those two drugs would yield the results he wanted—and it did. The fact is, drug abusers are an ideal demographic for the SDC—a population that does nothing but take without giving, and one whose grisly death does wonders for inspiring others to stay clean.

Kean's crime, I've decided as I box up my things to move them to the corner office, was arrogance. He thought he was untouchable; he thought he didn't have to answer to anyone. He ignored the warnings and did whatever he wanted. And for that, he had to go. Nobody on the executive team has to meet the same fate, necessarily.

My possessions successfully crated up, I take them down the hall to the big office on the end, the one that—until Saturday—had a nameplate on the door that read Phillip Kean, Executive Director, Washington Bureau. Guess that's me now. I should let Division know officially, seeing as how I essentially promoted myself. They may balk, deny me a raise or a change of status. I don't care; those things don't matter. Change is what matters, and that's why I'm here.

At five minutes before 10:00, I enter the empty conference room, with its large, rectangular table and sixteen chairs, its videoconference equipment and its wall-size whiteboards, rigorously wiped clean after each meeting. My colleagues are always punctual but never early, so I have a few minutes to catch my breath and prepare in my mind what I want to say to them. The wall is lined with windows, which gives me a view of the world outside. I've missed Washington; lately, it feels like I've been everywhere else.

At exactly 10:00, the seven of them file in, laptops in hand: Paulson, the ambitious one; Drake, the quiet one; Wernicke, the dreamer; Johannsen, the practical one; Biggs, the yes man; Hirsch, the man of action; Aronoff, the supportive one; and bringing up the rear, Sheehan, the shit-kicker. Seeing me at the head of the table, Sheehan is the first to speak as they take their traditional seats. "So, the rumors are true." In his voice I hear a mixture of disbelief and a hint of a challenge. *Did he have aspirations to the directorship?*

"Something you'd like to share, Mr. Sheehan?" I ask, vocally lifting my leg and urinating all over the room to mark it as my territory.

He doesn't back down. "Scuttlebutt over the weekend is that Phillip's out, and *somehow,* you're in as director."

"So much for item one on today's agenda," I reply with a little smile, already hating him. "Though I'm not normally a fan of the rumor mill, today it's accurate. Mr. Kean has tendered his resignation, effective immediately, following the failure of Case 224MKI in North Carolina. I was on scene for containment, and I can attest personally to his wishes and intentions."

At this, I watch as Sheehan says something quietly and privately in Aronoff's ear, beginning while I'm still talking. "Something else you'd like the rest of us to know, Mr. Sheehan?" I invite further.

"Well, with all due respect, *sir,*" he says, with the final word coming out with all the warmth of *fuck you,* "a mental review of the chain of command doesn't seem to put you next in line for this position."

"Consider it a battlefield promotion," I reply, containing my seething resentment, "because that's what Raleigh was on Friday afternoon, a battlefield. The briefing will be available by day's end. I was there, helping to contain the damage and the violence brought about by this ill-conceived plan. I helped save Phillip Kean's life, and his gratitude extended to nominating me for the position, which I accepted." *It's almost the truth.* "If you have any discussion on the matter, I'm sure the group would be willing to listen."

He's on the spot, and he knows it. I continue to stand while they all sit, my gaze fixed solidly on him. "It's just that …" He looks to his cohort for support and doesn't appear to find what he needs. "Word on the street is that you've gone soft on the mission statement."

"Is it?" I ask calmly, doubting it whole-heartedly. "That's very interesting, because the word I've heard on the street is that you're fired."

"What?" he asks, looking genuinely surprised. I admit I'm a bit surprised myself that I'd tolerate so little defiance from him before getting rid of him. But fuck it; I need to make a statement, and he volunteered.

I press the intercom button on the phone. "Security, code six, main conference room."

"You can't do this," he says.

"I think I can."

"I call for a vote of no confidence."

"Okay. It'll take a minute or two for security to get here. Call your vote."

Looking startled by my willingness to play along, he quickly says, "Motion is on the floor to poll the group for a vote of no confidence against Ephraim Shays. All those in favor, please raise your hands."

Not a hand goes up, save Sheehan's. Is it fear? Is it respect? I'm not sure, but it's exactly what I need. Two security officers arrive just in time to hear Sheehan say, "Fuck you all, you spineless pussies. You deserve everything this man will do to you."

One of the officers asks the group, "Someone called for security?"

"Please escort Mr. Sheehan to his office and stay with him while he gathers his personal belongings. He's not allowed to touch his computer, his files, or any other agency property. When he's done, collect his ID, his company credit card, and escort him out of the building."

"Yes, sir."

Sheehan turns to give me a wilting glare. "You're willing to destroy my career for the sake of making a point?"

Though I don't owe him an explanation, I offer one anyway. "You're the one destroying your career, Mr. Sheehan. Your performance has been erratic and your decision-making questionable at best. Insubordination isn't the best choice for frosting your career cake today. Despite what you may think, I haven't gone soft. If I wanted to be gauche, I could order the killing of your grandmother to demonstrate, but I don't consider that an appropriate display of authority, do you?"

His eyes tell me the answer that he won't express in words. "Let's go, sir," the security officer orders. Sheehan follows, certainly cursing my name silently as he goes.

Once he's clear, I take my seat and address the group. "My apologies. That was not on the agenda, certainly. Sometimes business presents itself unexpectedly. I'd like to thank you all for your support—or at least your lack of vocal opposition. As you've deduced, I will be running the Washington branch, at least in the interim. If anyone has concerns they'd like to voice, the floor is open at this time."

No one speaks. I notice that they don't all look as if they have something they'd like to say but they're keeping it to themselves out of fear. Just to be sure, I add, "You can also see me privately to discuss this if you'd like. On to the next item of business. Over the weekend, I read the briefings for the period during which I was away from the agency. While I agree that many of our initiatives are going well, I also feel we're starting to lose our way in some others. You all know about the breakdown of the cancer-centers initiative in August." Several of them nod. "It's unfortunate, but we were also seeing issues arise beyond the scope of what we anticipated. There was some collateral damage and some uncontrollable factors that led us to terminate the project early."

"Are there plans to start that type of initiative up again?" Paulson asks.

"We're going to keep looking at it," I answer. "For cancer and other terminal illnesses. We'll also work with Congress on right-to-die legislation, which as you know has been difficult in the past. Obviously, the most beneficial demographic to approach is the one that's ready and willing to die of their own accord."

"Yes, but what about the debacle with the suicide hotlines a couple years ago?" Hirsch says.

"That was poorly planned. And it was too closely monitored by outsiders. We didn't get the traction we needed there. In hindsight, though I was part of the planning committee, I'll admit that it was a bad idea. There was no opportunity for quality control, and the fact of the matter is, there's no subtle way to tell someone calling a suicide hotline that they should really go with that impulse after all."

This evokes some nervous laughter, allowing me to segue into the main topic. "I'm taking us back, gentlemen. Way back. The original mission statement of 1868, when this agency was known as the Resource Allocation Commission. Yes, circumstances were very different in this country at that time, but our mission was new, innovative, pure. The war was over, and there was turmoil. People scrambling for resources. Look around you. We may not have battlegrounds on our shores, but the scrambling is definitely there. I'd say even worse than it was in 1868. Back then, there were 36 million citizens. Today, we've topped 300 million. So, why are we here? Why do we get up every morning and come to this office?"

Silence. Maybe they think the question is rhetorical. "Somebody chime in. Why are we here?"

Aronoff takes the lead. "Because … because there are more people in the country than we have resources to support."

"Agreed," I reply. "What else?"

"Because some people are just taking up space," Hirsch adds. "They use up resources, and they don't contribute to society."

Johannsen says, "Because we tend to forget that survival of the fittest applies to our species as well as all others."

"Because survival isn't a right, the way we're led to believe it is," Drake says, earning turned heads from his colleagues unused to him speaking up.

"Precisely," I respond. "Despite what others may have led us to believe in the past, it can't be about targeting an ethnic group, a religious group, or even a particular socioeconomic status. It has to be about pinpoint accuracy. As such, I've come up with a list of potential projects for 2008. I'll begin by presenting them, and then we can engage in discussion regarding their merits. The first initiative involves a level of cooperation. I'm sure you've all seen free spay/neuter clinics for pet owners who can't afford this operation for their dog or cat. It stands to reason that there's a percentage of the human population who don't want children, but they can't afford the analogous surgery. I propose we offer government-funded clinics for this population, giving them a voice in their right *not* to reproduce."

Quiet murmurs from around the table signify a level of respect for the idea. It's a good start. "We also need to work on gun-control issues. We want the gun-loving crowd to start buying more, and the best way to do that is to make them believe that much stricter gun-control laws are coming. We've found that this population is more inclined to shoot themselves and each other, rather than innocent civilians, and we're okay with that. Yes, there will be some consequential casualties to outside populations, so we're going to be very careful in examining the feasibility of the program.

"Prison populations are another area of interest, particularly the lifers. While they aren't typically reproducing, they are rampant consumers without contributing to society. So we're going to see what we can do in that environment. We also have a strong interest in the welfare population, especially those individuals who have been on welfare for many years. Our focus will start by trying to encourage them to be participating members of a productive society. Their unwillingness to do so could lead to other avenues of exploration."

A quick glance around the table tells me they're still with me, so I continue.

"America's drug subculture is also a prime area for expansion. Every month, it seems there are new illegal substances on the streets, gobbled up by a population that—let's be honest, gentlemen—nobody would miss if they were gone. It would be akin to a public service if these individuals drugged themselves to death. Obviously, Raleigh taught us this weekend that we have to be careful, but there's plenty of room for progress. Methamphetamine is a gold mine on that front. People are voluntarily ingesting poison for a temporary, powerfully addictive high, and there's very little regulation of what gets made and sold. Any idiot with a chemistry set can be a producer. We're trying something unusual in the next few months. We're going to fund a new dramatic series on basic cable television about the production and distribution of meth. To a reasonable and discerning viewer, the stories will expose the horrors of the drug. But to those with an addictive personality and a craving for the newest thrill, it'll look like an hour-long candy commercial. We're also considering articles and news programs downplaying the dangers of this drug.

"Taking what we've learned from the cancer study, we want to continue to focus on the terminally ill and nursing-home populations. What we lacked before was subtlety. We treated it like a military offensive, rather than a widespread act of kindness and mercy. And that is why we failed."

"I thought we failed because of your cousin," Paulson chimes in.

Touché. But I can't let him have the moment; not entirely. "It's true that my cousin did take it upon himself to investigate and sabotage our operation. He had met a participant in the study who committed suicide in his presence. He also received a phone call from a former SDC operative, encouraging him to take these actions. It was a very specific set of circumstances, ones almost impossible to duplicate. Still, it exposed sloppiness in the system. This is not a criticism of anyone; simply a statement of a strongly held opinion, mine and others'.

"It also circles back to my belief that we've lost our way, that we've become some sort of covert hit squad for the federal government. I'm curious. By a show of hands, if you weren't bound by security clearances and confidentiality statements, how many of you would talk to your friends and family about what you do for a living?" *As I suspected.* "Not one of you. But why not? Aren't we doing this country a good service?

Performing a valuable job in the best interests of the population as a whole? Or have we lost sight of that? When you look at an operations initiative, do you see anything but the loss of life that's often needed to carry out the job?"

Their silence speaks volumes. "It's all right," I tell them. "It's understandable. And yes, I sometimes feel it too. But we can be better than that. It means some initiatives have to go. We'll go over it in detail. Most of all, I want us to be able to feel proud of what we do again, and to achieve that, I'll need support from all of you."

The remainder of the meeting goes well. I can't quite tell if their loyalty is motivated by fear of me, but in the end, the loyalty is what matters. On my way back to my office, Maggie stops me long enough to hand me a phone message—one of those pads where you just have to fill in the details and check the proper boxes. I see that she has checked the boxes for "You received a call," "Please call back," and "Urgent." The time shows 10:06 a.m., and on the line denoting who phoned, she has simply scrawled, in large capital letters: HIM.

Since I'm not expecting a call from Jesus, that leaves only one other possibility, and—all things being equal—I'd be better off having to call Jesus back. I look at Maggie's eyes. "How was his tone?"

"I can never tell for sure."

"I'll call from my office."

Few things in this life frighten me, but this man frightens me. I'm loath to even mention his name in discussing him, as if giving it thought or voice could somehow conjure him. Aware of my now-elevated heart rate, I enter my new office and close the door behind me. Sitting at my desk, I allow myself three deep breaths. I can't show any fear, weakness, or uncertainty in my voice when I speak with him; he'll seize on them. Unfortunately, this is as ready as I'll be able to get.

I open the folder with the contact protocols. There is no direct dial to reach this man, no friendly secretary to banter with and say, "Hey, the big guy wanted me to call him. Is he in?" Instead, there is a complex automated-routing system that relays who's trying to call and determines if the conversation is allowed to take place.

I dial the ten-digit number, followed by the fourteen-digit access code. Through the phone, I hear the redialer and the routing software connect me to two more places. When prompted, I enter a seven-character password. At the beep, I speak my name. Then I wait in silence. No hold music; no helpful voice telling me I'm fourth in line; no one to tell me my call is important and I should continue to hold. I'm well aware that my call is important, and short of my own untimely death in this chair, there's no question that I'm going to hold.

Six minutes and forty-seven seconds later, the void of sound is replaced by a voice, which begins by speaking a single word. "Ephraim."

The sound is beautiful and deadly, like a poisonous butter melting into the folds of my brain. "Director. Good morning, sir. Thank you for taking my call."

"Under the circumstances, I believe it's important that we speak."

Agree. Agree. Agree. Agree. "Absolutely, sir."

"I read your briefing on the events that transpired in North Carolina. I've also spoken with Phillip Kean."

"Did he call you, sir?"

"I sent for him. He's here with me."

A wave of cold passes through me. After all these years, I still don't know the physical location of the man I'm speaking with. To be summoned before him is about the worst fate I can think of. I shudder to think that I'm responsible for that outcome. "Respectfully, sir, I hope that my report didn't cast Mr. Kean in too unfavorable a light. I believe there were elements of merit to his initiative."

"He's here for information-gathering purposes only," the SDC's highest-ranking official tells me calmly. "Your willingness to speak in his defense is admirable. Given the events of the past seventy-two hours, you would be justified in seeking the strictest disciplinary measures against him."

"Thank you, Director. I … given the turn of events, I didn't want you to think that I was motivated by any … personal misgivings or unprofessional motives. In the moment, I did what I felt was best for the agency, and Mr. Kean did as well."

"I didn't call to talk about Phillip Kean, Ephraim. I called to talk about you."

"Of course. Forgive me, sir. Please go ahead."

"There's been a great deal of discussion today over your self-proclaimed ascension to the directorship of the Washington bureau. You're aware of this, are you not?"

"Yes, sir. I've already met with senior staff, and I have their affirmation of loyalty and support."

"Does that include Nathan Sheehan?" he asks, clearly already knowing the answer.

"Sheehan's track record was spotty at best, Director. I can cite a history of questionable judgments, poor performance ..."

"I'm aware of what's in Sheehan's jacket. What concerns me is the unilateral nature of your actions, Ephraim. You walked away from this agency for almost three months."

"With respect, sir, I exercised my unpaid leave option for the sake of taking care of an ailing family member."

"I'm well aware of that. I'm also aware of who that family member is. Tristan Shays, your cousin, and the man who infiltrated the Swift facility on your watch, causing the dismantling of a very time-intensive, labor-intensive, and cash-intensive initiative that was showing an ongoing success rate."

"There were problems, sir. Cracks beneath the surface that we didn't see. Participants in the study were turning violent against family members. Staff were starting to question the facility's intent. Then there was the issue with Kolodziej. He turned against us, subverted the system from within. I won't go so far as to say that Tristan did us a favor, but I believe the operation's foundation was crumbling and wouldn't have been sustainable for much longer, even if he hadn't been allowed to infiltrate."

"I question your capacity for leadership, Ephraim." The words send a wave of nausea through me.

"Yes, sir. I understand."

"Do you? Because beneath your cowed tones of subservience, I hear a deeper level of arrogant cockiness, the same one you've displayed since the day you started here."

"Not my intention, I assure you, Director."

"Intention doesn't enter into it. It's at the core of who you are. Your primary function is security. Because of your willingness to contribute, you've been given a voice in planning sessions. Nowhere is it written that you are marked for a leadership position."

"No, sir."

"Your appointment was presumptuous, and you circumvented protocols and procedures."

"I understand."

"I could relieve you of command and ask for your resignation right now."

The smart thing, the very smart thing to do is to agree, thank him for his wisdom and his understanding, and throw myself on what passes for his mercy. But I know my helping verbs, and his choice intrigues me.

"Could?"

I got him, and he knows it.

"Could," the Director repeats. "Not *will.* For reasons that are my own, I'm going to give you a chance. A probationary period of fourteen calendar days, during which time your title will be *Interim* Executive Director, Washington Bureau."

"Thank you, sir. That's more than fair."

"You're goddamn right it is. During that time, you will file daily reports to me of all activities of your branch. You'll also be monitored by individuals of my choosing. At the end of the fourteen days, I will make a determination as to your fitness for leadership moving forward. Until that time, you will continue at your present salary."

"Beyond generous, sir. I assure you."

"Be very careful, Ephraim. You're walking a fine line, and I think you know that I'm not to be toyed with."

"Wouldn't dream of it."

"Spend the next two weeks showing me that you can lead this

organization without making the kind of mistakes that Phillip Kean made, and we'll talk again about your future."

"Very good. Thank you, sir. Thank you for this opportunity. I mean that sincerely."

No good-bye, not another word. Just the silence that follows the orders of a man whose conversations are over when he says they're over. I've been taken to task, but all things considered, it could have been worse. Much worse. I can only imagine what Phillip Kean must be going through as he answers the Director's very pointed questions. That could just as easily have been me. I was in that park too, watching as human beings our organization altered ran rampant against an innocent population.

Fourteen days to prove myself. Fine. I can do that.

For several minutes, I simply sit, going over the details of the call in my mind. Like many of the events of my recent past that involve Tristan, I had no advance memory that this would happen. It's disrupting my understanding of my future, but if I were paying closer attention, I might realize it's teaching me fascinating things about the nature of time and fate. If only I could give it that level of attention.

Eventually, sufficiently returned to a state of calm, I rise from my chair and exit my office, heading back into the main reception area to let Maggie know I'm available once again. She knows better than to ask how the call went, but her face conveys a tangible level of sympathy and understanding. Based on the fact that I'm not dropping off my ID card and leaving the building, she infers that it couldn't have gone too badly.

"I'm available now," I inform her.

"That's good, because you have a visitor."

I look around the otherwise unoccupied lobby. "I do?"

"Yes. She arrived about five minutes ago, and I told her you were on an important call and couldn't be disturbed. I offered to make an appointment, but she insisted on staying. She's in the conference room now, expecting you to meet her in there."

"Did this person give a name?"

"No."

"Charming." I pick up the hand-held panic button from the desk and put it in my pocket. "Be watching. If this goes off, send backup."

"Yes, sir."

It's no wonder people hate Mondays, I muse to myself as I make my way back down the corridor to the conference room. I can't imagine who would insist on seeing me without an appointment, but courtesy seems to be a dying practice in this day and age, so very little surprises me.

I open the door to the conference room to find a woman on the other side of the table, her back to me as she looks out the window at the streets of Washington below. She is tall, dressed in a gray pant suit, and clutching a leather briefcase with one hand.

"I was told you wanted to see me," I say to the back of her head.

At that moment, Karolena Prizhen turns around, like a life-size ice sculpture on a rotating base. A soulless smile visits her face as she looks directly at me and replies, "Hello, Ephraim. I think you and I should talk."

Chapter 11

Monday, November 12, 2007

Tristan

There's not much to say as Ephraim stands at my front door, his possessions all packed up and at his feet. It's strange that after all the fuss I've made about being independent and not needing him here, I really don't want him to go. I can't tell him that. Well, actually, of course I can. I can tell him anything I want, but looking at his face, it's clear that he's completed the task he set out to complete, and it's time for him to be on his way.

I need to say something. As the *(former, goddamn it)* CEO of a major corporation, I should have no trouble conversing with someone, and yet as I stand here before my cousin, I am straining to find the proper words. "Thank you," I manage.

"Pleasure's mine," he replies simply. "I'm glad I could help you."

"You did. You really did." I shake his hand. I really wish we were a huggier bunch, but I just can't bring myself to do it. "What now for you?"

"Greener pastures. Back to the SDC; see what I can do there."

"Will I …" The question sticks in my throat. "Will I see you again?"

He offers a knowing little smile. "I think that can be arranged."

"Take care of yourself."

"You do the same, Tristan."

With that, Ephraim exits my home and my life, and for the first time in weeks, I am alone in the world. It should feel as natural as breathing, since the solitary bachelor's life has been one of my choosing for years. Yet I've grown so accustomed to the presence of Ephraim—and Genevieve before him—that as I stand in my foyer, mere seconds after my cousin's departure, I feel an emptiness I can't even explain. All at once, I am bored; I never get bored. Worse, I am aware of the oppressive silence of the house, which is absurd, because Ephraim had been very quiet when he was here. It's not like he ran around in army boots, singing Italian opera at the top of his lungs.

I miss him already.

No, no, snap out of it, you pathetic dolt. You're fine, and you will continue to be fine. You've been alone for ninety seconds, and you're acting like the last puppy in the pound. Distraction, you simply need distraction.

The television—that will do. It makes sound and shows mindless pictures. The perfect remedy for thinking too much. Finding the remote, I switch on the living-room set and begin to flip through the roughly eight hundred channels I've subscribed to, for some reason, in my overpriced cable (or is it satellite?) package. I really need to pay closer attention. I bypass old movies, newer movies, news, infomercials, dramas, Spanish dramas, stand-up comedians, lying-down naked people, science fiction, true science, and six basketball games. Nothing speaks to me—not even horizontal naked people—painfully cognizant as I am about how long it's been since I've personally been horizontal and naked.

A book, that's it. I'll lose myself in a book, and I won't even spare a thought for anything else. Standing at my well-stocked living room bookshelf, I pick up volume after volume, but nothing says *read me.* Everything from classical to contemporary passes by with no interest in delving in.

I could clean the house, I decide. *That's a good use of time.* But a quick inspection of the place tells me that thanks to Ephraim's help, everything is quite clean. I swiftly dismiss the notion of dirtying it and then cleaning it up again immediately as just too ridiculous to entertain.

The anxiety I'm feeling, though nowhere near panic-attack level, is nonetheless unsettling. Am I now incapable of being alone? Have my circumstances changed this drastically that just a few minutes in my own company leaves me desperate and insecure? It shouldn't be possible, I decide as my eyes light on … *the phone.*

"Hi, Esteban. It's Tristan."

His voice is warm and cordial, though I can hear beneath it how busy he is. "Tristan, good to hear from you. How are you feeling?"

"Much better than the last time I saw you, thanks. My memories are completely restored, and I'm feeling fine, physically and mentally."

"Well then," he says, "that's the best news I've heard all month. To what do I owe the pleasure of your call?"

"Just wanted to say hello, see how things were going. See how the mantle of command is treating you."

"Thank you. I tell you, when you first promoted me, I was a bit scared. I had moments of self-doubt, and I didn't know if I could run things after you'd done so for years. But once I believed in my abilities, it's the greatest thing that ever happened to me. The employees are fantastic, and projections for the quarter and the fiscal year are ahead of plan."

"Well, that *is* great news. Would you like to have lunch today, catch me up on things?"

"I'd love to," he says, "but I have a lunch meeting with a potential client. Rain check, though?"

"Absolutely."

Why do I feel like "Cat's in the Cradle" should be softly playing somewhere? This musing leaves a discernible gap in the conversation, and Esteban—as politely as he does with everything—prompts the next move.

"Anything else I can do for you today, my friend?" he asks.

With an embarrassingly forced little laugh, I joke, "Yeah, are you hiring? I'm also available on a consultant basis."

I hate myself for saying it. It's a terrible thing to do, and I wish I could take it back, but it's out there—just serious enough that Esteban is forced to formulate a reply.

"Tristan, you know there's nothing I wouldn't do for you. But we've talked about this, remember? What would happen if you started to miss the job, miss this place. We agreed that even if things slowed down for you in your other pursuits, coming back here wouldn't be the answer. I need you to respect my right to the position. I can't do the job if I'm always going to be looking over my shoulder. I hope you understand."

"I do," I answer with a little cough, born of a tickle in my throat. "Of course I do, and I'm sorry." Two more coughs as the tickle becomes a scratch, and then—something more. "Esteban, I've gotta go. That slowdown in my other pursuits? I think it's over."

I don't know if an official good-bye passed my lips or if I even hung up the phone. All I know is that like a shot, a pain surges through my mouth, throat, and lungs, as if I've just power-slammed a drain-cleaner smoothie.

This is new. Unlike the spicy-food pain I felt before, this one attacks the very air I'm breathing, making every breath an adventure in agony. *Fuck what passes for my life, why do they have to do this to me every time?* Mercifully, the onslaught pauses long enough to let me clear my head and get the details of my next assignment.

Baltimore. A man named Nick Swartz, fifty-six years old. In three and a half hours, he's going to have an accident in his home that will kill him, unless I can stop it from happening. *Baltimore—it's like a trip around the block, compared to recent destinations.* "Yes," I say aloud, perhaps for no other reason than to shut down the pain, "I'll do it. I'll take it."

For reasons I still can't explain, the pain does subside a bit at this declaration. Three and a half hours doesn't give me a ton of time, and I suppose I could once again try my luck at calling my intended contact.

But I clearly have nothing better to do, and a change of scenery will do me good, so I head out to my car. Fortunately, it isn't that far to go, as there's no one to split the driving.

Mercifully, there are no weapons to pack this time, no drug-crazed flesh-eaters to vanquish. Years from now, will I look back on that assignment as the "good old days"? I hope to hell not.

Late-morning traffic is a breeze, and at fifty-five degrees, it's unseasonably pleasant out, so I cruise down the highway with windows open a bit, enjoying the scenery of Maryland. The anxiety I was feeling in my home is melting away, and the tranquility of classical music on the stereo, the open road, cool breezes, and a bottle of iced green tea with citrus are soothing my soul. Yes, I have to go tell a stranger that he's scheduled to die today, which could reasonably be called a downer. But on the plus side, I get to tell him that a simple decision will prevent this fate. All he has to do is choose to believe me, and he gets to enjoy life for a while.

The miles pass swiftly, and with them the hours; before long, I am pulling into Baltimore. Close as it is to Ocean City, I don't know much about Baltimore, aside from what I've seen in John Waters movies. It has its affluent neighborhoods and its run-down neighborhoods, its arts district and its downtown area. In short, typical trappings of any medium-sized American city. Today's assignment takes me to a middle-class vinyl village subdivision in one corner of town. On a corner lot stands a modern-looking two-story home with gray siding and a black roof. It's not large, but if I understand the details of my assignment, the owner lives alone, so there's plenty of room for one person. A six-foot-high wooden fence encloses the backyard. The front lawn looks well-manicured, particularly for November, a time when homeowners traditionally let things go for the winter.

I spot the homeowner's car in the driveway, so I assume he's home. Not to be overly familiar, I park my own car at the curb and approach the front door. A check of my watch tells me I've arrived in time, but not by much. In only seven minutes, this man will make his very bad decision unless I can convince him otherwise. Remembering all of Ephraim's training, I ring the doorbell and wait.

Within a minute, the door opens, and a heavyset man in his mid-fifties looks out at me. He was probably handsome once, but a solitary life with no one to impress and no one to keep him diligent has encouraged him to slip into what Pink Floyd so eloquently called "alcohol-soft middle age." The hair he still has is gently unkempt; his clothing likewise. I can't smell his breath, but if I could, I suspect I would get a hint of Cheetos, for some reason.

He greets me with a monosyllabic and suspicious, "Yeah?"

"Mr. Nick Swartz?" I ask pleasantly, trying not to sound like I'm about to ask him if he's accepted Jesus as his personal savior.

"That's right."

"My name is Peter Kellogg, and I've driven here from Ocean City because I have a message to give you."

He looks confused, but he replies, "Okay," and holds out his hand.

"No, it's not that kind of message. It's a spoken message."

"Okay, so speak it," he says, as businesslike as a man at home in the middle of a Monday afternoon can be.

"I know this is going to sound hard to believe, but I receive visions—warnings of people who are in danger, and I'm burdened with the task of letting these people know before things go wrong. I received a vision of you today. In just a few minutes, you're going to go up on your roof to tack down some loose shingles, and if you do, you're going to fall off of the roof, and—I'm sorry to say this—you're going to die as a result of the fall."

He looks at me as I'm telling him this. When I finish speaking, he stares silently for a few seconds and then says, "Fuck off."

"Excuse me?"

"Which word was unclear?"

"Neither. I'm just a bit puzzled by your reaction, given that I just drove three hours to warn you, in an effort to save your life."

"Yeah, well, that'd be great … if I was planning on going up on my roof in the first place. But I wasn't."

"You weren't?"

"No. Not even in a one-of-these-days kinda way. Because I don't even have any loose shingles."

"You *are* Nick Swartz, aren't you?"

"Yeah, as in Nick Swartz who doesn't go up on roofs if he don't gotta." He steps out of the house. "Cause, as you might have noticed," he says, stepping toward the curb to look at his roof, "the shingles are just—" He hesitates. "Shit."

"What?"

"There's a loose strip. A big one."

I step over next to him. "Yeah, I'd say there is."

"Okay, now I know what this is."

"Huh?"

"You're a goddamn roofer."

"I'm *what?*"

"That's exactly what you are. I'll give you points for your little speech there, but it's the old scam. You drive around neighborhoods, looking for roofs that have holes or loose shingles, and you tell the person that they shouldn't fix it themselves, but you could do it quick and cheap. Then you get up there, and I end up with a bill for three hundred bucks for ten minutes of work. Well, no thanks."

"I assure you, Mr. Swartz, I'm not a roofer, and the last thing I want to do is get up on your roof and tack down your shingles."

"You're goddamn right you won't. Because I've got a ladder, and I can do it myself in ten minutes for the cost of a couple of nails."

"What? After what I just told you, you're planning to go up there and do the thing I cautioned you would kill you, just to prove a point?"

"Well, since what you told me was some screwed-up sales pitch, I really don't have anything to worry about. And you're gonna stand here and watch me do this, so you can see that it's not right to scam honest people."

"Why don't you just leave the shingles loose?"

"What the hell kind of roofer are you? If I leave them loose, they'll just pull others off, and pretty soon, I won't have any left up there. You wait here. I'll be back with a ladder and a hammer."

This is crazy. I'm invited to stay here and watch this idiot die. I should go. I should just get in the car and go. I delivered the message. The fact that he's choosing to ignore it is not on me. But I *always* go. I never stay to see if what I've said is right. What if I do have bad information? What if he gets on that roof, tacks those shingles down, and survives? This is my chance to check the accuracy of my warnings, and despite every reasonable instinct in me telling me to drive away from here at top speed, I'm somehow compelled to stay and watch this bizarre encounter play itself out to its logical conclusion.

Three minutes later, Nick Swartz emerges from his garage with a twenty-foot ladder, a tack hammer, and a small box of roofing nails. The look on his face is one of pure defiance. "Three hundred bucks, huh?" he says. "You just watch me. A man takes care of his property. He don't need some stranger to come and do it for him."

As he leans the ladder against the front of the house, I feel compelled to ask, "Is there *anything* I can say to discourage you from doing this?"

"Yeah, I don't think so," he answers, beginning his ascent.

"Not even the fact that, according to my vision, in three minutes, you'll plummet off of that roof to your death?"

"Ten bucks says you're wrong."

I should do something, I know I should, but I honestly don't know what to do. I've done what I consider to be due diligence in trying to talk him out of it. The pain I was experiencing is definitely gone, so I've fulfilled my celestial obligation, at least. And, truth be told, he's kind of a dick. But am I backing away from further persuasion, just for the sake of standing over his soon-to-be mangled corpse and saying "Told ya so"? Not that I would admit, certainly.

Mr. Swartz reaches the apex of the ladder, his steeply pitched roof, and begins pounding nails into the strip of shingles that has worked its way loose. The hammer strikes reverberate off of the surrounding houses, sounding to my distracted and gently guilt-ridden brain like a coffin being nailed shut. *Here lies Nick Swartz. Died needlessly to prove that he was smarter than someone he'd just met. Requiescat in stupidismus.*

Or maybe he really *will* show me. After all, he's made it this far. He got up on the roof, and he seems to be in control of his tool, so to speak. I like to think that my warnings are accurate, that I'm sent places because I can be persuasive, make a difference, save lives. But who's to say that there's not a bigger mechanism at work? Perhaps my warning to Nick Swartz today was more of a metaphor, saying, "Be careful in dangerous situations," and the warning about a specific time and place just meant he should start right away.

I'm really starting to warm to this explanation when I hear vocal evidence of a lack of surefootedness. The hammer drops to the ground, and seconds later, Swartz loses his footing and plummets to the pavement several feet away. I'm startled by the sound and uneasy about what I'll find, but I rush over to him and kneel at his side. He is a mess; not the splattered-insides kind of mess he'd be if he'd fallen from a much greater height, but he managed to land on his head and neck, resulting in—well, let's just say dude didn't bend that way yesterday.

Despite what I know from my warning, there may still be a chance to save him. I try to find a pulse somewhere on him, without any luck. I'm just about to open my phone to call for help, when—to my absolute shock—I hear a voice behind me say, "Whoa, is that me?"

I look up into the eyes of what appears to be Nick Swartz, standing over me. His question comes out with a great deal of calm and control, more than I suspect I could muster in his place. The fact that he's there to ask it, however, robs me of any calm or control I may have still had. I stand up in a rush, taking a step away from the newly arrived Mr. Swartz. "Holy shit!" I offer quite unhelpfully.

"Looks like you shoulda taken the bet," he replies. *How can he be so unfazed by this? And while we're on the subject, how the fuck is he here talking to me?*

With a look of pure stupor on my face, I'm sure, I reach out to the man—the one on his feet, not the one in the impossible yoga pose—and try to touch his arm. In a moment that surprises me less than it should, my finger goes through him like he was an overweight, middle-aged cloud.

"You're dead," I say quietly. "That's you. You fell off the roof."

"Now you're just rubbin' it in," he jokes, further disrupting my world view.

"How can you be here?"

"I dunno. I've never died before. Maybe this is just what happens. You're the expert."

"No. No-no-no-no-no. I'm not the expert. But I'm pretty sure that after you die, you don't get to stand around tossing off one-liners."

"Not *exactly,*" says yet another voice in this increasingly unexpected scene. Cloud-Nick and I turn around to see a young man with red hair and a short beard standing behind us. He's wearing a blazer and a green Oxford shirt with a pair of jeans—which isn't particularly relevant, except to note that the latest participant in this incomprehensible moment is a snappy dresser.

"And you are?" I prompt.

"Joshua Harcourt," he answers pleasantly. "I'm here for Mr. Swartz."

"Ah, well there's a bit of a complication, in that Mr. Swartz has just had a rather serious disagreement with gravity, and the upshot is … that's him on the patio."

"I know," Joshua replies. "That's why I'm here."

Curiously, Cloud-Nick and I both have the same reaction to this news: "Time out."

"I'm here to escort Mr. Swartz to the other side," Joshua explains, which really does little in the way of helpful explanation. He greets our blank looks with further detail. "I'm one of a group of individuals who assist newly departed spirits in crossing over from this life to the next."

"Weird," I reply.

"Cool," Swartz offers. Of the two of us, he's the one I'd expect to be more disturbed by this turn of events, being—you know—dead and all.

As such, I turn to him and ask, "You're okay with all of this?"

"I mean, it sucks being dead, I guess," Cloud-Nick admits, "but I wasn't exactly doing much with my life, let's face it. And now I know that this isn't the end. Something's waiting for me."

"Yeah, but what if it's something awful? Fire and pitchforks and … stuff?"

He turns to Joshua. "Is it?"

Joshua quickly responds, "I'm sorry, I don't have information about any of that. I don't actually go there. I just show you to the door."

"So how did you get *that* job?" I ask him.

"How did you get yours?" he counters. "The fact that you can still see and talk to Mr. Swartz means that you're among, shall we say, a privileged group."

"I don't know how I got mine. I woke up one day, and there it was."

He smiles pleasantly. "Same situation. I woke up one day, and I knew who was going to die that day, where and when they'd be, and I knew that I had to escort them to a specific place."

"Wild."

"So what's your gift?" he asks me.

"Gift?"

"Your special ability."

"Jesus, I never thought of it as a gift," I mutter. "Well, I get warnings about strangers in peril, and I go and alert them before it's too late."

"Hmm," he offers. "And yet, here we are. Didn't get to Mr. Swartz in time?" The question is devoid of any hint of accusation.

"No, I was on time. *Somebody* just chose not to believe me."

"You know, I'm right here," Cloud-Nick says, sounding offended.

"No," I correct, pointing to the pavement, "you're right *there,* where you wouldn't be if you had listened to me."

"Hey, whatever. Can we go now?"

"Just a minute," I answer before turning to Joshua. "Could I speak to you for a moment in private?"

"Sure."

I lead him a few steps away from the corporeal and the incorporeal Messrs. Swartz. Confidentially, I tell Joshua, "I lost someone recently, someone very dear to me, quite unexpectedly."

"I'm very sorry to hear that," he says. He's so polite, I feel like a finishing-school dropout in his presence.

"I'm not coping well." To my surprise, I feel a hitch in my voice, and it stops my words as I try to compose myself. Sensing my pain, he puts a comforting hand on my shoulder. "Thank you. Anyway, umm, she was a psychic ... a channeler, and I tried to contact her on ... you know, the other side—but I didn't have any luck. I thought that was the end of it. But seeing you here and hearing your story, it makes me wonder—"

"Be careful. It's easy to become overwhelmed by grief and make dangerous decisions. I'm just a person who volunteered to do an unusual job, just like you. I have no special insight into what comes after. All I have is my faith and my personal beliefs. Thanks to this gift, I know that death isn't the end, but as to what happens next, I really couldn't say."

"But this is weird, isn't it? Me being here, seeing our buddy over there. That usually doesn't happen, does it? Usually, only you can see them, I'm guessing."

"Usually," he says. "But for the past few months, things have been strange. I've talked with other servants who have told me the same thing."

"Servants?"

"It's what I call people who do the earthly work of the unseen forces. Do you have a name for your position?"

"*Schmuck,* maybe. But I suppose *messenger* would be appropriate. So you've met other people who do the kinds of things we do?"

"Several, yes. You'd be surprised how many of us there are. Things that people call miracles or divine intervention? I suspect that's handled by a member of the team. As living people, we can walk the world and intercede in matters of a more ethereal nature. I believe it's been going on since the days of the Bible. There are so many stories in it of prophets and seers, of angels. My guess is, these were people like us."

"I never thought about that," I admit. "You said something changed a few months ago. That was the time when I first started getting these assignments. Do you know what happened, what changed?"

"Personally, I don't, but I talked with someone who might. He told me that somehow, a door was left open between this world and a place he called Yenne Velt."

"This world and what?"

"Yenne Velt; that's what he said. It refers to the world beyond this one. That door was left open, and certain people and things got through. It's causing disturbances here, giving special abilities to individuals who wouldn't otherwise have them. So it doesn't surprise me that someone stepped up recruitment."

"I notice you're hesitant to use the name *God,*" I observe.

"It's difficult to be an atheist when you're in that being's direct employ. But because I don't know precisely who's sending me, I refrain from jumping to conclusions."

"This door you spoke of, do you think it's still open?"

"Yes, and from the look in your eyes, I feel like I know why you're asking."

"Joshua, I miss her more than I could possibly tell you. I don't want to leave this world to be with her, but if you can take me to that door and let me stick my head through, just for a minute, so I can talk with her …"

"It's more dangerous than you know. This is a place you and I aren't authorized to see. Not yet. Even if you could find that door, you might not recognize her if you saw her. Your first commitment has to be to yourself. Stay safe, and don't walk in places you don't know. It's a lesson I've learned to live by."

Knowing at my core that he is right, all I can do is thank him.

"You're welcome. I realize I don't know your name."

He's right; I never gave it. "I'm Tristan."

"Stay strong, Tristan. Believe in the reasons for things, even if you can't see those reasons." He turns back to Cloud-Nick. "Mr. Swartz, if you're ready, it's time to go."

The post-mortem embodiment of Nick Swartz joins Joshua, and together they start to move away from the house. A thought occurs to me. "Do you want to call the police or should I?"

"Would you?" Joshua asks. "Too many calls from me starts to look suspicious."

I watch for a minute as they head down the block. Gradually, Cloud-Nick begins to fade from my view, leaving Joshua walking alone, his assignment completed. I watch carefully, but I see no doors, no bright lights, no beams from above transporting Swartz to his next destination. One moment he is, the next he is not; just like all of us.

I get out my phone and call 911. I tell them I was visiting a friend in the neighborhood, and I saw that a man was sprawled out on his front patio. When I went to see if he needed help, I saw that he was badly hurt, and I wasn't even sure if he was alive. I give the address, and they ask for my name. I fake a bad connection and then disconnect the call. Calls to 911 from cellular phones are notoriously hard to trace, and my part in this whole bizarre day is over.

On the drive home, though, I have to wonder just what my part actually was. Alone with my thoughts, I go over the details in my mind. I was sent to Baltimore, I believed, because Nick Swartz was planning to go up on his roof and make repairs, and I was the only one who could stop him. But when I got there, it was pretty clear that he had no intention of going up on his roof. He wasn't even aware that the shingles had come loose until I said something to him about it. He had looked perfectly content to sit on the couch, drinking beer and watching *Judge Judy.*

Of course, when I did tell him about it, his first instinct was to get up there himself and fix it. *Yes, but only because he thought I was trying to scam him out of a repair fee.* I gave him a good warning, I know I did. I told him I didn't want his money, and I told him what would happen if he went up there, and he chose to go up there anyway. Which means that the next time he looked up at his roof, he would have seen the loose shingles and gone up there to fix them; I wouldn't have been there, and he would have fallen anyway.

Something else is bothering me, though—Joshua's presence. God—or whoever the hell is sending us—not only sent me, he also sent a soul chaperone. Meaning that he expected me to fail, or—

No. No, no, no, no, no, no! That can't be possible; that's too awful to consider. But it makes sense. What if I was sent there with the specific purpose of failing? What if Nick Swartz had to go, and he was taking his own sweet time about it? What if I was sent with the knowledge that this was just the push he needed to do something reckless enough to kill him? After all, Joshua was there fully expecting to escort him, so whoever sent Joshua knew I wouldn't be able to save Swartz.

What does that make me? Heaven's hit man? The concept is repugnant. I gave up my career and my life as I know it for the sake of helping people. Saving lives. I can't get up each day and drive for hours, only to help snuff out somebody who's too dumb to die on their own. How many times in the past was I causing harm instead of preventing it? I don't think I have a way to know. What about the ones yet to come? Will I constantly have to wonder if that's the hidden intention?

I pause long enough to take a few deep breaths as I drive. I can't let this possibility psych me out. I could be way off base on this, and even if I'm not, there's got to be a reason for it. At this moment, I really wish I had Ephraim here to put things in perspective. Instead, all I have is my own thoughts, which are more conflicted than I've ever felt in my life. I've handed my career over to a friend, for the sake of what I thought was philanthropy. Now I'm starting to doubt that too. And even when I do save someone's life, they're never grateful. Everyone's so full of doubt and suspicion and cynicism, they can't put that aside long enough to thank me.

So what do I do now? Talking to Esteban made it pretty clear that I can't just return to work and pick up as if things haven't changed. And I can't exactly stop taking these assignments, not unless I want to suffer from uncontrollable, overpowering pain for the rest of my life. *The rest of my life*—it's a sobering thought. Will I still be doing this when I'm eighty years old? For that matter, will I even live to see eighty years old, or will one of these assignments put me in the path of danger, allowing some stranger to live while I don't?

I would have thought nothing of giving my life to save Genevieve's—and Esteban's too, for that matter. But the others? Would I have sacrificed myself to protect that church in Georgia, or the child at the museum, or the airplane full of refugees—or Phillip Kean? I find myself unable to say yes to those questions, and I wonder what that tells me about myself. Why was I chosen for this job if I'm not willing to lay down my life in the service of others? Words like *selfishness* and *cowardice* come to mind, making me feel even worse about myself.

With nothing to do but think too much, the drive home feels very long. I arrive in Ocean City in the late afternoon, and the sun has already set, leaving the air considerably colder than it was earlier, when I succeeded or failed at my assignment—depending on what the outcome was meant to be.

I open my front door, step inside, close the door behind me, turn on the light, and sigh loudly before going any further. I nearly jump out of my skin when a voice from the living room asks, "Rough day?"

Ephraim stands as I look in his direction. *Has he been sitting here in the dark, waiting for me? If so, for how long?*

"Yes," I answer. "I didn't expect to see you here. Where's your car?"

"Down the block. I didn't want to alarm you by putting it in the driveway."

"No, of course not. Scaring the piss out of me in my living room is much less alarming."

"Point taken. Want to talk about that rough day?"

"Not particularly." I venture further into the house, joining him in the living room. "It hasn't even been a full day since you left. Did you miss me that much?"

"Twenty-four hours haven't passed," he corrects gently, "but I won't say it hasn't been a full day. That's why I came back. I was on a mission of my own, and it was successful. To complete it, I need your help. I've found Karolena. We need to go take care of her."

My heart races at those words. "By *take care of her,*" I reply as calmly as I can, "I trust you don't mean clean her house and pick up her groceries."

"I meant kill her, but if you want to do those things first, we can work it in."

"No, that's okay. Killing's good." It scares me a little, how easily I can say these words—and mean them. I want her dead, and more than that, I want to be the one to do it. Fuck nobility; I want to cut the bitch.

"I know you're just back from being out," he says. "Assignment?"

"Yes."

"Long drive?"

"Baltimore."

"Okay. Few hours. I can take the first driving shift. Because we need to leave now."

"Where are we going?" I ask.

He hesitates a moment, his face solemn. "I've convinced her to meet me at Gnothautii headquarters in York, Pennsylvania."

My heart feels brick-heavy in my chest at the mention of the name. The Gnothautii—the ones responsible for my injuries and Genevieve's murder. The very place where it all happened. My next question comes out as a frightened whisper. "Why there?"

"It was important," he answers apologetically. "The place has been shut down, but she still has access. She proposed the place, and I accepted. I need her to feel like she has an advantage."

"What if she brings reinforcements?"

"Leave that to me," he says confidently. "Are you going to be all right, being back in that place, after what happened to you there?"

It takes me a moment to answer. "I don't know. I think so."

"I know how much it means to you to be with me for this, to know that she's been defeated."

"Yes," I reply. "Thank you for that. I can do it; I can be there."

"Then we should go. It's close to a four-hour drive from here. We can get something to eat on the way. We'll take my car."

And so, just a few minutes after returning from my last mission, I depart for my next. There's nothing noble or divine about this one. It's all about revenge, plain and simple. She killed someone I love, and now I'm going to kill her.

Thirty-five minutes into the drive, Italian beef sandwiches in hand, we continue north to whatever this night will bring. "I can't help noticing," Ephraim says, "that you seem a bit sullen. Did today's assignment go poorly?"

I tell him about my encounter with Nick Swartz and the way it ended and about meeting and talking with Joshua. I share with him my concerns, confusion, and frustration, and he listens with great interest.

"So you met an escort," he says. "I didn't know they really existed. Fascinating."

"You've heard of them, then?"

"Only stories. Remember, I did a lot of research when I was building up my own personal talents and abilities. I'm told there are more extraordinary people out there than you may realize. Some are like us, gifted with foreknowledge. Others are like your new friend, helping the souls of the departed. There are others with gifts that would amaze you."

"How is it that this isn't common knowledge?" I ask.

"Through deliberate actions taken by the government."

"Seriously? It's an official government conspiracy?"

"Imagine what could happen if groups of these people got together, focused their efforts, and rose up as a unified force. That scares the government officials, and they're doing everything they can to make people who offer claims of psychic ability sound like crackpots. Doing a pretty good job of it too. They've even made some people doubt their own gifts. But we know better, don't we?"

"Yeah, I guess we do," I answer, surprised by all of this.

"Today really bothered you."

"Yes, it did. I mean, it would be one thing if I didn't go and warn him, and he died because of it. But I did go. I was there; I gave my warning, and he fell off that roof."

"Despite our best efforts, tragedy sometimes happens."

"So why send me?"

"To give him the warning."

"So why send Joshua?"

"To help him when the warning wasn't heeded. You're looking at this as an either/or situation—either you're needed or this Joshua person is needed. I suggest that both of you were needed. Dig deep, to the very root of why we're sent. We're not told to restrain people from the activities that will hurt or kill them. We give them a warning—advance knowledge that few people in this life get—and after that, they have to decide if the activity is worth the risk."

"So I'm not God's assassin?"

"Of the two of us," he says, "I think I'm a lot closer to that description than you."

"SODARCOM. So you've gone back to them?"

He nods. "With Phillip Kean out of the way, a more sensible governance can proceed."

"And nobody has to die?"

I get a disapproving sidelong glance for that one. "I'm not turning it into a Starbucks, Tristan. We'll re-examine the original charter and determine areas of greatest need. The need is still there. This country is dangerously overpopulated, and natural selection is being thwarted by misguided but well-intentioned individuals. And you can't tell me you've never met good candidates for my organization's work. *Wastes of space* is a common expression for them. People who do nothing but take, while giving nothing in return."

"I plead the Fifth."

"Your silence is my confirmation," he says, sounding self-satisfied.

After a few moments, I admit, "I've missed this."

"You couldn't miss it *that* much. Our last road trip together was yesterday."

"Yes, well, I was *prepared* to miss it. Thinking you weren't coming back."

"Well, don't get used to this. I'm not back to stay. I'm here to escort you to a one-time bitch slaying. Then I'm on my way."

Though his tone is casual, even a bit playful, his words strike me with the deadly seriousness of tonight's work. *We're going to kill someone. Yes, someone who sorely deserves it. But all the same, tonight's goal is to ambush a human being and end her life.*

Works for me.

"You okay with that?" he asks.

"I've never done anything like this before. Does she know ahead of time that I'm going to be there?"

"Can't imagine that she does. She thinks I'm there to work with her, to help her. She doesn't know I was the one who saved you from her the last time. As such, I'll want you to hang back and let me do the talking."

There's a difficult question yet unasked, and now is the time to ask it. "Do I … have to be the one to kill her?"

"Have to be … or *get to be?*" he replies.

"Either."

"No," he says, and I can't tell if I'm relieved or disappointed at that answer. "For a variety of reasons, it should be me who does it. But I'll make sure she knows that it's being done on your behalf and exactly why she deserves her fate."

"Thank you," I answer quietly.

"Don't thank me. This isn't a gift. It's a terrible responsibility that it's important you witness, and I hope you never have to do anything like this again. Don't become one of those people who get a taste for killing, Tristan. It turns who you are inside-out."

As he says these portentous words, all I can do is stare out at the road ahead, the road to an encounter that will very likely change my life forever.

Chapter 12

Monday, November 12, 2007

Ephraim

Halfway through our drive to Pennsylvania, Tristan takes the wheel, giving me time to think about what's ahead. Neither of us has much to say; I think we both know how brutal this night will be for everyone.

He relies on my directions to get us there. The last time he was here, he didn't leave under his own power, and he has no recollection of the specific route. I, on the other hand, have committed it to memory, and it will be with me for the rest of my life. North on 83, left onto Queen, left onto Tyler Run, and right onto Palisade. He parks us right out front, by the main door to the building. We're far enough off the beaten path that there's nothing to be gained by hiding the car. There's not another vehicle in sight, but I know we're not alone. A quick check of my watch tells me that it's almost 10:00 at night. Wonder if I'll have to call in sick tomorrow, on the first day of my probationary period.

"What should we do?" Tristan asks.

"We should go in, scope the place out, and wait."

"Will we be able to get in?"

"I'll get us in," I assure him.

He is visibly uneasy as we make our way to the front doors. He pulls on the doors and finds them locked, which doesn't surprise me at all, given that the place has been abandoned for months. I step over to a concrete planter a few feet away, lift the artificial ficus out of it, and reach inside to pull out the key that I knew would be there, courtesy of Karolena. I insert it into the lock, turn, and open the door, pocketing the key after we relock the door behind us.

"You are full of surprises," Tristan says quietly.

"If you only knew."

I lead the way past the vacant reception desk, through the lobby, past numerous meeting rooms, and into the heart of the building, to a room very familiar to us both—the same room where the Gnothautii tried to kill Tristan and succeeded in killing Genevieve Swan. We hesitate outside the door to that room, and I see in Tristan's eyes every horrific memory of what he endured within. He turns to me, his eyes silently pleading *anywhere but here.*

"Does it have to be in this room?" he asks.

"I'm afraid so. For what we have to do, this is the place. Are you with me?"

His answer is slow in coming, but when it does, the words are resolute. "To the end."

I open the door to the former operating theater of the Gnothautii Society and turn on the lights. As promised, everything is still in place, just as it was when I let my vengeance loose upon the place in August. Any evidence of carnage has been cleaned up, mercifully. Tristan has enough reminders of what happened here; he doesn't need one more. He enters first, stepping slowly into the room. Several paces behind him, I close the door, staying near it for now. I watch his face as he looks around. It's clear that he's uncomfortable being here, that he's reliving some of the worst moments of his life. I wish I had words of comfort for him, but there's no comfort here. Not for him or for me; just the matter at hand.

After several seconds of uneasy silence, he begins to ask, "So what do we—" but before the rest of the question gets out, another voice interrupts.

"Tristan Shays, how nice of you to come back here."

He turns rapidly to watch Karolena emerge from the shadows in a corner of the room, where she's been waiting patiently for our arrival. "Ephraim!" Tristan calls out in a panic. "There she is! Get her!"

Ignoring him, I speak to Karolena directly. "I brought him here like you asked."

"Bring him to me."

"First things first. Where's my money?"

She produces a medium-sized gym bag and places it at my feet, unzipping it to let me look inside. I was expecting a briefcase, but that'll teach me to be so traditional. Inside, as promised, is 1.5 metric shit-tons of money.

"Thank you," I say with a little smile. "Have you had a chance to hook up the equipment again like I asked?"

"I followed your directions to the letter. Everything should be ready for him."

If I had physically ripped my cousin's heart out and held it up to show him, the look on his face would not be more shattered than the one he wears now. "Ephraim, no," he says, straining not to cry. "Not like this. Not after everything we've been through. I can't believe that it was all lies, all trickery."

"Be quiet," I snap at him. "This isn't personal; it's just business. If you want to blame someone, blame yourself for being such a trusting, sentimental idiot. You offered the scorpion a ride across the river on your back, and you knew what the scorpion could do. This is my nature, Tristan. This is who I am. You think you know me? You think because I lived in your house and ate your food and helped you when you were in trouble that we're allies? That we're family? It's called the long game. I played you from the very beginning, and you believed me."

He looks at the gym bag. "I'll give you ten times what she paid you."

"It's not just about the money. Karolena and I are defying God himself. By taking down the messengers, stripping them of their ability to see the future and change things, we're correcting an aberration. Forcing the creator of this world to take responsibility for his actions. It's unfortunate that you have to suffer for it, but that's what you do. You take the pain so that others can thrive. So now, you're going to do what I tell you and accept what's happening to you. Cooperate, and I'll make this as painless as possible."

I see the despair in his expression turn to silent resentment, and there's nothing I can do about that. Wheels are in motion, and I have to see this through to the end. "What do I have to do?" he asks, containing his emotions.

"Behind you is a modified sensory-deprivation tank. It was one of the pet projects of the Gnothautii. They were exploring the device's many potential uses, but their work was interrupted. Tonight, we're going to move that work forward. These devices have been used for decades as a means to induce a hyper-relaxed and tranquil state, through the removal of sensory stimuli. The Gnothautii postulated that the opposite effect could be induced through the introduction of intense sensory stimuli, carefully monitored and regulated. Individuals could be brought to a state of superhuman awareness. Or their minds could be manipulated to the point that every thought, every memory, every ounce of personal awareness is forced out, leaving an empty shell that can be rewritten, filled with whatever knowledge, whatever identity the user wants. You are privileged to be our test case. Karolena will sit at that control panel, hook her own mind up to the machine, and with my guidance, she will unmake you and re-create you in whatever image we see fit. You should feel honored."

"I can think of a dozen reasons why you shouldn't do this," he replies, clearly not feeling honored.

"I'm sure you can. Primary among them being a sentimental fondness for your sense of self. You lost it for a while, and now that you have it back, you're reluctant to give it up again. It's a very reasonable response. Unfortunately, I can't let that dissuade us. You're a member of a very troublesome group, Tristan. The messengers are living evidence of the fallibility of God, and we can't let that continue. We're seeking them out, even now. All of them. And in this room or rooms just like it, one by one, they will be relieved of their burden. That's what you wanted, isn't it? A life free of this responsibility?"

"Not like this. What if it kills me?"

"Sacrifices are always present in the advancement of science."

"I trusted you."

"Not now, Tristan."

"I trusted you, and this is how you repay me."

"Take your clothes off," I instruct.

It serves to stop his anger briefly. "What?"

"The tank contains water, and for proper electrical conductivity, your clothes have to be off. So take them off, please."

"Buy me dinner first," he retorts humorlessly.

"I did buy you dinner, three hours ago. Now you're wasting time. Take your clothes off, or I'll have Karolena take them off of you like you were a petulant six-year-old who won't go to bed."

I turn my head as he begins to disrobe. Karolena offers no such courtesy, going so far as to comment when he's done, "I had no idea. I may have to keep him around and remake him as my personal plaything. Seeing as how he's ... *unattached* at the moment."

At these words, Tristan takes three very purposeful steps in her direction, but for his own safety—however fleeting—I put myself between him and her. It is enough to stop his intentions. "Get into the tank," I tell him. "Let's go." Standing behind him, I walk him up the three metal steps to the dark metal tube. I would call it coffinlike, except it's twice the size of a proper casket. I swing open the lid, exposing the interior, half-filled with warm water.

"Lie down on your back," I instruct. "The chamber is lightproof and soundproof, so this is the last opportunity to communicate until it's over. Is there anything you'd like to say?"

"Nothing that's fit for mixed company ... *cousin*."

"Inside, please."

His eyes never leave mine as he lowers himself into the chamber, constantly burning an accusation of betrayal. Even as I close and secure the lid, I still feel him looking through me. But I can't think about that now. There's work to do.

Quickly I descend the steps and return to Karolena, who is now seated at the control panel for the device. "I didn't think you could actually do it," she says. "I know that you and I have had our differences."

"Money cures a lot," I reply.

"Of course. Now then, you said I would be able to control what happens to him?"

"If you've connected the controls correctly, then yes."

"I trust you're not doubting my abilities," she says, imperious as ever.

"I wouldn't dream of it. But quality control is important, so if you'll grant me a cursory inspection of the hardware, we can get started."

I look over the control interface and see that before Tristan and I arrived, she did indeed make the connections I specified. Fortunately, during the time that I was the Gnothautii's test subject, I had familiarized myself with the machinery they were using. Karolena has it calibrated properly.

"Perfect, as you said it would be. Now, in order to control what happens inside the tank, you'll need the neural interface on your head." She picks up the device, a rather imposing-looking ring of wires and electrodes, and pushes her hair aside to allow it to make contact with the skin of her forehead. "Very good. It's also important that you don't move around during the process. It can break the connection, and we'd have to keep restarting. So if you'll strap yourself into the chair there, we're just about ready to begin."

She fastens what looks like an automobile's lap belt around her waist, securing her to the chair. "I'll begin the sequence of commands," I further instruct, "but once they're started, you will be directly linked to Tristan with your thoughts. Whatever you want to happen to him, just think it, and the machinery will make the necessary changes in his brain."

"I love it," she says. "Money well spent. Ephraim, this is brilliant.

With this at our disposal, we can eradicate anyone who stands in our way. Not destroy them, but rewrite them to be willing participants in anything we devise. We'll remove their resistance but retain their knowledge base and their experience. And I want you involved in the planning and execution stages, by my side, through it all."

"It would be my pleasure."

"So, our little friend is all tucked in over there. I think we should see what this device can do. From this point, all commands are thought-based? No controls for me to touch?"

"I'll direct the controls," I respond, "while you think about what you want to happen. There's one more step to make the link stronger." I remove a small device from my jacket pocket. "This is a jet injector, the kind used for immunization without the need of a hypodermic needle. Inside is a combination of serotonin and dopamine, which will react with the neurotransmitters in your brain, facilitating your control over Tristan's thought processes. You might feel a slight sensation of euphoria."

I press the jet injector to the back of Karolena's neck and activate the trigger, releasing a small vial of iridescent blue liquid through her skin at the base of her skull. "All done," I say pleasantly. "Didn't even hurt. Good thing, too, because I don't have a balloon to give you if it did."

"What happens now?" she asks, the anticipation evident in her tone.

"Give it a few seconds. You'll start to feel it very soon."

I watch as the smile slowly leaves her face, replaced by something resembling discomfort. "I feel strange," she says, tight-lipped.

"It's okay. That'll happen. Just stay focused. Can you hear me all right?"

"Yes."

"Can you move in your chair?"

"No," she reports, a hint of panic in her voice.

"Then let me help." I sprint over to where she is seated and turn her in her swivel chair until she is facing me. "I'm afraid I may not have been entirely truthful in what I told you today. That fabulous new hat you're wearing—well, it's actually inducing a temporary paralysis of your extremities. Can't have you thrashing about, after all."

"What … is this?"

"What is this? Why, Karolena, I'm hurt that you don't recognize good, old-fashioned payback when it's rammed up your ass. Very thoughtful of you to orchestrate the whole thing by inviting me—and to this very room, of all places. Your private little amusement park of human experimentation and torture. The room where you killed Genevieve Swan, the woman my cousin loves. The room where you ordered your butchers to dismantle Tristan. The room where your doctors destroyed any hope I ever had for living a normal life when they tampered with my brain."

Her eyes widen at this; not what I expected. "Surely you knew what they did to me here years ago. Or were they afraid to report their failure to you? Of course; that makes sense. Can't tell Mommy that her kiddos fucked things up so badly. Well, they did, and now here we are. Good to be back, actually. Didn't know if that would be possible after somebody burst in here last summer, rescued Tristan, and shot up the place. Now, who would that have been? Oh, that's right—it was me."

"Y-you?"

"I've gotta say, Karolena, for someone who prides herself on being the evil mastermind of a powerful organization, your intel is for shit today. Yep. Me, all me. Didn't relish the thought of killing your boys, but I didn't lose sleep over it when it was done. Because I was hurting you. Hurting you the way I wanted to hurt you for years. For the longest time, I was so afraid of you, but little by little, I saw behind the mask and found a person there. A miserable excuse for a person, devoid of any of the decency that permeates most people—but still a person. Fallible. Touchable. Credulous. So I strung your ass along, using my poor cousin as bait. He's in that tank right now, cursing my name because I couldn't even hint to him that this place wasn't a trap for him; it was a trap for you. I know how strong your little mind tricks are. I can hide my thoughts from you, but he can't. So I lied to him. Good news is, he's in that tank right now, listening to soothing music and seeing muted pastel lights. Probably wondering when the torture's going to start." I lean in close to her ear and whisper, "It starts now."

On the control panel, out of her reach, I turn a dial from zero to three. Immediately, Karolena cries out in pain and surprise. "What … d-d-did you inj-ject me with?"

"Oh, that? A little gift from Florida! Your associates down there were doing bang-up work on your pal Anatoly, and they just happened to have extracted a few CCs of his cerebrospinal fluid. Now, in most people, that stuff's harmless, helpful even. But with the radiation coursing through his body and the genetic mutations he's undergone, it was a little tube of just-what-I-needed. And now you get to feel the things he feels. Congratulations, Miss Prizhen. You wanted a weaponized human being; enjoy the weapon."

"Please," she says, struggling to retain control. "You don't … ha-have to do this."

I turn the dial higher in response, evoking a louder shout from her. "I don't have to do this? Are we going to resort to clichés now? Okay, since you're having trouble talking for once, let me run down the list for you. 'You don't have to do this.' Mmmmm, yeah, I really do." She gets a jolt. "Let's see. 'I'll give you anything you ever wanted.' Got it right here." Another jolt, another scream of pain. "What else? Oh, here's an oldie but goody: 'I'll make you rich!' Believe me, Karolena, an hour or two watching you squirm in agony is worth more to me than any bag full of money you can offer me. Which I'm keeping, by the way. You won't need it where you're going."

She emits a squeak of surprise at this. "Surely you don't think there's a way out of this for you?" I ask, disappointed in her. "I'm going to use this equipment to do to you the same things you were going to do to Tristan. I'm going to strip the evil right out of you over the course of a couple of very painful hours, during which you'll suffer mentally and physically, with unspeakable hallucinations and waking nightmares. After that, I'll release you from that chair, and you'll be purified like a newborn baby. At which point I could tenderly escort you from this place and allow you to live out the rest of your life in kindness and gentility.

"But I'm not going to do that. Do you know why?" She shakes her head just a bit, as much as her impaired muscles allow. I lean in close to her face and shout, "Because *fuck you,* that's why! You would kill me and everyone I've ever loved without thinking twice about it, and that's why, when I'm done separating you from everything that made you the monster you are, I'm going to take you out of this building, douse you in bacon grease and sugary cereal, and leave you in the woods for wild animals to eat. Because that is exactly what you deserve."

Three hours and thirty-two minutes later, I re-enter the Gnothautii's operating theater and look around in disgust. The place served its purpose well tonight, but something tells me that an unfortunate electrical fire wouldn't be a bad idea. A strange smell hits my nose, and I lift my hands to my face to sniff them. Bacon grease. I tried hard not to get any on me, but when you're dealing with a half gallon of it, accidents will happen. It's all about preparation. I picked up the supplies I'd need before I even picked Tristan up. I knew my plans for tonight. Unfortunately, he didn't, and that's the next awkward order of business.

I make my way up the steps to the sensory-deprivation tank, release the latch, and swing the metal lid open. Tristan sits up immediately and glares at my face. "You dick."

"I feel I owe you an explanation."

"Ya think? Here, let me start it for you. I've had an indeterminate amount of time to rehearse it: 'Tristan, I'm sorry, but I had to get your hopes up about killing Karolena and then take you to the very room where people tried to kill you. Oh, and then I'm going to turn on you, team up with Karolena, shove you into the tube of death, and leave you to wonder why the torture hasn't started yet.' How's that?"

"You know, for someone who's just come out of a sensory-deprivation tank, you're a lot more tense than I expected."

"Would you *please* help me out of here and get me a towel?"

I take him by the hand and ease him back to his feet before retrieving a large towel I find in a nearby locker.

He looks around. "Where's Karolena?"

"Communing with nature," I answer.

"Is that a euphemism for something unspeakably awful?"

"Yes."

"So I take it that the double cross was a ruse to trick Karolena into a ... what? Triple cross? Or would that take it back down to single cross?"

"Triple, technically. And yes, you're correct. I'd like to take this opportunity to tell you how genuinely sorry I am that I had to deceive you that way. Remember, Karolena's a powerful psychic. If she saw the truth of the matter in your thoughts, things would have ended very differently. Besides, there was always the chance that I wouldn't prevail, and then my original story would've fit anyway."

"I had some very uncharitable thoughts about you in that tank."

"I can only imagine. I tried to give you soft music and pretty lights while I was working out here. I hoped that would help."

"I'll grant you," he says, "it was a confusing, very subtle form of torture, and after a while, I did my best to relax."

"Would it help you to know that she suffered a lot worse than you did?"

"No," he says. "Well, okay, yes."

"So you're all right?"

"I wouldn't go that far, but I'll say that I'm going to be. What time is it, anyway?"

"Almost 2:00 in the morning."

"Any chance we could find a hotel around here for the night?" he asks hopefully.

"No such luck. I have to be at work in the morning. And the local authorities are likely to make a disturbing discovery soon, so I don't want us anywhere near here when they do. Besides, this place can't be allowed to remain standing. I can rig things so that the wiring will short out and reduce the place to cinders in the next eight hours."

"It's almost too bad," Tristan says. "This equipment could have been used for good things, advancements in neuroscience, instead of finding new and creative ways to hurt people."

"Someday maybe. Just not here and now."

"So that's it, then. Nothing to do but head home?"

"Not quite," I answer. "There's one more thing to do, and it'll take about an hour."

"Okay. Let me get dressed, and I'll help you."

"Actually, in order to help me, you shouldn't get dressed."

He looks appropriately confused. "O-o-o-o-kaaaaaay, gonna have to ask for clarification here."

I was hoping to avoid this conversation and just do what I have to do without even telling him it was happening, but the process with Karolena took too long, and I had to let him out and tell him what was going on. Besides, he has a right to know what needs to happen to him. "Tristan, what you've been through in the past several months is life-changing. You've seen and done things that almost no one alive will get to experience. I also know the physical and emotional traumas that you've gone through. I'm not proud to admit that I've been the cause of some of them."

"I forgive you for that."

"Thank you. That means a lot to me. But there's a remedy, and it needs to go beyond mere forgiveness and moving on. That's part of the reason I arranged for tonight to take place here. You have important work to do, more important than you can possibly know. More important than I'm at liberty to tell you. And in order to complete that work properly, certain aspects of your past are better … obscured."

A moment of realization overtakes him as he understands what I'm suggesting. "No …"

"Tristan, please. It won't be anything like what you went through before."

"I can't. I—I can't let go of my memories again; not after what they did to me."

"Not all your memories. Just a few. Most of them are painful memories anyway. Things you'll be glad to be rid of."

I can see in his face that he wants to believe me, but there's a lingering veil of doubt. "What things?"

"Karolena. SODARCOM. The Gnothautii. The pain they put you through. I can block those things, hide them away where you'll never have to think about them again. Never lose another minute of sleep or have flashbacks or post-traumatic stress."

"What about the pain that comes with the assignments? Can you get rid of that?"

"Unfortunately, no. I don't have the medical skill for that, and the people who might have had it fell when I rescued you. I'm sorry."

"What else?" he asks. "What other memories do you want to block from me?"

I have to tell him. "As it happens, one of the memories you need to move forward without is me."

"What? But you're my family. You're on my side. I want you to be a part of my life moving forward. I rely on you for guidance."

"Yes, you do," I reply, a smile masking the inner conflict I feel at having to do this for him. "And that's part of the reason. What's coming ahead for you is bigger than me. More important. And believe it or not, it's your insight, your creativity, your problem-solving skills that will be needed to prevail. My presence in your life will only cause unnecessary complications. Because of that—and believe me, it pains me to tell you this—I have to be part of the memories that are closed off to you."

"So … I'll never see you again?" I hear such sorrow in his words.

"I won't say that. I know some of what lies ahead for you, and that means I'll still be able to keep an eye on you. Make sure you're doing well. You just may not know who I am when I do. I could be delivering sandwiches or disguise myself as a homeless man on a park bench. I care about what happens to you, Tristan, and I won't let you go through this alone."

"But wait, we still have to go home together tonight when this is over. How will that work if I don't know who you are or where I am?"

"When the process is complete, I'll introduce a safe, gentle sedative into the tank, which will allow you to sleep for the next eight hours or so. After that, I'll dress you, put you in the car, drive you home, and put you in your bed. You'll wake up by noon, feeling refreshed, and without the memories of the worst parts of the past few months."

"And some of the best parts."

"If you mean to include your time with me in that statement, then thank you. I have to agree. I know I've been a challenge sometimes, but this time with you has been remarkable, and you're going to be very good at this, even when things are at their worst."

"I'm trying not to get very nervous about all these upcoming difficult times you're talking about," he says.

"You see, this is precisely why I need to be chased out of your memories. I'm nothing but a string of complications."

"Ephraim … what about Genevieve?"

The question was inevitable. Most of the conversation up to this point was probably just a way of postponing the difficult query. And while it gave me time to formulate an answer, it doesn't make the answer any easier. "Ahh, Tristan, it's very involved. Very difficult."

"Please don't take her away from me."

I wish he hadn't said it like that.

"I lost her once, and then I lost my memory of her, which felt like losing her all over again."

Cruel as it feels, he's just given me my opportunity. "And when you got those memories back, what did it bring you?"

"Pain," he answers in quiet anguish.

"I'm sorry, my friend, but that's the truth of it. She's tied in with so much of what brought you grief and hardship. If you let her stay in your memories, the good things will stir up the bad things, only you won't know why. This most recent mission of yours, you talked with Joshua, the escort, about trying to contact Genevieve. For your protection, I should block your memory of that mission as well. Otherwise she'll start to be associated with unexplainable twinges of suffering for you. You don't want to do that to her memory."

"I hate this!" He shouts the words, which reverberate off of every solid surface in the room, raising the hairs on my arms in recognition of how powerful his mind is.

When enough time has passed to be respectful, I quietly ask, "But you'll do it?"

"If it's the only way."

"It's the best way."

"You promise you won't hurt me the way they did the last time I was here?"

"Tristan, I swear to you on everything I hold sacred in this world that I will safeguard your life and your well-being during this procedure."

"Thank you."

With nothing else to say, he drops his towel and allows me to escort him back to the tank. As he climbs back in, he says to me, "I may have urinated in there earlier. I'm not sure. Does that change anything?"

"Just try to keep your mouth closed during the procedure."

"Ephraim?"

"Yes?"

"Can I ask you a question?"

"Of course."

"Why do you smell like bacon?"

"It's not important."

A click of the latch, and the lid is once again secure. I return to the control panel and disable all controls that have anything to do with administering harm. That part is over. Now I have to focus on the task at hand. In a way, it was easier working on Karolena. I had the neural link directly on her head, I had Anatoly's juicy, radioactive goodness coursing through her veins, and I had the knobs I could turn up to eleven. But this? This is microsurgery without the benefit of a cutting tool.

To be accurate, I won't be able to remove the memories from Tristan's mind. All I can do is hide them away behind layer after layer of protection, with inserted misdirections that will lead him to other thoughts if he should accidentally happen to get too close. If this works—and I pray it will—he'll be able to look me in the face from inches away and believe we've never met.

My arsenal is two-pronged: a cocktail of psycho-reactive drugs in aerosol mist, combined with the equivalent of an industrial-strength series of post-hypnotic suggestions, for lack of a better term. The drugs will sedate him to the point of hyper-suggestibility, and after that, I should simply be able to whisper into his soul and hide the painful parts away for the rest of his life. It's tempting to hide his newfound burden away, his knowledge of his task as a messenger. But I can't; it's not fair to him, and it's not fair to the people who will need him. Because the assignments will keep coming, and he'll need to be prepared. I have memories of things yet to come, daunting situations that Tristan will have to face. For some of them, I will be there to witness, maybe even to lend subtle assistance, but I know I can't carry him. Not like I did, not like before.

I release the sedatives into the tank and give them a few minutes to take effect. I'm able to hear him in there but not see him. I listen closely and hear regular, distress-free breathing. Gently I say into the microphone, "Tristan, can you hear me?"

Softly, peacefully, "Yes."

"You're safe, and you're in a good place, a place where your thoughts can be at peace. Nothing and no one can harm you here. I want you to let go of your surroundings and concentrate on only the sound of my voice. If you understand, say yes."

"Yes."

"You're doing very well. Keep your eyes closed and breathe in and out regularly. Feel the warmth and comfort of the water as it supports you. I want you to picture your home in your mind. See your house and the ocean behind it. Imagine yourself walking in the sand."

The process is intricate, extremely involved. I must watch every word I say, lest a stray statement indelibly obscure a vital aspect of his life. After an hour and a half of very precise guidance, I feel confident that it has been a success. Switching off the microphone, I introduce more of the sedative into the chamber and allow him some much-needed sleep.

Once I'm sure that he's properly under, I return to the tank, wrap my soaking-wet, unconscious cousin in a towel, and lift him out of the tank, resting him against me as I guide him down the stairs. "It's all right," I tell him, though I doubt he can hear me. "You're going to be fine. It's over."

Making him forget about me was the most difficult part, because I will miss his company and his conversation. I've never been terribly close with family members until he came along, so the thought of erasing myself from his memory is not one I relish. I feel confident that he won't recognize me if we meet again, but I did give him a suggestion that if he sees me, he'll know that I am dear to him.

With some effort, I dress him and lead him out to the car, placing him safely in the passenger's seat and closing the car door behind him. *Just one more piece of business to conduct.* I return to the building and gather the materials I'll need. Some salt water, some slow-dissolving plastic casing, a few conductive chemicals, and the main breaker box for the building. A recipe for an easy and delicious, set-it-and-forget-it electrical fire that should be ready to go in about eight to ten hours. Good riddance to a place of such potential that was turned into a chamber of horrors.

As I pull out of the parking lot, the clock on my dashboard says 4:22 a.m. It has been an incredibly long day, and the thought of six hours in a comfortable three-star hotel is the quintessence of bliss at this moment. But I have a package to deliver, and right now, he's sleeping peacefully. He needs to wake up in his own bed, in his own house, with no recollection of who I am.

And me? I'm going to be a bit late for work today, I suspect. Just in time for my first day of probationary service as interim director. What's the worst thing that could happen? They fire me, and I have to find a job that doesn't involve determining how many Americans have to die in a given fiscal year. *Pauvre moi!*

Fortunately, I'm able to stay awake and alert on the deserted highways of Maryland—which get considerably less deserted as the morning rush hour approaches. Thanks to some consequence-free speeding in the dead of night, I arrive in Ocean City just after 8:00 in the morning and park near the front door of stately Shays Manor. It's a hell of a nice house, and I'm going to miss it.

My traveling companion continues to slumber under the effects of the sedative, so I help him up and support him like Maryland's best-dressed town drunk. I use my key to open the front door and bring him inside. Fortunately, there are no neighbors nearby to be made suspicious. I don't relish the thought of navigating the stairs with him on my hip, but I have to make his waking experience as normal as possible. That means he can't awaken on the living-room sofa. So it's up-up-up the stairs we go, slowly and clumsily as he and gravity conspire to pour his dormant form back to the first floor in a heap.

With coordination skills I didn't know I had, I manage to get him all the way up the stairs without dropping him, down the hall, into his bedroom, and seated on his bed. Knowing that he probably wouldn't fall asleep fully dressed, I manage to strip him down to something resembling sleepwear, put his head on the pillow, and even get him tucked under his blankets. I realize that I would give about a thousand dollars to fall asleep here too for the rest of the day.

I stand over his sleeping form for a moment. "I guess this is goodbye then. I wish it didn't have to be this way, but we both know how things worked out. It was a pleasure taking care of you, helping you when you couldn't help yourself. And I'm sorry for the shit I put you through. Some of that wasn't ... well, it wasn't very nice. But you dealt with it, and you came out stronger, and I respect that. You're going to be very good at this.

"What else can I say? Watch your back. Drive whenever you can, instead of flying. The guy with the gun in Charleston will be hiding behind the red car. That'll make sense in about eight months. Hmm, what else? Remember to eat regularly, and come home in between missions whenever you can."

I start to walk away from the bed, but I have one more thought to offer, so I turn back. "Oh, yeah, if it's not too much trouble—don't fall in love."

Epilogue

Twenty-two months later
Thursday, September 10, 2009

Tristan

So much travel. My life is made up of so much travel. Sure, I like the open road, and it gives me the chance to see new places, but I still have to wonder, after more than two years of this, when I'll get something as indulgent as two weeks' vacation. Not this week, certainly. Maybe with a vacation, I could get some proper sleep. Lately I'm plagued by dreams—visions of things that may have happened to me when I first started receiving assignments. It's strange; they feel like memories, and yet I don't remember experiencing them.

I see a man, but I don't know who he is. Sometimes he's trying to help me; other times he's trying to hurt me. I don't know his name or what he wants. In other dreams, I see a woman. She feels so familiar, though I feel certain that I haven't actually met her. Who are they, and what do they want with me?

There's one other dream—a dream of floating, not on air but in water, in a small metal box. Almost like a coffin half-filled with water.

In it I can see no light. It's like being buried, but above ground. And when the box opens, my senses are overloaded with light and sound. The man is there, and he comforts me. "It's all right," he says gently. "You're going to be fine. It's over." *What's over?* I can't even ask him in my dream; I'm too weak. He puts me in a car and drives me home.

It's over. So why does it feel like from that point, everything actually began?

Fourteen hours from home, I feel gently weary. This is one of the longer trips I've taken since this all started for me. All the way from Maryland to Florida. And not just northern Florida, no. That would at least be a reasonable distance. But all the way to Key freakin' West, thank you. And for what? To give a warning—a much more vague and nebulous warning than I'm used to, actually—to a stripper in some club. For a few minutes there, I had really considered *not* taking this one. I mean, it's not like she's a world leader or something. And yet I did take it; against my wishes and my better judgment, I gave in. What was the thought process on that? How did *that* even begin?

How did it begin? Christ, that's the one answer I *do* know.

It began, as it always begins, with pain. Two days ago, in the privacy and comfort of my home, I suffered a searing firestorm of pain that started in my right leg and worked its way up through my abdomen and into my chest, radiating out through both arms. When it struck, I dropped to my hands and knees and struggled to stay focused. Because I knew that with the agony came vital information. It was how I learned about Rebecca.